ROSES

REUTS PUBLICATIONS

roses

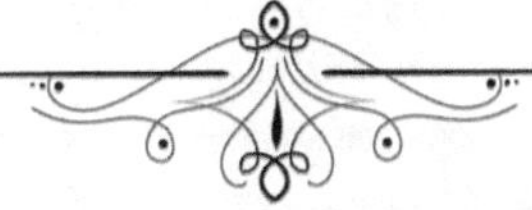

Cover design by Ashley Ruggirello
Interior formatting by Ashley Ruggirello
Edited by Michelle Hoehn and Kisa Whipkey
Cover Art Copyright 2017 vampstock/SamKross-Stock/mistyt-stock on DeviantArt.com

Paperback ISBN: 978-1-942111-47-4
Electronic ISBN: 978-1-942111-46-7

REUTS Publications
www.REUTS.com

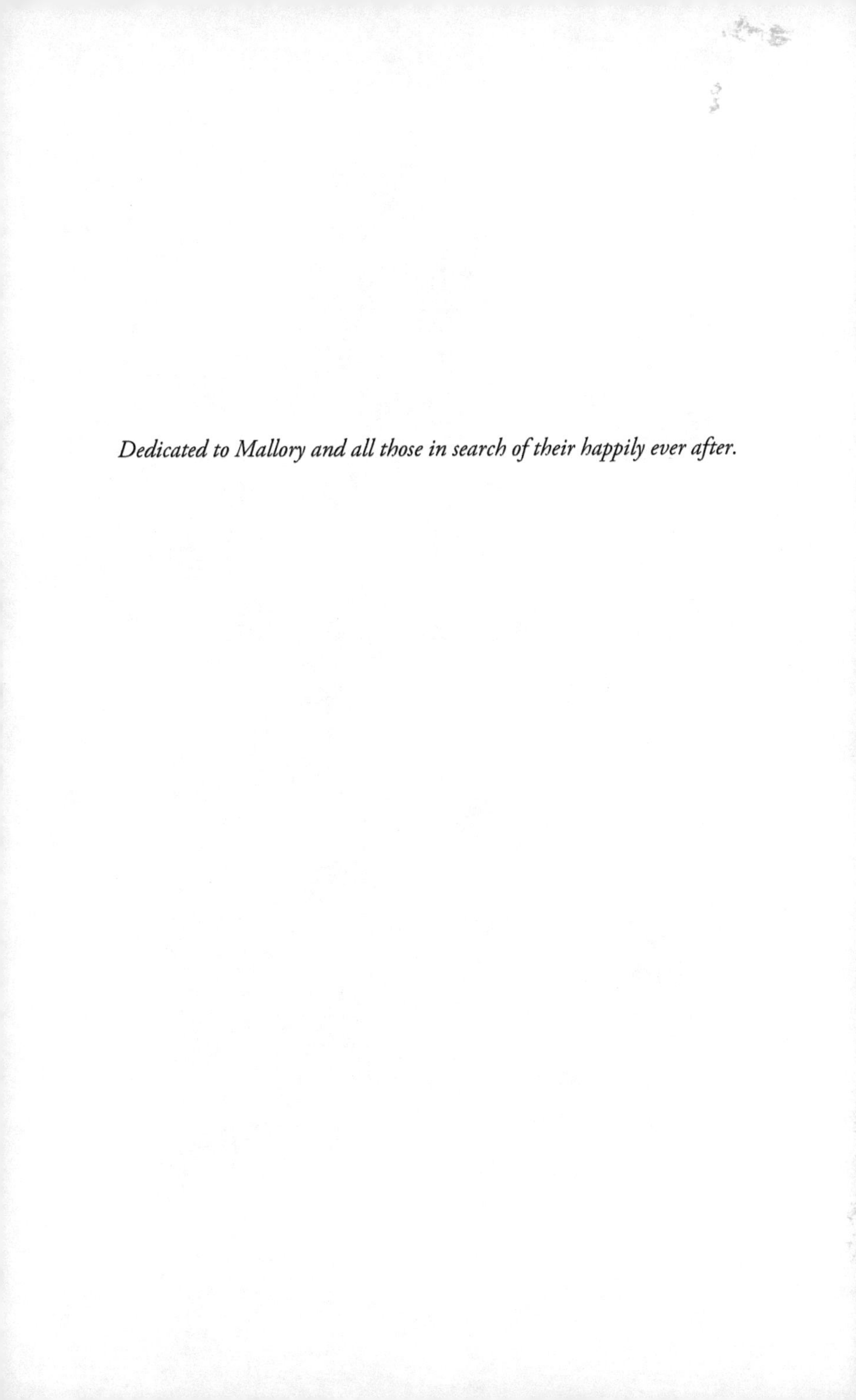

Dedicated to Mallory and all those in search of their happily ever after.

CHAPTER ONE

Snow fell lightly all around Poppy as she gazed about the cemetery. She was small, much shorter than usual. A warm hand held hers tightly, engulfing her tiny fingers. When she looked up, she smiled. It was her grandmother.

She looked around and saw that they were the only two people in the cemetery. She knew then that she was dreaming not just a dream, but a memory, and one she dreamt of often. She didn't mind; this memory held comfort, and she let herself be taken by it.

"It's all right, Poppy." Her grandmother's rich voice warmed her. "Don't be afraid."

She wasn't, but she gripped her grandmother's hand as they walked among the headstones. They stopped before a familiar grave, and Poppy stared solemnly at the spindly letters carving out the name: "Phoebe Pruette, Loving Wife, Devoted Mother."

"Grandma," she heard her young voice say, unable to control the words. "What happens when we die?"

"We turn into flowers, darling," her grandmother said softly. "That's why we're put into the ground. So we can grow into beautiful flowers."

They stared in silence for a moment, watching the snowflakes fall across the cold bare stone.

"There aren't any flowers here," Poppy said. "It's because it's too cold, right?"

Her grandmother squeezed her hand.

"Come spring, I'll make sure to tell the caretaker to let her flowers grow."

For some reason, that answer made Poppy angry. Her mother's flowers should be able to grow whenever they wanted, not just when it was warm enough or when a caretaker decided not to trim them.

"I wish Mom was still here," Poppy said bitterly, tears forming in her eyes.

Her grandmother sighed and knelt to look her in the eye.

"Oh, Poppy. I know." She wiped a tear from Poppy's cheek with a wrinkled finger. "You must be careful, though. Wishing is a dangerous habit."

Poppy sniffed, taking in the features of her grandmother's gentle face.

"Why?"

Her grandmother smiled and cupped her cheek.

"Another time."

She stood, and they looked back at the headstone.

"Grandma? What flower is Mom?"

"A rose, dear. Why?"

"Can I be a rose too, like my real name?"

"Of course, darling. Everyone in our family will be roses."

Raindrops slid down the bay window of the kitchen nook where Poppy Pruette sat, as still as the day was wet. Last night's dream seemed magnified now as she replayed the memory of it over and over in her head. Her phone pinged again with another news update. The headline from the local news site read, "Murder in Miner's Way." Just a few minutes earlier, her father had brought in the actual paper. There, on the front page, the picture of an elderly woman gazed back at her. She knew the face well, with its gentle smile and caring eyes—had known it all her life. Even now, the woman watched over her from the black-and-white print as she had for twenty years.

This is the worst day of my life, Poppy thought.

She had experienced the death of loved ones before, but nothing had ever felt this damning. The sour taste in her mouth, the feeling of suspended time, the breaking of her heart. It was a struggle to breathe, to think. Her world was over; life as she had always known it had stopped. The only person who had loved her shamelessly, more than anyone else, was gone.

A man's voice drifted into the room. "Poppy?"

Poppy looked up and saw her father standing in the kitchen doorway. He looked deathly pale and unsettled, his eyes red with emotion. Standing behind him was Samantha, his longtime girlfriend. She looked even worse than he did.

"The detectives are here."

Poppy nodded, unable to say anything as her father turned away. She brushed a few red strands of hair out of her face, unsticking them from the paths her tears had left.

How in the world can this be happening, she thought as fresh tears fell on the newspaper, *and why?* Who in the world would want to murder her grandmother?

It has to be a mistake, she tried to tell herself. Roseanna Pruette was loved and known by everyone in the quaint hamlet of Miner's Way, Virginia. She was the mayor's mother, and took great pride in everyone's accomplishments. She'd been more like the entire town's grandmother than just Poppy's, which made her death all the more shocking.

There was a gentle knock at the doorway. Glancing up, she saw the familiar face of the sheriff. He had a white mustache that curled at the corners and bright green eyes, though today, they were clouded with blatant pity. Poppy had known Sheriff Roberts her entire life, and she wasn't surprised to see his red-rimmed eyes. He was younger than her grandmother, but Sheriff Roberts and Roseanna Pruette had been friends for as long as the Pruettes had lived in Miner's Way.

"Hello, Poppy," he said as he came into the room. He was followed by two young men she'd never seen before. The first was somewhat handsome, but looked uncomfortable, dressed in a cheaply made suit. The one behind him had large, sympathetic eyes and a mop of curly hair. "This is Detective Peirce and Detective Fields of the Michigan State Police. Detectives, this is Poppy Pruette."

Poppy nodded as she returned to look at the paper, ignoring her curiosity as to why the Michigan State Police were here. She didn't want to answer any questions. It had only happened a few hours ago.

No, she corrected herself. It had been the night before, sometime after her grandmother's birthday party. A neighbor found the body just before eleven o'clock.

Just enough time for it to make the press, she thought bitterly, tossing the newspaper aside.

A sinking feeling hit Poppy in the stomach as she remembered her grandmother's request to have lunch the next day. Poppy had said she'd already made plans to go shopping with a friend who was visiting. She'd known her grandmother was disappointed, but had shrugged it off, knowing she'd make it up to her.

I'll never make it up now, she thought, guilt weighing on her shattered heart.

She spun the ruby ring her grandmother had given her when she graduated high school. It was her favorite stone, almost identical in design to a rose quartz ring her grandmother wore.

Used to wear, she corrected herself again. The rose quartz ring was a family heirloom and had been passed down for almost a dozen generations. She turned her thoughts back to the present as memories of her grandmother retelling the old story threatened new tears.

"These men would like to ask you a few questions, Poppy," Sheriff Roberts said. "Do you think you could answer just a few?"

Poppy nodded slowly, not looking up. Her mind was suddenly busy replaying everything she'd ever done that had made her grandmother upset with her, like the time she cut all the prize-winning roses in the garden and had put them in vases around the house. She'd only been seven years old, and her grandmother had forgiven her long ago, but Poppy couldn't stop the fresh waves of guilt from washing over her.

The younger detective pulled out a chair from beneath the table and sat down.

"I'm Detective Peirce," he said.

Poppy looked up at him through blurry eyes and shifted instinctively back in her chair. She hadn't really looked when they'd walked in, but now that he sat directly before her, she could see a familiar translucent glow around him. She was used to noticing the auras of their kind, but she'd only ever seen them around blood relatives, not complete strangers. They only lasted a few moments before fading away to nothingness, and even as she watched Detective Peirce, his glow began to fade.

His eyes narrowed as he noticed her reaction, but he said nothing of it. "This is my partner, Detective Fields," Detective Peirce said in a gentle voice, nodding to the curly-haired man who stood behind him.

She shot a quick glance at the other detective and, seeing no aura, relaxed a little. *So, it's just you I have to worry about,* she thought, settling into defense mode. Her grandmother had always warned her to be cautious of those with visible auras, regardless of who they said they were.

"How are you feeling?"

"Destroyed," Poppy said harshly, hoping her message to him was clear: *I don't trust you or your partner, so back off.* "I'm *feeling* destroyed."

"Uh, Poppy," Sheriff Roberts chimed in, obviously taken aback by her attitude. "Detective Peirce is just trying to help."

"It's all right," Detective Peirce said, not taking his eyes from her. He patted his pockets. "Roberts, I seem to have left my cell phone in the cruiser. Can you grab it for me?"

Sheriff Roberts looked confused, but nodded.

"Sure thing." He paused before he left the room, adding, "Try to be nice, Poppy."

"Teddy, do you mind helping the Sheriff?"

Detective Fields barely nodded as he followed the sheriff out of the kitchen. Poppy didn't acknowledge either of them and continued to stare daggers at the detective before her.

"Your full name is Rose Poppy Pruette, but everyone calls you by your middle name," he said matter-of-factly, pulling out a notepad from his pocket. "Why is that?"

"I would get confused when I was younger. I spent a lot of time with my grandmother, so whenever anyone would call her Rose, I thought they were talking to me. I've been called Poppy since I was four."

"Interesting. Family name?"

Poppy glared at him before answering.

"It was my great-grandmother's name."

He nodded.

"Nineteen years old—oh, no, twenty. You just had a birthday." Poppy remained silent, so he continued. "Honors student and graduate of Miner's Way High School, member of the Junior Science Squad. The only child of Phoebe and Peter Pruette, Mayor of Miner's Way, and only grandchild of Roseanna Pruette. When you were four, your mother passed away in a car accident, and though your father has dated, he's never remarried. He has a longtime girlfriend, Samantha Gomez, whom you get along with, I assume?"

Detective Peirce had watched her the entire time without looking down at his notes. Poppy nodded, feeling increasingly uncomfortable with the fact he had memorized so much about her.

"You attend Washington and Lee University and have plans to go back there sooner than the fall semester because you're taking some summer classes, correct?"

She nodded again.

"You've had two serious boyfriends, one of which you've recently parted with, and the only person in the whole town who has anything negative to say about you is the retired janitor, Mr. Barr."

"Mr. Barr?" Poppy interjected, momentarily distracted. "He's senile, and he's never liked me, not since the third grade."

"Because you knocked over several paint cans in the hallway."

"That's wasn't me—wait." Poppy stopped suddenly. "Why do you know all of this?"

"I'm a detective, Poppy. It's my job to know all of this."

"To know that I spilled a couple of paint cans a hundred years ago?" she retorted. "Don't you think that's excessive?"

"You said it wasn't you who did it."

She fell silent, scowling. The hint of a smile played over Detective Peirce's face, and her eyes narrowed further. She decided she didn't like him at all.

"Is there something you wanted to ask me about my grandmother, or are you just here to recite my life story?" she asked coolly. His smiled vanished.

"Who wants you dead?" he asked frankly.

Poppy was taken aback for a moment.

"No one," she said quietly, confused by the question.

"No one that you know of," he said. "But I don't believe your grandmother was the intended victim last night. I don't think she was supposed to die—at least, not first."

Poppy stared. "What do you mean, 'not first'?"

"I think you were."

The growing knot in her stomach twisted. Why would he think she was supposed to be the victim? His aura had disappeared completely, making her even more uncomfortable. It was easier to stay on her guard when his aura was visible . . . without the reminder, he could be just any normal detective. She changed the subject and spoke directly, as she usually did when she was nervous.

"Why are you here?"

"To investigate this murder—"

"No, why are *you* here?" she interrupted. "You two aren't detectives in this town. Why does my grandmother's murder matter to *you*?"

Realization passed over his face.

"So, you know who I am?" he asked slowly.

"I know *what* you are, not who you are," she corrected. "But it wouldn't matter if you told me or not. I would expect someone like us to lie. And even if you did tell the truth, our kind are never what they seem." She paused, looking down at her grandmother's picture, amazed that she seemed to remember every detail of her warnings and wisdom now that she was dead. It was like every conversation they'd ever had was under a magnifying glass.

"Do you know who you are?" Detective Peirce asked, tilting his head in a surprisingly condescending way. "Who you're connected to?"

She bristled at his tone. "I know which story involves a grandmother being attacked," Poppy said, doing her best to give him her I'm-not-an-idiot look, but as she said the words, her confidence faltered. "We're from the Hood line; that's what my grandmother called it, at least. She told me this wouldn't happen, though. That we had an arrangement, and this wouldn't happen."

That got Detective Peirce's attention.

"You've got protection?" he asked. His face was stern and serious, which only added to his naturally handsome features. His dirty-blond, light brown hair was cut and styled to perfection; his strong, square jaw and bright hazel-green eyes reminded her of a generic good-looking guy, but the severity of his disposition made him look every bit the authority figure.

Being a detective suited him.

"You didn't tell me who you were," she said, ignoring his follow-up question.

"Who did you receive protection from?" he countered.

Poppy realized that he wasn't going to answer her until he'd learned everything he could. Folding her arms across her chest, she leaned back, challenging him. Two could play that game.

After a few moments of staring her down, Detective Peirce relented.

"Prince Charming, from the Charming line," he said quietly, his tone distasteful.

Poppy raised her eyebrows, unconvinced.

"Look, I don't care if you believe me or not, but you can Google me if you want."

"Prince Charming?" she asked sarcastically.

"No, the Peirce family of New York City. I'm all over the Internet."

"So? Is your family's popularity supposed to vouch for you?"

Detective Peirce looked surprised, and Poppy was amazed at how much younger he looked when his tough exterior was down. Of course, just as quickly as he had dropped his facade, it was back.

"No, but it should serve as a background check," he said, a hint of something she couldn't quite place in his voice. "And that isn't why I'm here."

"You mean you'd still be here if I wasn't who I was?" she asked in disbelief. "I doubt it."

"I would be," he said.

"Not likely."

"Look, I'm here to investigate a murder. That's my job. If you have an issue with who I am, you're going to need to get over it, because I have to find out who killed Rose Pruette." He caught himself as her eyes widened at his bluntness. "I'm sorry, I didn't mean to be insensitive."

"Yes, you did," she answered. "Because, like you said, it's just your job. My grandmother wasn't anyone to you, but she was someone to me. She was someone to a lot of people in this town, and now you're rattling her off like some victim in a *Law and Order* episode?" Poppy stood up abruptly, making her chair scratch sharply across the floor. "Are we finished?"

"Far from it," he said, standing as well.

She muttered something rude under her breath and walked around the kitchen island to the pot of coffee she'd made an hour earlier. This nightmare had begun at six this morning, when her father woke her with the news. Her grandmother's body had been found in her driveway by a neighbor who'd been getting up to go to work. Her father had avoided most of the details, but she'd learned enough: her grandmother had been trying to get away, and had made it as far as the end of her driveway before collapsing.

Poppy closed her eyes as her mouth began to taste of cold metal, and she tried to fight down the nausea. She'd been sick in the sink earlier, after learning even that much, while her father's assistant, Rupert Powers, had held her long hair back. Rupert had known about the murder before her father—as he usually knew most things first. That's what assistants were for, she guessed, but Rupert was more than an assistant—he was part of the family, like a close cousin, since she didn't have any.

She had a ridiculous vision of an awkward Detective Peirce holding back her hair should she be sick again and took a shuddering breath. Absolutely not.

She spun the ruby ring on her finger to distract herself.

"Her ring," she said suddenly. Sheriff Roberts had given them a bag of everything found on the body, but she couldn't remember seeing the ring.

"Sorry?" Detective Peirce said, puzzled.

"Was there a ring found—" She choked on the next words before getting out, ". . . on the body?"

He glanced over his notepad and shook his head. "No mention of a ring."

"It's a little sterling silver ring set with a rose quartz crystal. She . . . my grandmother never took it off. It should have been there." She realized she'd rambled that off rather quickly and bit her lip.

Detective Peirce gave her a sympathetic look and she shook her head sharply. She didn't need his sympathy.

"Never mind." She turned back to the coffee.

The house had been crowded ever since six, and as Poppy made herself a third cup, she realized she hadn't left the room once. Maybe she hoped that if she didn't leave this room, she wouldn't have to enter a world where her grandmother didn't exist anymore.

"Do you want coffee, Detective?" she asked loudly, trying to quiet her thoughts.

"Sure, thanks. You can call me Owen, by the way," he said, coming to the other side of the kitchen island.

"Okay . . . Owen." Poppy poured him a cup of coffee, added a spoon of sugar, and stirred. She handed it to him as she pulled out one of the white stools beneath the island. Everything in the kitchen was white and stainless steel. She'd always thought it was a bit nautical for a country kitchen, but her mother had designed it, and they would never change it.

"How'd you know I take my coffee black with one sugar?" Owen asked, looking at his cup.

She stared at him a moment. "I don't know," she answered honestly. "It's how I make mine."

He quirked a brow, but didn't answer. The silence stretched as they stared across the island at one another, drinking coffee.

Finally, she said, "So, you don't think it's someone like us? Or you do? I honestly don't know what you were getting at before, so let's not beat around the bush."

Owen tilted his head. "You seem pretty comfortable with all this," he said, a hint of suspicion in his voice. "I mean, knowing who you're related to."

"I've always known," she said as she shrugged. "My grandmother has been telling the story since I was born. She said there were others, but we had nothing to worry about."

"Because you were protected?"

"Because she met the Vanns," Poppy said, sidestepping his question.

It was true. Poppy's grandmother had told her that she'd sought out protection when she was a young woman, but that was sort of a family secret. They never discussed it, but once, when her grandmother was sick a year earlier. When her grandmother recovered, they never mentioned it again.

"Your grandmother met the Vanns?" Owen asked.

"Yes, years ago. She wanted to meet them, since a member of their family murdered a member of ours all those years ago, but they weren't too interested in bringing up old memories. Grandma said we needn't worry about them." She paused for a moment, taking a sip of her coffee, and looked pointedly at Owen. "Was she wrong?"

"No," Owen said. "The Vanns aren't involved, I can assure you of that."

"How?"

Her lack of faith seemed to bother him.

"Because I know them personally," he said, annoyed. "Their son, William, helped me with a case about a year ago."

"A murder?"

"A kidnapping."

"Oh," Poppy said. "You sure get interesting cases. Why'd you need his help?" She kind of liked doing the questioning and seeing him grow restless.

"Because it was a delicate case for our kind . . . "

"So you *do* get assigned to cases involving our kind."

He shifted his weight and scowled. "No. That was special. So is this case. I don't *just* get assigned to these, though." His tone went back to one of stern authority. "We aren't discussing that. I need to know about *you*."

"You don't think the person who did this to my grandmother is like us?"

"No," he said. "That's what worries me."

"Why?"

"Because we're dealing with someone who's off our radar. When something happens to someone in our world, we usually know all the facts. This is different. I believe that this person didn't intend to murder your grandmother. This person wanted you, and I can't figure out why."

A sudden low, buzzing noise filled the room. Owen reached into his pocket and took out a phone. Poppy lifted an eyebrow as he read the name and ignored the call, placing it back in his pocket. *Hadn't he left his phone in the car?* He caught her eye and immediately looked away, clearing his throat.

Sheriff Roberts walked in then, followed by her father.

"I couldn't find your phone in the cruiser, Peirce," Sheriff Roberts said.

"That's all right," Owen said smoothly. "I found it. In my pocket the whole time, can you imagine that?"

Poppy snorted and all eyes turned to look at her. She sipped her coffee innocently and refused to meet anyone's gaze. No one else saw how obvious it was that he'd wanted to talk to her alone? This was something she would have to talk about later with her grandmother, and laugh at how mindless some people could be. Another crack split in her heart when she realized that she would never get the chance. Her grandmother was gone. Loneliness flooded her heart as Owen stood up and spoke with Roberts.

"Honey." Her father put a hand on her shoulder. "How are you doing?"

"Fine," she said, barely keeping her next words from spilling out. *Don't call me honey.* She didn't want Owen looking at her like a little kid.

What does it matter how he looks at you? she scolded herself silently. What was wrong with her? The man was here investigating her grandmother's *murder*, and she was worried about looking mature? She was thankful at that moment that people couldn't read her thoughts.

"I'm fine," she repeated. "Where's Samantha?"

"She ran out to grab some food," he said. "She's a bit of a wreck."

"Well, they were pretty close," Poppy said, swallowing hard. Samantha had come into their lives about five years ago, during her father's first run for mayor. Her grandmother had taken an instant liking to her, glad that her son had finally moved on. Poppy had taken longer. Her grandmother was the reason Poppy and Samantha had grown close at all. "Have they learned anything else?"

Her father didn't answer right away, but looked back at Sheriff Roberts. It was then she realized the sheriff was wearing plastic gloves, holding what looked like a note in one hand and a flower in the other. Owen reached into his pocket and pulled out a plastic glove. He put it on and carefully took the piece of paper from Roberts to read it.

"What is it?" Poppy asked, her eyes locked on the flower. It was a rose, blood red and beautiful. She reached for it and frowned when Roberts pulled back.

"That's from my grandmother's greenhouse," she said.

"Yes," Roberts said, his tone serious. "We just found it with a note."

"At the crime scene?" her father asked.

"No," Roberts said, looking a little flabbergasted. His eyes settled on Poppy. "We found it on the property. It was stuck under the windshield wiper of your silver Nissan."

"My *car*?" Poppy exclaimed. "What does it say? Who is it from?"

"There's no name," Owen said without hesitation.

"You mean to tell me that a note and a rose cut from my mother's greenhouse was just discovered on my daughter's car and no one saw who did it?" her father burst out angrily.

"It could have been there for hours, Peter," Roberts suggested.

"This is ridiculous," he retorted. "What does it say?"

Poppy felt goose bumps cover her skin and her eyes locked on Owen. He looked up from the note and held it up for her. She grabbed for it, but he shook his head.

"Fingerprints," he said.

She took a deep breath as he held the note in front of her so she could read the elegant cursive writing:

Roses are dead.

Fear seized her as she stared at the words. She caught herself as she staggered backward, trying to breathe through the sudden feeling that a hand clenched her throat.

"Poppy?" Her father steadied her, his tone alarmed.

"Roses are red; poppies are, too. All save one; that in the forest grew," she murmured, forgetting the others for a moment.

"What?" Owen asked after a brief pause.

"My grandmother used to recite that to me," she said dully as her father read the note. The murderer had taken a line from the poem she'd heard her entire life and twisted it into something sinister and ugly.

Poppy felt ill.

"Do you need to sit down?" her father asked, his voice tight.

Poppy shook her head.

"Maybe you should," Roberts said.

"No. No, I'm fine," she said without conviction. Owen was staring at her intently when she looked up again. "The murderer wrote that."

"That's an assumption," Owen said.

"Her name is . . . was Roseanna. Everyone called her Rose for short. We're Roses. And you said the murderer was after me."

"Wait," her father interrupted. "This bastard is after Poppy, too?"

Owen hesitated, struggling with an answer.

Her father glared between Sheriff Roberts and the detective. "Well?"

"In my opinion . . . " Owen paused, giving them a serious look. "And this is not on record, but in my opinion, Poppy may be in serious trouble."

They all stared at him for a few seconds before her father erupted.

"That's it! *Rupert*!" he shouted. "She's leaving!"

"What?" Poppy said, turning to look at her father.

"Yes, sir?" Rupert said as he entered the kitchen. He was a tall young man, who moved with surprising grace considering he was a little on the heavier side.

"Dad, what are you doing?" Poppy asked.

"Poppy's leaving town for a while," her father said, ignoring her. "Arrange it, and tell no one."

"Yes, sir," Rupert said, a blur of jet black hair as he weaved effortlessly from the room.

"Dad, I'm not leaving."

"Yes, you are," he said.

"No, I'm not. I can't leave you here," she argued.

"I'm not arguing it, Poppy," he spoke over her. "You're leaving, and that's final."

"But, Dad—"

Her father turned to face her suddenly, both hands landing on her shoulders.

"I can't, Poppy—I won't . . . " he said, visibly choking up. "I'm not going to lose you, too. Not after your mother, and now your grandmother."

Owen broke in before she could answer.

"Sir, if I may, I don't think taking Poppy out of the only home she's ever known is such a good idea."

"This isn't our only home," Poppy's father snapped. He stopped himself and took a deep breath. "I'm sorry, Detective Peirce. I'm going to do what I think is best for my daughter."

"Which is send me away?" Poppy fumed. "I'm not leaving. School starts in a few weeks, and I don't feel comfortable leaving you here alone."

"School can wait until September, Poppy. As for now, you'll go to Windgate—"

"Windgate? I'm not going to Connecticut!"

"Yes, you are."

"No, I'm not," she said through gritted teeth. Rupert came back in, phone to his ear.

"It's not up for argument, Poppy. You'll stay up there with Rupert—"

"Rupert isn't my bodyguard!"

"I'm not fighting you on this. You're going to Windgate, and that's final. I'll be up there in a few weeks. We'll arrange protection. Rupert? Get on that."

"Yes, sir," Rupert nodded.

"This is insane," Poppy said, frantically trying to come up with a better solution. "I'm twenty years old. You can't just ship me around—"

Owen interrupted suddenly.

"Sheriff, call the station. I want that note in forensics as soon as possible. Mr. Pruette? Can I speak with you in private?"

Her father glanced between them before nodding and following Sheriff Roberts from the room. With a backwards glance, Owen gave Poppy an encouraging nod. For a fleeting moment, she forgot everything else and trusted that nod. He would talk sense into her father, make him see he couldn't send her away, not now.

Grandma wouldn't let him . . .

Poppy squeezed her eyes shut to stop the thought. For a second, she'd forgotten, and now she felt the crushing weight of reality settling around her again.

She was alone. Truly alone.

CHAPTER TWO

Roseanna Pruette was laid to rest on Wednesday morning, which brought with it a light drizzle. Though it was a warm summer shower, Poppy felt frozen. She rode in silence in the middle of a police escort with her father, watching the empty streets of Miner's Way roll by. Most everyone in the little town was in attendance, following them from the church to the cemetery. She dreaded the thought of witnessing the burial, so she let her mind settle on other things equally angering and desperate.

She'd won the argument to stay long enough for the funeral, but barely. While her father had talked with Owen for long hours into the night over what the best procedure would be, the outcome was not at all to her liking. As far as everyone in town was concerned, she'd be leaving tomorrow to go back to Washington and Lee, starting her summer classes. The trusted inner circle of her father, Samantha, Sheriff Roberts, and Rupert knew she'd really be traveling to Windgate, the family cottage on the coast of Connecticut. Her father had gladly accepted that Detectives Peirce and Fields would be her escorts and bodyguards, and the exhausting yelling match she'd had with him after she'd found out had done nothing to change that. She'd be under constant supervision in Windgate until the murderer was apprehended.

"There isn't anyone better for the job, honey," her father had said. "Detective Peirce knows our kind, and knows more than anyone what kind of people we're dealing with." Poppy rolled her eyes at the memory, not wanting to admit to even herself the small comfort she'd felt at the idea she'd have someone of their kind with her, even if she didn't trust him.

They arrived at the cemetery, and Poppy got out of the car slowly, not really focusing on anyone or anything as the crowd moved to the designated family plot. She let her eyes wander over the many faces. Most she knew as locals from town; those she didn't recognize, she knew not to trust.

She'd seen their auras the moment they'd arrived at the church earlier, blended together in a muted haze. There was an old woman who looked vaguely like her grandmother and who hadn't stopped crying since the church service; a gangly, older gentleman who looked rather sick; and a man her father's age who kept rubbing his face, attempting to mask the occasional tic. She'd stay away from them—family or no, they were strangers to her. Some had to be related to Rose, as the faint auras that hung above their heads glowed softly in a odd, muddied mix without color. Poppy wondered if this was due to their feelings. Maybe auras changed with emotion. It didn't matter though, as Poppy was wary of her grandmother's advice regarding trust and anyone with an aura.

Her eyes moved past the relatives and swam over the rest, unable to stop herself from wondering if someone here had done it. It was a gruesome thought, but one she couldn't avoid. It was Owen's theory, after all; it had to be someone close to the family to know of her grandmother's poem. The note had been with the police department since it was found, but Poppy hoped she'd be able to get it back once they had dusted for fingerprints. She wasn't sure why she wanted the horrible piece of evidence, but wanted it she did.

The minister began his sermon just as the rain let up. Poppy guessed there were over two hundred people in attendance, plenty of suspects to consider. A sea of people dressed in black, and Poppy could name almost every single one of them. A man caught her eye as she looked over the crowd, standing next to one of the cemetery's old oak trees. She rolled her eyes when she realized it was Owen, shoulders stiff and chin up, looking tense even from where she stood.

Owen shifted, and his eyes locked with hers. He nodded curtly and her stomach flipped as she realized she'd been staring. She turned back to the minister, feeling guilty. About what, she didn't know, but Poppy hadn't stopped feeling guilty since this nightmare began.

The burial lasted about an hour while Poppy tried to block out the constant pats on her shoulders from the people who sat behind her, handing her tissues. She had cried so much in the past few days she seemed to be all out of tears. She hoped no one noticed that she wasn't crying; then again, neither was her father. She stole a glance at him. He looked statuesque next to her, as if he was trying to be as motionless and cold as the cherubs that posed on the headstone next to his mother's grave. Poppy looked forward and tried to imitate him. Maybe everyone would think lack of public emotion was a family trait, and not just that she was heartless.

Her mind started to race. *Calm down*, she told herself. She was retreating into her mind and worrying about what everyone around her was thinking. It was exhausting, and another unfortunate habit that did her no good.

A warmth crawled up her neck and cheeks. Her throat suddenly felt as if it was full of stones, making it difficult to breathe. She closed her eyes, trying desperately to calm herself down by breathing steadily. This was beyond any feeling she had ever experienced. An irrational fear crept through her, and for a moment, she felt she would either faint or die. . . .

What am I afraid of?

The thought hit her just before the wave of terror reached its peak and she remembered how to breathe. The stones loosened and she swallowed gratefully, realizing her whole body was shaking.

For several minutes, she kept her eyes tightly shut, desperate to return to a normal state of mind. She jumped slightly when her father touched her arm, letting her know the service was over. Opening her eyes, she let him pull her to her feet, and together, they placed their roses on the casket. Her legs were steady again as she lined up with her father and Samantha to shake the hands of parting attendees. She was more than a little relieved—she didn't want to appear weak to anyone here.

These traditions are silly, she thought as people filed past. They'd shaken hands at the church, now here, and almost everyone was coming to the house afterward anyway.

Poppy felt like she had been standing for hours when she saw the last person in the line. She smiled as her oldest friend, Sean McCray, gave her a hug.

"Hey," he said softly. "How are you doing?"

"Fine," she answered automatically, as she had a thousand times that day. No one really wanted to know how she felt.

"Don't lie to me," Sean said in his light Southern accent.

Poppy gave him a half smile. Sean had been her best friend since he moved from Georgia to Miner's Way in the sixth grade. He'd graduated high school and moved to New York to pursue a degree in criminal justice—like his father and his grandfather—but Poppy also knew he was trying to become an actor. It was a pretty big secret, since Sean's family was very traditional in a Southern sense, but not nearly as important as the fact that Sean was gay, though no one suspected it. He'd had girlfriends throughout high school and didn't have much trouble hiding his sexuality. He was Southern, after all, and from a pretty prominent family. One's sexual orientation was talked about as much as polar bears, which wasn't often, as one might think.

He had come out to only two people as far as Poppy knew, and she was one of them. The other was his older sister, Carrie, who lived in Austin, Texas, with her husband. Poppy and Sean had been inseparable through most of high school. Sean was a throwback, Poppy always thought, a Southern gentleman in a modern time. She'd always chalked it up to his love of writers like Tennessee Williams and Margaret Mitchell, as he imitated the smoky warmth and pride that radiated in the hazy South. Poppy enjoyed the thought of Sean drinking a glass of scotch with William Faulkner, though he hated hard liquor and often commented it would be a snowy day in Savannah if he was ever caught in an ivory-colored suit. Before he left for New York, Poppy had told him that he would be a wonderful actor and had noted the sad look in his eyes that told her he had been acting his whole life.

"I'm miserable," she said quietly as Sean took her arm.

Her father was speaking to the minister, and he nodded at Sean as they began to walk toward the cars. The wind blew and Poppy felt a shiver down her spine, suddenly feeling as if she was being watched. She sighed moodily as she remembered Owen, probably following close behind them. She shook off her worry as Sean guided her down the slope that led to the parking lot.

"It's awful," Sean said as they walked. "I just got in this morning, otherwise I would have been here sooner."

"I know," she said quietly. "Don't worry about it, though. This is the first minute of privacy I've had since Sunday."

"I can imagine," he said. "Poor Aunt Rose."

Poppy smiled sadly. Sean had been scolded the first time he'd met her grandmother for calling her Mrs. Pruette, and she had insisted he call her Aunt Rose. Her grandmother had often said that there was something special about Sean. "He's a good soul, that one," she'd said fondly. Poppy wondered if she'd known his secret all along.

Shaking her head, she yearned to talk about something else.

"How's New York?" she said, sighing heavily. "Warmer, I hope?"

This made Sean smile. "It is not my fault that the one and only time you came to New York was in January," he said. "It's beautiful in the spring."

"You sound smitten."

"You know I love the South," he said, eyebrows raised. "But New York is my home away from home. You should come stay with me sometime soon. This summer, maybe?"

"I'd love to," she said happily. Her heart sank seconds later when she remembered her current situation. "I can't."

"Why not?"

"Because," a male voice said, surprising them both, "Poppy is returning to school early this year."

Poppy glared at Owen like a mortal enemy. *Who in the world does he think he is, listening in on a private conversation?*

When he saw her reaction, Sean's grip tightened slightly and he stood a little straighter. Poppy noticed the fake but pleasant smile Sean often gave people he didn't like. He'd always had too much class to look anything less than in control.

"Hello," Sean said, stretching out his free arm to shake Owen's hand. "Sean McCray. Nice to meet you."

"Owen Peirce," Owen said, shaking Sean's hand. "Same here."

The contrast between the two was like night and day. Sean was always impeccably dressed, with his well-kept, dark chestnut hair and dark eyes. He always had a smile on his face—whether it was sincere or not depended on the company. His Southern drawl wasn't so strong that he sounded like a cartoon character, but was just enough to demonstrate where he was from. Owen, on the other hand, was the exact opposite. With his dirty-blond, light brown hair and sharp hazel-green eyes, he looked disheveled and tired. Handsome or not, Poppy noticed that his mannerisms seemed forced, as if he had learned them only to imitate them.

"And I'm about ready to go home," Poppy said, not bothering to hide her aggravation. "Sean, will you take me?"

"Sure."

"I'm afraid that's not going to happen," Owen said. "Poppy needs a police escort—"

"I don't need one," she snapped, stepping away from Sean. "Stop it. I can ride with Sean. It's fine."

They stared daggers at each other before he turned around abruptly and walked away. Surprised that her words had actually worked, she felt a little underwhelmed as she turned back to Sean.

"Rude, wasn't he?" Sean said, watching Owen as he walked away. "But . . . whoa, he's attractive. Have I seen him somewhere before?"

"Attractive?" Poppy said bluntly. "What are you, crazy?"

"If I know anything, Poppy, it's an attractive guy, and we all almost just died from the tension between you two. What was that?"

Poppy rolled her eyes.

"You're as mad as a hatter," she said as they walked to his car.

"And you're as blind as a bat."

Sean was out of his mind if he thought there was anything but a battle of willpower between her and Owen. There certainly wasn't any sort of chemistry there, especially when all she felt for him was annoyance.

They had just reached the older model black Cadillac that Sean's grandfather had given him as a graduation gift when they heard her father call out.

"Poppy!" he yelled, halting her in her tracks. "Stop right there."

She turned around and saw her father walking down the slope toward her, followed by Rupert and, to her fury, Owen.

"I haven't heard him call you like that since we were kids," Sean said, slightly amused as they stomped closer.

"You'll be going with Detective Peirce back to the house," her father said, stopping before her.

"Why?"

"You know why," her father said. "I'm sorry, Sean."

"Not a problem, Mr. Pruette."

"Dad—"

"Not right now, Poppy." Her father gave her a stern look. "See you at the house, Sean."

"Yes, sir," Sean said, winking at Poppy as he got into his car.

If Poppy had pulled all her memories of anger into one pool, it wouldn't equal what she felt in that moment as she stormed toward the police cruiser.

"You arrogant jerk," she hissed at Owen as she got into the passenger side. "Do you know who that was?"

"A suspect?" Owen answered calmly as he started the car.

"A suspect! That was Sean McCray, son of Garrett McCray, of McCray and Sterns law firm! They're the most well-respected family in the county, not to mention Sean is my best friend."

"I know the McCrays," Owen said. "And I know he's your best friend, but I'm not in the business of pleasantries. I'm in the business of keeping you safe."

"I can look out for myself, thanks, and I trust Sean a hell of a lot more than I trust you. Besides, it's common courtesy, something you obviously know nothing about!"

"You're right. I'm not too interested in that either."

"You son of a—"

"I thought Southern belles had a better handle on their vocabulary."

White-hot anger flared within her. *What kind of antebellum mindset is this guy in?* "Who the hell do you think you are?" she shouted. "Insulting me and my friend, making a fool out of me in front of everyone at every chance you get—"

Owen stomped on the brakes, causing her to jolt forward.

"First off, put your seatbelt on. Second, I'm the guy keeping you alive, Poppy Pruette," he said hotly as he turned on her. "In case you forgot, there's a person out there who wants you dead, and I'm sorry if you find me and my ways rude or disrespectful, but that's not my problem. I take my job seriously, and if it means ruffling your feathers a bit, I'm not too worried about it, as long as you come out alive on the other end. Now, you may not like me, and honestly, I don't think I'm going to like you all that much either, but I'm not going to have you kicking and screaming at every turn. I don't care how well you know the people in this town, because the killer knows you better. So quit acting like I'm trying to ruin your life when I'm trying to protect it."

Her anger bubbled like boiling tar and a slight ringing filled her ears. She opened and closed her mouth without making a sound as outrage was replaced with fury, then shame, then fear, and then anger again. It was like mixing every emotional ingredient into one large pot.

To her mortification, her eyes teared up. She hated when this happened. It was a ridiculous reaction to being too flustered to speak, and she struggled to stay calm. All she could do was let out a frustrated breath as she looked away.

Owen instantly softened.

"Look," he began, but his phone buzzed. "Damn it, hold on."

He shifted his weight, reaching for the phone in his front pocket. He seemed agitated when he read the caller's name and ignored it, putting it down beneath the car stereo. Poppy read the name as the ignored call flashed across the screen before going black:

Ajax

Owen inhaled and was about to continue speaking, but she held up her hand to prevent him.

"Stop," she said shortly, trying to even her breathing. After several moments of inhaling through her nose and exhaling out her mouth, she spoke. "I know you are only here for my protection, but I'm on a bit of an emotional roller coaster right now, so if I snap at you, don't take it personally. . . . I just wish this was all a bad dream."

"Wishing is a dangerous hobby."

She glanced at him sharply, every fiber of her buzzing. "What?"

He gave her a sad smile. "I know this must be difficult."

"You know nothing about it," she snapped, still thrown by his all-too-familiar comment. "My grandmother was the only person in this world I ever connected to. She loved me more than anything, even more than my father. I know it's going to sound terrible, and I won't be able to say it the right way, but I was everything to her. That may sound incredibly conceited, but if she were here right now, she'd tell you the same thing. And when someone loves you like that, there's no other comfort in the world like it. But now, she's not here, and I'm not myself anymore. So if I yell and fight you, know that I'm not me. I don't know who I am right now."

Owen watched her for a moment before nodding as he began to drive again. She hadn't wanted to say that to him— she hadn't wanted to tell him anything important, but it was all she had. She felt numb, and doubted there was a soul in the world that understood. Who could? Her greatest friend had been her grandmother, which might have been pathetic in some way, but it was the truth. It was just one of those things.

And on top of processing her grandmother's death, she had to worry about a murderer after her, which just sounded like something out of a movie. She was no longer herself. How in the world was she going to do this?

Poppy didn't notice they'd reached the house until Owen opened her door. She felt oddly content walking beside him as they made their way through the crowd assembled all over the property, from the car-filled driveway, to the smokers on the porch, to the friends in the foyer. Everyone tried to smile and make small talk.

"Feel better, Poppy," an old teacher said, patting her on the back.

"Sleep well," her elderly neighbor said, his light eyes flashing sympathy.

She tried to utter the same routine responses she'd used all day, only her voice seemed to have stopped working. Owen stepped ahead, guiding her through the house and up the stairs as a hush came over the crowd behind them. They were watching her, thinking about her, pitying her, but she didn't care. She had released her first bit of real emotion on Owen and felt completely exhausted in return.

She pointed at her room as they walked the hallway and he opened the door, stepping in before her. As she stood silently near the bed, Owen checked the room. She nearly laughed. It was frightening to think she now needed rooms checked for her. He nodded at her when it was cleared, closing the door as he left her alone. She sat to take off her shoes, barely able to think anymore.

Poppy lay back on top of the covers, ignoring the hushed voices outside her door, and fell quickly into a much-needed sleep.

CHAPTER THREE

Owen closed the door with a quiet click behind him, stopping Mr. Pruette, Samantha, and, to his annoyance, Sean, as they came up the stairs.

"How is she?" Mr. Pruette asked, looking over Owen's shoulder at the bedroom door. "Is she all right?"

"She's fine, sir. Just tired, I think," Owen said. "She's just . . ." He wanted to use the word "broken," but thought better of it. "Very tired."

Mr. Pruette looked longingly at the door.

"I'm just so worried about her," he said. "She and my mother were very close."

"Yes, she told me."

"Did she?" he asked, a hint of hope in his voice. "I'm glad. She holds things in so much that I worry about her. She shut down after her mother's death. The only person who could ever get her to open up about things was my mother. She's okay, though?"

"Yes," Owen reassured him. "I would be surprised if she wasn't sleeping already."

"Okay, then. I'll head back down."

"Are you hungry or thirsty?" Samantha asked, her kind brown eyes looking hopeful to help. "A cup of coffee, maybe?"

"No, ma'am. I'm fine."

"Well, let me know if you need anything," she said as she turned to leave, following Mr. Pruette.

"I'm just going to talk to the detective for a minute," Sean said as they headed downstairs.

"Oh, all right, but quickly," Mr. Pruette said. "And quietly."

"Yes, sir," Sean said with a smile.

Owen stifled a groan as Mr. Pruette left. He knew Sean wasn't a threat, but he still didn't want to be bothered.

"Owen, was it?" Sean asked.

"Yes."

"Owen Peirce?"

The faint upward inflection in his tone made Owen stand a little straighter.

"Yes," he repeated.

"The same Owen Peirce who was in the *New York Star* a few years ago?"

Great, Owen thought. "Yes, why?"

Sean smiled. "I thought you looked familiar." He shook his head. "What are you doing here?"

"My job. Now, was that all?"

"Of course, I didn't mean to bother you. I'm just worried about her," Sean said, his fascination melting away to genuine concern. "She's not good, is she?"

"No," Owen said, a note of finality in his tone. Sean may be Poppy's best friend, but Owen didn't know him and wasn't in the mood to be polite. Sean took the hint and left, his eyebrows raised.

When he was out of sight, Owen leaned back against the bedroom door and slid down, placing his elbows on his knees as he rubbed his hands over his tired face. He had been up since daybreak, watching Poppy's every move, which was more difficult than he'd realized.

For someone who had a killer after her, she certainly didn't seem too concerned.

Not fair, he thought to himself. From her brief description of her relationship with her grandmother, Owen had gotten the sense that nothing else really seemed to matter to her at the moment.

He thought of his own grandmother and how he would feel if she was suddenly gone, but the thought had barely formed before he had reminded himself of what his grandmother thought of him. They had been on the outs for at least five years, ever since he'd decided to skip out on his last year of college to attend the police academy instead. She'd said it was nonsense to try and distort his fate by becoming a cop, but he hadn't cared at the time. He still didn't.

But his family had been right in the sense that he could never fully escape who he was. Only a year after joining the force, he had attempted to arrest his best friend, Roderick, a descendant of one of the Others, as they were known in his world. There were the Good, like him, and the Others, like Roderick and William Vann.

He shook his head. William hadn't turned out to be quite as bad as he'd thought, though he was a descendant of the Vann family, or the Big Bad Wolf line, as they were otherwise known. Yet, it was because of William that, after three years at the NYPD, he had been transferred out of state. Of course, things like that didn't just happen. NYPD cops weren't transferred out of state, and yet, by some twist of fate, he had found himself in Michigan, in the same town where his grandmother's best friend lived with her husband and their granddaughter, Hanna Loch.

Owen shook his head. William hadn't been the real reason, since it was the Hertzes who had attacked and kidnapped Hanna, but Owen had still had a hard time accepting that William Vann wasn't a bad guy. It went against everything he had ever been taught about their world, but he had been wrong before, and he had been wrong when it came to William, much to his continued annoyance.

It had all been too perfect, too much of a coincidence that he'd be placed so close to someone like himself, and the minute he'd picked up William for his expired license, he'd known that his grandmother had somehow managed to send him there to watch over Hanna, though it still baffled him how she'd known a Vann was going to be in Michigan at all.

He shook his head, trying not to think about it. It was almost too confusing to comprehend, and he had lived through it, only to once again be summoned to some godforsaken town in the middle of nowhere to help another of his own.

His phone vibrated in his pocket. Pulling it out, he saw Teddy's number.

"Hello," he answered in a tone that suggested he was anything but tired.

"It's me. I need you down at the car. I have a lead on Roberts."

Owen had had Teddy do a background check on everyone in Miner's Way, including the local law enforcement.

"I'll be right there," he said, hanging up and struggling to stand. His legs fought to stay still for a few moments longer, and he winced as he stretched them out.

With one last look at Poppy's door, he ventured downstairs, where he met Mr. Pruette talking to a group of older men in suits, each with tiny flag pins attached to their lapels.

Politicians.

"Is there something wrong?" Mr. Pruette asked when he saw Owen.

"No, sir. I just have to check in with my partner." Owen glanced at the men surrounding the bottom of the stairs and looked back up to the second floor. "I know this is probably the wrong time," he said, his voice hushed as he attempted to speak only to Mr. Pruette, "but I don't want anyone going up these steps until I get back."

"No," Mr. Pruette said. "No one will. I'll have Sean see to it."

"Not Sean," Owen said, trying to keep the annoyance from his voice. "I know you probably have to mingle, but—"

"I'll stay," Mr. Pruette said quickly. "I can protect my own daughter."

Owen nodded and walked away, careful not to insinuate anything.

Squeezing through the crowded doorway, Owen felt an uneasy pull in his chest. If his instincts were correct, the killer was there, somewhere between the tears and peach cobbler pies neighbors kept bringing into the house. Owen hated large crowds, had hated them his entire life. There were always too many secrets being told behind cupped hands. It made him distrustful of everyone, especially now, when there were a handful of family members from the Hood line hanging around.

Looking around as he headed across the yard, he saw small knots of people. A few more politicians, speaking with one another while pointing at the house. A handful of children, bobbing and weaving in between the guests, too young to understand that funerals were a time for quiet reflection. An elderly woman Owen had observed at the burial was crying openly as she turned away from a balding man whose back was turned. Owen's eyes lingered on her for a moment as her aura wavered, almost like a candle about to flicker out. *Grief does strange things to people like us*, he thought as he crossed the street.

Teddy had parked their unmarked Dodge Charger on the opposite side of the road a few houses down. He was an average-sized man, with dark eyes, curly hair, and a friendly smile, though Owen had witnessed firsthand the lightning-quick change in Teddy's demeanor when situations got sticky.

They had been partners for four months after Owen had been promoted to detective and moved to Lansing. They had worked on only two cases before being called on by the State Police of Virginia for Rose's murder. Teddy had questioned him the entire flight to Dulles Airport; he didn't understand why or how they had been tapped to figure out a murder in another state. Thankfully, he was a tireless man when it came to his job, and Owen had given him so much work that he had held off on most of his questioning, for now. He handed Owen a coffee as he reached the car.

"What have you got?" Owen asked, taking a sip of his coffee.

"Sheriff Roberts was involved in a payoff cover-up a few years back," Teddy said, handing Owen a few papers. "Turns out, he was having an affair with a married woman—a legal assistant. Her husband was a contractor and found out.

Things got pretty heated for a while—Roberts threatened to get the husband thrown in jail on trumped-up charges, while the husband threatened to oust him during the reelection for Sheriff. Roberts's uncle, a judge a few counties over, paid off a few people and the matter disappeared."

"How?"

"Don't know. The affair ended, and the husband moved out of state. Looks like there might have been an assault charge at one point, but it was expunged."

"By the uncle?"

"Looks like it."

"So the sheriff is a hothead. Interesting. Anything else? What about McCray?"

"Clean as a whistle. Comes from a rich family, all lawyers; he's enrolled in NYU as a pre-law student. Looks pretty straightforward."

Owen grunted.

"You don't think so?"

"There's just something about him that I don't trust. I think he's hiding something."

"I'll look again, but I don't know if we'll find anything. As for everyone else on the list . . . a few parking tickets, a couple of DUIs, but nothing out of the ordinary."

"Well, keep looking. There's got to be something, somewhere." Owen looked up the street. "Someone's hiding *something*."

"You think our killer's there now?"

"I don't doubt it for a second."

Teddy shook his head.

"It doesn't make sense. Why would someone kill an old woman for no reason? And a woman loved by everyone in the community, it seems. Nothing was missing except an old silver ring; there wasn't even sign of a break-in."

"This wasn't a senseless act. Someone had a motive. We just have to figure out what."

"About that. Why do *we* have to figure it out? Come on, man, you know why we got assigned this case. What's the deal?"

Owen inhaled slowly and exhaled even slower. He didn't want to bring it up, but Teddy was his partner, and the only person he trusted for a hundred miles.

"Remember when I told you I was from New York?"

"Yeah." Teddy smiled.

"And how I originally came to Michigan as a favor for a friend?"

Teddy nodded.

"Well, my family is pretty powerful, and my grandmother in particular likes to think I'm her own personal police officer. She's got her eyes and ears everywhere, and Rose was an old friend, so she heard about her death before most of this town, I'd bet. She wanted me on the case, pulled some strings, and we were on the red-eye here a half hour later. I don't like it, but I go where I'm sent, and if those in charge are fine with taking her orders, then there's really nothing more I can do but my job."

"Really?" Teddy asked, slightly shocked. "What are you, some kind of Rockefeller?"

"If only," Owen said, knowing the Rockefellers were lucky not to be like him. "Anyway, I'm going to head back to the house. The girl is alone, and I don't like it with all these extra people around."

"How's she doing?"

Owen shook his head.

"She's a tough one, but I don't envy the position she's in. She's devastated." Owen frowned, aggravated. Poppy had just barely turned twenty and should be worrying about finishing papers for classes, about which party she and her friends were going to attend, not looking over her shoulder for a murderer.

No one should, he thought.

Teddy nodded, as if agreeing with Owen's thoughts. Just then, Owen's phone buzzed. He glanced down at the name, even though he knew who it'd be:

Ajax

Cursing under his breath, he ignored the call.

"Telemarketer?" Teddy joked.

"Unfortunately, no." Owen shoved the phone back into his pocket, avoiding Teddy's eyes. Ajax was the last person Owen wanted to talk to or explain to anyone right now.

"Okay . . . well, what do you want to do here? You look like you might need to sleep. When are we heading to Connecticut?"

"Tonight," Owen said, rubbing his eyes with his thumb and forefinger. "We should probably head out around midnight. I should sleep. How are you feeling?"

"Good. I can take over. You going to sleep in the car?"

"Yeah," Owen said. "Mr. Pruette's at the bottom of the stairs. Just make sure no one goes up there. Give me a few hours, and I'll hash out the details with Mr. Pruette."

"No problem. You need some rest. I'll come get you in a few."

Owen nodded his thanks as Teddy headed back to the Pruette house. He opened the passenger side of the Charger and slid inside. He leaned the seat all the way back, closing his eyes as he shifted in place, trying to get comfortable. Images of faces passed through his mind as he tried to create a mental web connecting everyone to Poppy. Her face stood out most. Her long, deep-colored red hair tucked behind her ears, her green eyes that had hints of yellow specks. Both were tattooed to the back of his eyelids. Hers would be the face he saw when he closed his eyes until the case was solved. And though he didn't like the reason for it, he found he didn't really mind.

CHAPTER FOUR

"Poppy . . . Wake up, Poppy . . . "

A voice floated around her, intruding into her mind and pulling her out of sleep. She hadn't dreamt while she slept and instantly missed the peaceful darkness that had engulfed her for the past few hours. She blinked as her eyes adjusted, confused by the dark windows of her bedroom and the warm glow of her end table lamp. A figure hovered over her and she shot up suddenly, startled that she wasn't alone.

The same panic she'd felt at the funeral seized her, as if some massive hand had wrapped around her throat, wanting to drag her down into complete terror. The figure materialized until she recognized Owen, and she willed herself to be calm.

"It's okay. It's just me," Owen said, reaching out, but stopping just before his hand reached her shoulder. "It's time to go."

"Where . . . why are you in my room? And why is it dark out?" she asked foggily, knowing she wasn't making sense. In the corner, she saw Samantha holding the old blue duffle bag she used to pack clothes for school.

"I packed a bag for you," Samantha said. "Your father didn't want to wake you, so he asked me to do it. I hope that's okay."

"Oh. Yeah, sure."

Samantha gave her a small smile and carried the bag out of the room.

"It's time to go," Owen repeated.

"I told you, I don't want to go to Windgate," she said, not caring that it sounded childish. "I just want to go back to school."

She swung her legs off the bed, looking down at her outfit. She was still wearing her black dress and wrinkled cardigan from the funeral earlier that day. A memory of her grandmother scolding her for sleeping in nice clothes rang throughout her mind.

"And I told you, there wasn't a choice," Owen said, his voice gentle, but firm. She noticed the bags under his eyes had diminished somewhat, making his face look younger. "Come on."

"I have to change," she nearly growled, still too tired to think clearly. "How old are you?" she asked, staring blankly at Owen's face.

He seemed slightly taken aback, but answered. "I'm twenty-seven."

"Aren't you a little young to be a detective?"

What looked like a grin crossed his face, and Poppy was surprised again by the change. He didn't look nearly as serious as he acted when he smiled.

"It's a charmed life."

"Ha, ha," she said sarcastically as she removed her cardigan. She stood up and walked over to her dresser, then paused a moment, waiting for Owen to leave. She turned to see him still standing by the side of her bed, unmoved.

"Um, can you get out?"

Without a word, Owen left. *He didn't even look ashamed,* she thought as he closed the door behind him. *I bet he doesn't know the meaning of the word.* She grabbed a pair of well-worn jeans, a tank top, and a navy blue cardigan from her dresser. She didn't want to leave Miner's Way, but everyone seemed bent on making her do what she didn't want to. She was an adult, after all, and should be able to make her own damned choices.

Stop being bullheaded, a voice sounded in her head. She knew it was her reasonable side, the side that often kept her in check when her emotions were running high. She hadn't listened to that side of her in a few days and tried to ignore it. It was easier to let her emotions dictate her actions, but it was draining.

She dressed quickly and hurried downstairs. She saw Detective Fields standing at the door with Rupert, talking about something she couldn't hear. Without so much as a nod to acknowledge them, she went down the hall and into the kitchen. Her father was standing with a travel mug, talking with Owen and Sheriff Roberts.

"There you are," her father said, handing her the mug. "I made it a little stronger than usual. I wanted you to be alert." Poppy nodded, the steel warming her hands instantly. It was a nice feeling.

"Now, I want you to listen to me," he said as he gently pulled her to a corner of the room. "I know everything is a bit hectic right now, and you have every right to be upset, but Detective Peirce and I agree this is the best option. If it were anyone else, I would refuse you leaving my sight, but he's . . . well, you know."

Her father disliked talking about their heritage. It wasn't so much that he was ashamed of it, but rather that he wasn't at all impressed by it. Poppy often wondered if his political career would be jeopardized if he went around bragging about being related to a fairy tale character, but her grandmother had always kept it under wraps.

"There are people in that world who aren't, well, as gentle as us," he continued slowly. "They're not part of the Good lines. We never had to deal with any of the Others, your grandmother made sure of that."

"Yes, I know." Her father had never tried to talk to her about this before. It was awkward, like when he'd tried to talk to her about boys on her thirteenth birthday. Just like then, her grandmother had beaten him to the punch and told her the history of the Good and Other lines. While there were many on both sides of the old stories, theirs involved the Vanns, who were Others and descendants of the Big Bad Wolf line. It was generally believed in their world that the Others would always be fated to destroy the Good, which was why her grandmother had made the deal she did with the Vanns decades ago.

Her father cleared his throat. "Okay, good. But perhaps thinking we were protected left us to be targeted. . . . I honestly don't know, Poppy, but I want you—no, I *need* you to watch your back. I can't have anything happen to you. You're all I have left," he said.

Poppy bit her tongue, refusing to let her eyes water. Her father wouldn't cry, and neither would she.

"I know you were always told to be wary of people like us, but I trust Detective Peirce. He's the right sort, I think."

"Because he's one of us?" she asked quietly.

"No," he answered, shaking his head. "Never put too much belief in the old stories. But it doesn't hurt to know the people he comes from. I just think he's a good guy."

Poppy looked across the room to where Owen spoke with Sheriff Roberts. She agreed, though she would never admit it out loud.

"I love you, Poppy."

"I love you too, Dad," she said as he pulled her into a hug. Next, she hugged Samantha, once again stifling a surge of emotions. "Love you."

"I love you too, and be safe. We'll be up in a few weeks after the media dies down. Okay?"

"Okay."

Her father looked over to Owen and nodded. She said goodbye to Sheriff Roberts and Rupert as she left her home and walked toward the black Charger in the driveway. She sat in the back, while Owen sat in the passenger seat and Teddy drove.

They drove in silence for nearly an hour before Owen unbuckled his seat belt and climbed into the back seat.

"What are you doing?" Poppy asked, shifting all the way to the right side of the seat.

"We're switching cars," he said as he pulled out a blanket from beneath the driver's seat.

"It's a bait and switch," Teddy said, speaking over his shoulder while his eyes were on the road. "Well, not switch, so much as take two."

"We're going to drive an identical car and go up the highway while Teddy takes the back roads. When we reach Philadelphia, we'll switch and take back way while Teddy takes I-84."

"Why?"

"To throw someone off if they're following us."

"You think someone's following us?" Poppy asked, turning around to look out the rear window. There were no headlights that she could see.

"Could be, could not be. But we're not taking any chances," Teddy said as he pulled into a gas station. He pulled up along the side of the building where the lights from the overhang didn't reach. An identical car sat parked in the shadows, barely visible. "Ready?"

"Ready," Owen said as he wrapped the blanket around Poppy. Teddy crawled into the passenger side.

"What are you doing?"

"You're going to wrap yourself up and come with me into the other car."

Again, Poppy looked behind her, searching the empty parking lot for a car or a person.

"I don't think anyone's following us."

"Better to be safe than sorry," Teddy said. "Should take about eight hours. Both cars are full of gas. Shall we say, nine?"

"On the dot," Owen said as he got out of the car. "Ready, Poppy?"

She gave him a sharp nod. Covering her head, she opened the door and followed Owen quickly to the other vehicle.

"Wait, my bag."

"Leave it," he said as he slowed, making sure she was in the car before he climbed in. Within minutes, they were back on the road, following signs for I-95. Poppy watched as Teddy followed them for a while before continuing straight while they took a ramp onto the highway.

Although it was a serious situation, she felt a little like a spy, rushing off in a getaway car. She was embarrassed to admit that it was exhilarating, though her heart beat uncomfortably.

Owen looked over at her.

"What's up?" he asked, his brow slightly furrowed.

"It's just so bizarre," she said as she aimlessly counted the street lights that lit the highway. "You know, a few days ago, I was normal." She paused for a moment, suddenly wishing she could just be a regular twenty-year-old. "A few days ago, I had this regular life, and now . . . "

"You're still normal," he tried.

"No." She shook her head and sighed. "No, now I'm the girl someone is trying to kill. That's not normal . . . although, maybe I was never really destined to be normal, huh? Maybe it's just caught up with me, the old story. What was the lesson? Don't talk to strangers?" She laughed humorlessly. "But you're convinced it's someone I already know, anyway."

"Destiny has nothing to do with it," Owen argued, changing lanes. "This isn't a fairy tale."

"I know," she said. She stared at him for a moment. "You don't like being you, do you?"

"What?" Owen asked, though she knew he understood.

"You don't like being a descendant of Prince Charming. You think the whole Good and Others thing is ridiculous. You don't like fairy tales."

"What I don't like is there being some predetermined map of how we're supposed to live our lives. Just because someone wrote 'happily ever after' hundreds of years ago, I'm supposed to follow the same path? As if those people's lives just stopped at the end of the story . . . like they're in this perpetual state of bliss for eternity. It's presumptuous."

"Wow," Poppy said. "You might be the most jaded Prince Charming I've ever met."

"Don't call me that."

"Why not?"

"Because I'm not a prince."

"Or charming."

His sideways glare made her grin.

"I want to live my life the way I want. I don't think there's anything wrong with that, but some people think I couldn't be more wrong."

"Who?" Poppy asked. When he didn't answer right away, she leaned toward him a little, resting her elbow on the center console. "Who?"

Owen sighed. "My grandmother."

Poppy didn't expect the sudden, dull burning in her chest. It was jealousy, but the kind of jealousy she'd never felt before. She was jealous that Owen still had a grandmother.

"Oh," she whispered, looking out onto the road.

"She's a difficult woman," Owen continued quickly. "Not like your typical grandmother, not the baking cookies type. She's bossy, and mean, and thinks she's always right because no one ever told her 'no.' Spoiled, really, is the best way to describe her. Oh, damn it."

His phone was buzzing. Poppy looked at the screen as he ignored the call.

"Who's Ajax?" she asked, curious.

"What?"

"The person who keeps calling you. Who is it?"

"You know, it's rude to look at someone's phone."

"You're going to lecture me on rudeness?" she said incredulously. He gave her a pointed look and she shrugged. "Fine. So, you and your grandmother aren't close?"

Owen sighed. "We were, a long time ago, but she became obsessed about my future. She was absolutely certain I had to live my life a particular way. It became suffocating. So I left."

"Where did you go?"

"I dropped out of college and went to the police academy instead. Worked for the NYPD for a few years—happily, I might add—before she started pulling strings. Had me sent to Michigan first, and now—"

"She had you sent here," Poppy finished his thought. "Why?"

"I believe our grandmothers went to school together when they were young. The older generations stuck closer together, especially the Good. We're more dispersed now.

She wanted me to be on the job, and what my grandmother wants, she usually gets."

Poppy nodded as she processed all the information. From what she gathered, Owen had become bored playing the rich kid and rebelled.

They drove in silence for a while longer before Poppy began to slip into sleep. She dreamt of Owen on a white horse, fighting another Owen wearing rags and riding a donkey. Her grandmother was cheering from the sidelines as they charged at each other with lances that looked as though they were made from rolled-up book pages. Soon, the dream faded into black and another replaced it, striking all the familiar chords of a memory.

"I am so sorry, Aunt Rose," Mrs. McCray said in her heavy Southern accent.

Poppy stood contritely, holding her grandmother's hand as they stood in the entranceway of the McCray estate. Her yellow party dress had chocolate cake smeared all down the front, completely ruined. She didn't care—she hated the dress.

"Sean and his sister don't usually behave like such maniacs." She glared at her children, ten-year-old Sean and thirteen-year-old Carrie. She was a thin woman, with dark, short hair and thin lips. An underestimated beauty, but intimidating when she wanted to be. "If this were the old days, I'd take a switch to both*

of them." She turned to Poppy, looking sadly at her dress. "I hope it's not ruined, sweetheart."

"Nonsense, my dear, they're kids," Poppy's grandmother said. "Kids get dirty, and besides, Poppy's going through a growth spurt. She wouldn't fit in this dress for much longer."

"Still, I'm just so sorry. Here," Mrs. McCray handed her a plate. "It's a piece of the cake, since hers ended up on her dress." She shot her children a look. "Goodbye, Poppy."

"Bye," Poppy said, waving as she followed her grandmother to the car. Once she had her seat belt on, she turned to face her grandmother. "It was an accident, Grandma. Sean didn't mean it."

Her grandmother smiled. "It's all right, dear. Did you have fun?"

She grinned. "Yes. I wish I didn't have to leave." She paused and watched the road for a minute. "Why don't I have any brothers or sisters?"

"Why would you want brothers or sisters?" her grandmother asked. "Sean and Carrie are going to be grounded for a month for starting that food fight."

"Yeah, but they never have to go home to separate houses. They're best friends and get to hang out all the time."

"Well, not all siblings are best friends. Although, I'm sure if you had one, you'd have made quite the pair."

"What sort of siblings don't like each other?"

Her grandmother thought for a minute while Poppy stared at her, waiting. "Well, the Three Virtues never got along with each other."

"Who are they?"

"They were three sisters, blessed with being kind, beautiful, and wise, while also cursed with fear, vengeance, and pride."

"This sounds like a story. Are these real sisters?" Poppy *questioned, doubtful.*

Her grandmother laughed. "Of course it's a story, but that doesn't mean they aren't real!"

Poppy smiled. "Oh. Why didn't they get along?"

"Well, at first they did. They loved each other more than most. But one day, as sometimes happens, they got into a fight. It was the worst fight they'd ever been in, and after, they decided it best to go their separate ways, never to speak to one another again."

"What caused the fight?" she asked, looking down at her ruined dress.

Her grandmother patted her hand. Poppy thought she looked sadder than a moment ago, and she could still remember the tiny tear that shone in her grandmother's eyes when she answered.

"Love did, my dear. A curse was placed on them, and all but one would survive, but that's another story for another time."

As the vision faded, Poppy wanted to stay, holding on to the memory with all her might. She had wanted to know the rest of the story then, but her grandmother had refused to tell her. Even after asking several other times, it was a story she never finished, always insisting that she'd tell Poppy at a later time, a time that would now never come. The car bumped and she opened her eyes. It felt like she'd only slept a few minutes, but the sky was the hazy gray it usually was just before the sun rose.

She looked over at Owen to let him know she was awake. He looked tired. They continued until they saw a sign for New York City while driving through Philadelphia and she thought of Sean.

She yawned. "Maybe I can visit Sean while I'm up this way."

"No," he said stiffly.

Poppy rolled her eyes as she stretched. "Oh, good, you're back. I liked the other Owen I met before much better."

He frowned and didn't answer. They stopped at a bagel shop as soon as they got off the highway, since they were now to take the back roads. Poppy's growling stomach was grateful.

They drove all the way up along the Delaware River, passing through little historical towns like Milford, Pennsylvania, until finally reaching New York, where Owen moved back and forth between the roads along the Hudson River and the highway. Poppy wondered if this was perhaps familiar to him, since he had grown up only an hour away in the city. It was all new to her, as they'd mostly flown to Windgate when they went every summer. They'd only ever taken the road trip once.

Driving into the coastal town of Stonington, Connecticut made Poppy nostalgic. She had spent nearly every summer of her life there, and a flood of memories came rushing at her as they passed a hundred places, each with their own unique smell and feeling. It was like driving back in time. She fidgeted with her ruby ring as they slowly drove through town.

The summer rush was in full swing as they passed through the tourist part of town. Though Poppy was technically a tourist, her mother had lived here, and when they finally reached the quiet, residential part of the coast, Poppy felt relaxed for the first time in days. The fear and panic that had been slowly eating at her seemed to vanish completely. This was her sanctuary. Her place of peace. Nothing could harm her here.

They drove by some large homes, which gave way to smaller houses. They turned down a dozen or so side streets, until finally, they came to the end of an empty cul-de-sac where an old iron gate sat, the word "Windgate" engraved on its front.

The long, white crushed-stone driveway led to a large, two-story cottage with a pitched roof that was flat on top and two protruding sides flanking the main entranceway. It was white, with dark blue trim and a gray roof, though it could barely be seen since two rather large pine trees sat in front of the house. It was nearly fifty years old, and had been renovated only a few years ago—the summer Poppy, her grandmother, and her father had driven instead of flown. As the car pulled up in front of the home, Owen stopped Poppy from getting out. She looked at him, waiting, and he pointed to the dashboard clock. It read 8:50 a.m.

"Teddy isn't here yet," he said.

She sank back in her seat. "So?"

"We have to wait for him so one of us can do a check while the other is with you."

She had hoped Owen wasn't actually as uptight as she had originally believed, but clearly, she was wrong. To check the house seemed slightly extravagant.

"I'm sure it's fine," she said, though she didn't make a move to leave the car.

"You could be right," he said matter-of-factly. "And you could be wrong. So we'll just wait for Teddy."

They didn't have to wait long before the identical black Charger pulled in behind them. All three got out. Instantly, the smell of saltwater surrounded Poppy. It was as if she'd been hurled back in time, to a place that only brought her happiness.

Teddy handed Poppy her bag, while Owen reached into his coat and walked away toward the front entrance. Poppy paled and turned to Teddy.

"He has a gun?" she asked incredulously. "Hey! The front door needs to be jiggled a bit!" she called after him.

"Of course he has a gun," Teddy replied, pulling his tan coat to the side to reveal a strap across his chest and around his waist, his own gun resting on his hip. "We always carry them with us."

"You're not going to use them," she said quickly. "You actually think you're going to need to shoot someone?"

"Calm down," Teddy said gently, his smile reaching his eyes. His dark curly hair moved gently with the breeze coming off the ocean. He was so much more relaxed than Owen. "We only use them if it's absolutely necessary."

"I don't think any situation is ever necessary for a gun," she said as Owen disappeared inside. Poppy had hated guns for most of her life, ever since one accidentally went off next to her ear when she was at a family party at the McCrays'. They were regular skeet shooters. She and Sean were running around, weaving in between people when she'd bumped into Sean's father. He was holding a gun that was thankfully pointed at the ground when it went off, but the shot sent pieces of dirt and rock everywhere. Needless to say, it scared the life out of her, and she had been an advocate against them ever since. "Don't cops carry stun guns nowadays, anyway?"

Teddy just laughed, which didn't make her feel any better, though he did have a lovely laugh. He wasn't nearly as serious and worrisome as Owen, and she decided then that she'd much rather hang out with Teddy.

Owen finally reappeared some twenty minutes later, nodding to show it was clear. Poppy grabbed her bag from the ground and headed up the path to the front door. The soft ocean breeze ruffled through her hair as she followed Owen through the doorway and into the bright white foyer.

She was home.

CHAPTER FIVE

*P*oppy went immediately to the master bedroom on the first floor, just off the kitchen at the rear of the house. It had a view of the ocean, with glass patio doors and large half-windows that she opened on her way in. The house always felt more alive when the breeze could move freely through it. Her childhood bedroom was just down the hall—the master bedroom had always been her grandmother's room. She looked around the room briefly before collapsing onto the large bed. Without much thought for Owen or Teddy, Poppy let sleep take her away once more.

She woke a little before noon, staring blankly at the ceiling for a moment before remembering where she was. After unsuccessfully trying to fall back asleep, she sighed and dragged herself into the kitchen for some coffee. She opened the cupboard for a mug, and on seeing the jars of multiple teas, grabbed one at random and put the water on to boil instead. Her grandmother had loved to sit by the ocean with her tea. She listened for voices upstairs, wondering if Owen and Teddy were catching up on rest as well.

Peeking down the hallway, she saw no movement in the other bedroom. There wasn't any sign that she was here with two detectives. The teakettle whistled and she grabbed it from the stove quickly, enjoying the quiet stillness of the seemingly empty cottage. Poppy opened the back doors to the deck and stood on the stairs with her tea. The sky was gray, and the water was choppy, crashing somewhere below the grassy mounds that sat above the waterline. It was just as she always remembered it: big, beautiful, and empty. It wasn't like the local beaches in the area, where soft sand stretched a hundred yards before the sea. Poppy had always insisted on going to the public beaches when she was young, since there was so much more to do. She had never really appreciated the quiet shore behind her house. Instead of soft sand, it had coarse dirt, with long, dry grass blowing in the rough wind and a few beach plum shrubs scattered here and there. Only a few yards of sand sat between the dunes and the sea, but it was private, and for once, Poppy cherished the solitude.

She sat on the last step of the stairs, sipping her tea. She took out her phone; several text messages from Sean, a missed call from her roommate back at college, and a voicemail from her father appeared. Without listening to the message, she called her father's cell.

"Poppy," his voice sounded in her ear. "How is everything? You got in safe?"

"Yes," she answered. "Just calling to say hi."

"Good, but now isn't the best time. I'm heading into a meeting."

"Already?"

"Government doesn't stop," he said. "I love you. And thanks for the call."

"Love you, too. Bye."

It may not have seemed like much, but it was a lengthy conversation for them. Her father was a quiet guy, and she had taken after him.

Her stomach growled loudly as she finished her tea and stood, stretching. Once back inside and on the hunt for something to eat, she opened the fridge and found a bottle of ketchup, baking soda, and a half-eaten sandwich wrapped in paper with Teddy's name written on it in black marker. She considered eating it before a better idea hit her. The far bedroom door was still closed, with no other sign of either detective.

Poppy grabbed her bag and left a brief note on a pad of paper from the junk drawer:

Went to get food. Be back soon.
—Poppy

It wouldn't take long to grab the essentials from the local market, and she'd probably be back before they'd even notice she'd gone.

We came here because it's safe, she thought as she walked down the hallway to the mudroom. After opening the door to the garage, she grabbed the only bike that had a basket on it. It was an ancient-looking thing, painted a dull yellow, but she always rode it, even rejecting her father's offer to buy her a new one. It had been her mother's.

She walked the bike outside, hopped on, and pedaled her way to the market. Soon, she found herself smiling as she rode down the roads and sidewalks. She hadn't ridden a bike in forever. The familiarity of it, along with that of the town itself, jolted her back to a simpler, happier time.

The local market wasn't much more than an old convenience store. It looked like a shanty on the outside, the dark, weathered wood splintering as the aging paint peeled away in chunks. She grabbed a loaf of rye bread, milk, eggs, butter, and a block of cheese, along with a box of pasta and some tomato sauce. It wasn't much, but she'd lived on far less at college. She brought her basket to the clerk, a boy with red hair and freckles all over his face who looked a few years younger. She guessed it was the elderly owner's nephew.

Subconsciously, Poppy wrapped a hand around her own dark red hair.

"Twenty-two, sixty-three," he said, his voice cracking. A deep blush quickly covered his cheeks.

Poppy smiled and handed him the money. She decided it was probably best not to start a conversation, just in case. Her stubborn side argued that there was no reason for such caution, as Stonington was a second—and at this point in her life, safer—home, but a second voice that sounded annoyingly like Owen's overrode the first, and she left without saying anything. Fitting everything into the basket on her bike, she adjusted her weight as she began to pedal home.

She nodded to the few people she passed—joggers, mostly, and a mother pushing a newborn in a stroller. By the time she made it to the driveway, she guessed twenty minutes had passed, at most. Her happy calm fled as she pedaled through the gate and saw Owen on the front step, talking frantically into his phone. Teddy must have been in the car, because the rear lights turned on just as she made her way along the side of it.

"Poppy!" Owen shouted the moment he saw her, his expression furious.

Great, she thought.

"Hey," she said as she leaned the bike against the porch. She turned when she heard the car door slam and saw an agitated Teddy coming toward them.

"That's all you have to say? Where the hell were you?" Owen barked at her.

"Excuse me?" Her heart beat furiously as anger flooded her. She grabbed the bags from the basket and pushed past him into the house.

"Owen, calm down," she heard Teddy say behind her.

"You are *not* supposed to leave the premises without one of us!" Owen continued shouting as he followed her, ignoring Teddy. "You could have been killed! Did you forget why we're here in the first place?"

"Killed? In broad daylight? Are you mad? I just went to grab a few things." She dropped the groceries on the kitchen counter and turned to face him.

"It could have waited!"

"I was hungry!" she yelled, her voice matching his. "And I am not a prisoner! I can go five minutes down the road for some freaking food!"

"All right, everyone just calm down," Teddy interrupted, raising his voice over them. "Owen, I need to talk to you."

"She can't just go out—"

"The other room, Detective!" Teddy snapped.

As if remembering his role, Owen turned on his heel and marched out of the kitchen. They heard the back door slam as he went out to the porch. Poppy shook with her anger as she put the groceries away. She hated being yelled at.

"You really can't go off like that, Poppy," Teddy said quietly. "You're in hiding."

"I know," she grumbled, slamming a cabinet door. "But he doesn't have to shout at me like that. Who does he think he is?"

"He just worries. You should know that Owen is a bit hard to handle."

"No kidding."

"Not without reason," he added, his eyebrows raised. "He takes his job very seriously, and you disappearing isn't helping him do his job." He sighed.

"Why's he such a jerk, though? So I went out and grabbed a few things. What's the big deal?"

"Poppy, if I can speak frankly for a minute: your grandmother was killed in her own driveway, surrounded by a town of people who loved her. Do you think she felt threatened, ever?"

Poppy was silent.

"I know you feel safe here, but whoever did this isn't going to stop until one of two things happens: we catch him, or he catches you. And Owen is a good guy, deep down. He just wants to keep you safe. He's got a bit of a knight-in-shining-armor complex."

The term struck Poppy as funny.

"Why would you say that?" she asked, watching him out of the corner of her eye.

Teddy waved a hand and chuckled. "It's something Hanna said to me once, and it's always stuck, I guess. I think that's how he sees the world."

"Hanna? Who's Hanna?"

"Hanna Loch? She's the girl from the kidnapping case."

Poppy looked out the glass doors to make sure that Owen wasn't anywhere near coming back. Unable to see him, she turned back to Teddy, eager to question him. She had wanted to know about that case since the morning she first met Owen, when he mentioned that William Vann had helped him.

"Hanna Loch was the girl Owen saved?"

"Right."

Poppy shuffled some bags on the counter, trying to sound innocent. "I heard there was someone who helped him with the case. William Vann?"

Teddy looked at her, his brow quirked.

"You heard, hmm?"

She blinked innocently and he smiled.

"Yes, that's right. He started as a suspect, but turned out to be pretty helpful. Why do you ask?"

"Just curious. Owen mentioned it briefly."

Teddy sighed and rubbed a hand over his face.

"Look, he's strung very tight. I think he's worried what happened to Hanna will happen to you."

Poppy frowned. "Something happened to her?" she asked in surprise. "I thought he solved the case . . . "

Teddy shook his head. "She's fine. But it was a similar situation. She was in her hometown, surrounded by people she knew and trusted . . . " He paused and looked out the glass door. "Hanna and Owen are very close, like family. Anyway, Hanna had been kidnapped as a child by three siblings, but before they could kill her, they were arrested."

"Kill her?" Poppy repeated, horrified. "Why would they kill a little girl?"

"She had witnessed a double homicide." Poppy felt her stomach churn as she placed her hand over her mouth. Teddy continued. "They wanted to cover their tracks, but Hanna was rescued before they had a chance to hurt her. A police officer died saving her."

"Oh my God."

"Yes, well, it was too much for Hanna, I guess, psychologically, because she blocked the whole thing from her memory. She didn't even know any of it had happened until last year, when they came after her again. William Vann—he's the nephew of the cop who was killed trying to save her—he somehow knew they'd be back to finish her off, and if he hadn't helped, I don't want to think what would have happened."

Poppy was silent for a long time as she tried to process the story. *What a terrible thing to have to deal with,* she thought. Teddy finished and Poppy felt sick as she processed the story. *How were fairy tales ever glamorized?*

He put a hand on her shoulder. "It's nothing to take lightly, this situation we're in," he said gently.

She swallowed hard, nodding. "I'm sorry," she said, looking down.

Teddy smiled. "Hey, what happened then is not going to happen now. This guy's not getting near you, we'll make sure of it. Just help us out a little." He winked, and she smiled back.

"Okay, deal." She grasped for something else to say. "So, Hanna . . . whatever happened to her?"

"Went to college in South Carolina. Moved in with William. Owen wasn't too excited about that, but I think he got over it." Teddy paused, looking out the sliding glass doors. "Speaking of which, we have to do a sweep in about five minutes. I should find him. You all right?"

"Yes, fine," she said, waving him off as he exited the kitchen.

Poppy leaned against the kitchen counter, picking absentmindedly at a grocery bag. She could understand Owen's reasons for being uptight, given what had almost happened—twice—to Hanna.

But I'm not Hanna, she thought, frowning. *Maybe that's the problem*, a little nagging voice said in the back of her mind. Sure, he was worried about her safety, but maybe it was more than just that. Maybe she wasn't the girl he wanted to be looking after . . .

She scowled and grabbed the box of pasta and sauce. *Stop it*, she told herself. *You're being ridiculous.* Poppy put water on to boil and the sauce on low to warm up, trying to ignore the underlying need that was growing inside her—the need to talk to this Hanna. Teddy had said they were "like family," so who exactly was she to Owen, and what made him so protective?

Poppy groaned as she made her pasta and tried to put the whole thing out of her mind. It didn't matter; he was here for a job and that was all. Best to just keep to herself and let them both do their jobs.

For several days, she did just that, keeping her distance from them both. When she did find herself in a position to converse with one of them, she chose Teddy. She discovered he was married within the last year, and expecting his first child in the next month or so, which only made Poppy feel guiltier, as she was the reason he couldn't be with his wife during the end of her pregnancy. When he admitted he was deathly afraid of pregnant women, though, she laughed and appreciated his effort to make her feel better about the situation. She liked Teddy and his easygoing way about life; he was always quick with a joke and genuinely pleasant to be around. She swore he was a little disappointed that he couldn't be with his wife, but he never made Poppy feel responsible.

Unlike Owen, who seemed to point out at least once a day that they were at Windgate because of her, as if it were her fault someone wanted to kill her. On more than one of the brief occasions she spoke to him, she told him to leave, but he never did, which only annoyed her more.

She tried to dissect and understand Owen's character from a distance. *He probably thinks I'm nuts*, she thought whenever he caught her staring at him, trying to see what made him tick. She was looking for the glowing aura that had nearly blinded her the first time they met, though she knew she'd have to be away from him for longer than a few hours in order to see it with fresh eyes again.

A week passed, and then two, excruciatingly slow, but to Poppy it could have been a year. She had already read half of the old romance novels her grandmother kept in the living room, and television couldn't hold her attention for more than an hour. The only interesting thing that had happened since arriving at Windgate was a few dropped phone calls. The one time Poppy answered, she could have sworn she heard breathing, but the line went dead almost immediately. Owen forbid her from answering the phone after that.

Poppy wanted to go out and do something, but even mentioning leaving the house got her a cold stare-down from Owen. When Teddy suggested going out to eat one evening, she nearly twisted her ankle jumping up and grabbing her jean jacket.

"Let's go!" she almost shouted as she raced to the front door.

"Hold it!" Owen called after her. She groaned loudly as he turned to Teddy. "I don't think that's such a good idea."

"It's been two weeks," Teddy said. "You're going to drive her mad with cabin fever."

"It's true," Poppy said, coming back into the kitchen. "I think there's a condition named after it. Stockholm syndrome. I'm feeling the symptoms."

"Stockholm syndrome is when a hostage feels sympathy for their captor to the point of defending their actions. This isn't that."

"You're right," she answered. "I don't feel any sympathy for you guys at all."

"Ha, ha." Teddy smirked. "Okay. Compromise. How about I go out and grab us food? I don't think I can eat any more pizza."

Poppy stifled a sigh. It was probably the best she was going to get.

"Seafood sound good?"

She perked up instantly. "Yes! Go to Crazy Pete's! They have the best lobster. And a couple of crab cakes! And ask for extra biscuits!" She wanted to get the most out of this.

"Geez, you sound as if we're starving you," Owen said, a touch of humor in his voice.

"Pizza is not a staple food, so technically . . . "

"Hold on a minute," Owen said as Teddy grabbed the keys.

"Try and keep the peace while I'm gone. Poppy, I'll try and find this Crazy Pete's, okay?" Teddy said, ignoring Owen.

"It's five miles up the coast, on the right. You can't miss it," she told him, grinning.

"All right, see you two soon."

Teddy left, leaving Poppy and Owen alone for the first time since the car ride up. Unsure of what to do, Poppy nodded in the most awkward way possible and went into the living room where she had left a historical romance novel resting on an armchair. Owen turned, as if to say something, when his phone rang.

"Hello? Yes, Captain . . . " he said as he moved outside for some privacy.

Poppy watched him out of the corner of her eye until he closed the door before tossing the book down. *This is some sort of torture*, she thought as she got up to make what felt like her millionth cup of tea. There was nothing else to do except read, drink tea, and stare at Owen, who decidedly did not like being stared at, since he would all but glower at Poppy whenever he caught her staring. *Well, too bad*, she thought. It was a free country, she could stare at anyone, anytime, for as long as she wished.

Plus, his face is getting rather dull, she thought spitefully. She had memorized the odd color of his eyes, which changed from blue to green, the length of his perfect, prince-like nose, and even the shape of his mouth. And his hair, which was a little longer than she imagined he liked, always fell rather flawlessly across his forehead. Yes, she could pick him out of a crowd without question now, and she almost believed that she had memorized all his features out of boredom and nothing more.

She had been staring absently into the living room, so when something moved outside the sliding door, she thought nothing of it. Owen was probably pacing back and forth, talking to his captain about how they were all going to die of boredom. When the doors opened, she finally looked and saw someone she had never seen before.

A man with skin the color of burnt gold stared at her, his eyes like black marbles. His black hair was pulled back, possibly in a ponytail, and he wore a maroon sweater beneath a gray jacket. There was something worldly about him, something frightening, and yet magical. He took a step toward her; she opened her mouth to yell, but before she could, the steely voice of Owen echoed throughout the room.

"FREEZE!"

The dark-eyed man stopped, never taking his eyes off Poppy, whose heart was racing. Owen appeared on the other side of the room with his gun drawn. Poppy looked back at him, but her gaze returned to the intruder when the click of Owen's gun, though quiet, shattered through the silence.

"I said, freeze," Owen repeated, his voice hard as ice.

"I heard you," the stranger said, his words laced with some foreign accent. *Is it British?* Poppy watched as Owen dropped his gun slightly, his face suddenly confused. Ignoring Owen's command, the stranger turned around to close the door behind him. "Will you put that away?"

"Ghess-goo?" Owen said, though Poppy didn't understand it. It sounded like he said, "guess who."

"It's been Guess for a few decades, Peirce."

"Um, excuse me," Poppy interrupted. Both men looked back at her. "Who the hell are you?"

Owen lowered his gun completely, placing it back within his holster beneath his jacket.

"Poppy, this is Ajax Guess. He's a . . . well, he's not quite like us. He's . . . "

The man named Ajax walked toward her, his hand extended.

"I'm a writer," he said, smiling, his white teeth a stark contrast against his deep golden skin. "It's nice to meet you, Poppy."

Warily, Poppy took his hand and squeezed it firmly.

"A writer?" she said suspiciously.

"Well, not by choice," he said, his accent curling around his words, mesmerizing Poppy. "I'm in public relations, actually, but in this little club," he said, twirling his finger around, "I guess it would help to say that I'm a relation of Scheherazade."

Poppy's mouth dropped a little in shock.

"Scheherazade. As in the *One Thousand and One Nights* Scheherazade?"

"The same," he said, shrugging slightly before turning back around to Owen. "And you are going to be late."

"I'm not going," Owen said firmly.

"Late for what?" Poppy asked.

Without turning back to look at her, Ajax spoke.

"He's going to be late for his story."

CHAPTER SIX

Owen came around the kitchen island and sat on one of the bar stools. He gave Poppy a look she didn't quite understand. Was he annoyed? Embarrassed? Or did he want her to leave so he could talk to this Ajax character alone?

Too bad, she thought to herself. Who was this guy, and why did he just show up out of nowhere, telling Owen he was going to be late? She was going to hear whatever he had to say. Turning to Ajax with an over-enthusiastic smile, Poppy turned on the coffee pot.

"Would you like something to drink? Coffee? Tea?" she asked sweetly.

"Tea, if you wouldn't mind," Ajax said, and he leaned on the island.

"Poppy, I have to discuss something in private with Ajax," Owen said, though she ignored him, busying herself with the teakettle. She only glanced up when he said "Ajax" again.

"She doesn't know?" Ajax asked, a little surprised.

"I think I have an idea," Poppy began, pulling out a mug and some tea bags from the cabinet. "Let me guess. Owen, or as we know him"—she winked at Ajax—"Prince Charming, has a damsel in distress to save somewhere?"

"Well, yes, for the most part," Ajax agreed. "And he's going to be late if he doesn't get on the next plane to California."

"I told you, I'm not going," Owen said, a hint of aggravation in his tone. "I told you, and I told my grandmother, it wasn't going to happen, and it's not. I'm not taking part in it."

"Why does this always happen to me?" Ajax asked rhetorically as he looked up to the ceiling. He rubbed his eyes and turned to Poppy. "I swear, had I known what this job was going to entail, I would have handed it off to my sister."

"What is your job, exactly?" she asked as the water began to boil. "You're a writer, but not by choice. What does that mean?"

Ajax sighed, pulling one of the bar stools toward him. He sat and inhaled dramatically, as if he had told whatever story he was about to tell a thousand times before.

Well, in his case, Poppy thought smartly, *a thousand and one.*

"You know about us and our world, right? Our *other* world?" he asked, pausing until she nodded. Her grandmother had used the term "other world" once or twice, and she was a little surprised that it was a known expression. "Good. And so you know that every once in awhile, history repeats itself? Well, in the beginning, when these stories were first put to the page, there were only a handful of people who could read and write—a talent in those days. The people who wrote these stories, though they probably didn't know it, became magically bound to the words they wrote and the characters they created."

"They didn't create characters," Owen interjected. "They were real people."

Ajax waved his hand and shook his head.

"You heard it your way, and I heard it mine," he said to Owen before returning his attention to Poppy. "Anyway, these original Storytellers lived in a time when magic wasn't all that hard to believe in. In some places, it even existed."

"Hold on," Poppy interrupted, raising her hand to stop him. "You're saying magic was real?"

"While I understand the skepticism in your voice, yes, that's exactly what I'm saying. Once upon a time, magic was real, and to some extent, it is still real to this day."

Poppy laughed. "You're cracked. You know that, right?"

"Why? Because I'm not so closed-minded as to think that up until a few hundred years ago, human beings believed in magic and that, in the history of the human race, the skepticism of magic is actually only a recent development? Or because you can't comprehend that something that's been made into a joke was actually something that shaped the world as you know it?"

Poppy's smile faltered a little.

"Listen, I'm not here to prove it one way or the other. The facts are this: magic existed. Thrived, even, at one point in time, and this"—he motioned with his hand to the three of them—"us three, sitting here right now, is because of it. There was magic in those stories, in those people, and the Storytellers who wrote them. A magic so old and so powerful that it exists today, though we can neither see it nor understand it. It's real, whether you believe it or not."

The teakettle began to whistle, shaking Poppy out of her frozen state. It was as if his accent-laced words had entranced her for a moment, and she fleetingly thought that he must be who he claimed. Only a Storyteller could hypnotize someone the way he had.

She took the kettle off the stove and poured the hot water over the tea bag. Handing it to Ajax, she nodded slightly, urging him to continue.

"Thank you," he said, taking the mug of tea. "Anyway, you know that the stories that are so popular with the masses aren't written the way they happened. I believe that in your own family history, the grandmother and granddaughter were brutally murdered, not saved by a huntsman, correct?"

Shocked by his sudden, blunt words about murders and grandmothers, Poppy inhaled sharply. Owen's hand fell on her shoulder. She looked at him, surprised she hadn't seen him get up from his stool. He looked at her with concerned eyes, almost as if to ask if she were all right. She half nodded, trying to brush it off.

Ajax didn't seem to notice, or perhaps he simply didn't care, because he continued. "Well, the first few times these stories began to repeat themselves, things got messy . . . "

"Messy, how?" Poppy asked, though she didn't know why she was so interested. Owen's hand tightened around her shoulder, but she shrugged, ignoring it.

"People died, groups formed, and pretty soon, there were whole movements against magic and its practitioners. Those who were touched by magic were pursued, including the descendants of fairy tales. Being connected, we descendants of the Storytellers felt responsible, and so the Good came together and it was decided that whenever a story repeated itself, a Storyteller would be there to watch over them, making sure that it all happened just so, or we would deal with the consequences."

"And we're the Good, right?" Poppy said, familiarity ringing in her consciousness. "My grandmother used that term a few times."

"Yes, there are the Good and the Others. Not very creative nicknames, eh? Don't worry, I don't think anyone really cares, except maybe the Others. The Good are, as you or anyone can guess, the good guys, the protagonists. The Others, as they decided to call themselves, are the bad guys, or the antagonists, for lack of a better definition."

"And what are the consequences?"

"Yes," Ajax said, turning his attention to Owen, who stood behind Poppy. "Consequences occur if the story isn't properly acted out."

"My life isn't an act, and nothing is going to happen," Owen said, though Poppy could hear a distinct lack of confidence in his voice.

"Aren't we all merely players on the world stage?" Ajax mocked.

"Not quite the exact quote, friend," Owen said, glaring. "And like I said, nothing is going to happen."

"Oh no? Remember the last time someone like you didn't follow through?"

"What happened?" Poppy asked, turning around and finding that Owen had walked away. "Is this about the girl in Michigan? Hanna?"

"No," Ajax said, his tone changing. "But thank you so much for bringing that up. That," he said, following Owen around the counter, "wasn't supposed to happen."

Owen turned on his heel, his eyes cold as he stared Ajax down. Poppy noticed the sudden change in the atmosphere of the kitchen.

"Don't get on me about that," he warned, his voice quieter than she had expected it to be. "That was a personal affair."

"I'm not saying I would have rather she died," Ajax said, "but you can't keep interfering in these people's lives, Owen. You of all people should know that. It's not your responsibility."

"Hanna was different. She didn't know about any of it. They should have told her, so she could have at least had a fighting chance." Poppy nearly had the entire upper half of her body leaning over the counter, listening intently. "And who cares if I was up there? Did you even visit the Vanns? They shouldn't have been near her either."

"You know I only meet with the Good. The Others never listened in the first place. They've always taken matters into their own hands."

"Well, then what about Hanna? She's fine."

"Is she?" Ajax countered. "Hanna is a rare bird, even in our world, and because of what happened in Michigan, Pearl La Roux can't get in touch with her now."

"Where the hell was Pearl before?"

"Question!" Poppy asked, holding her hand up. Both men looked at her, as if surprised she was still in the room. "Who's Pearl La Roux?"

"A Storyteller," Ajax said. "Hanna's story was one of her responsibilities."

"She's an airhead," Owen countered, "who didn't even show up in Michigan until after Hanna's kidnapping."

"Don't call her an airhead, Owen." Ajax pinched the bridge of his nose, as if to defend Pearl out of obligation and nothing more. "She's technically family."

"Well, it's her own damn fault that Hanna is considered an Other now."

The look on Owen's face was startling to Poppy, and a thought suddenly popped into her head. *Did Owen love Hanna?*

"Shit!" Poppy yelled as she knocked over her mug of hot water. She quickly grabbed a rag as Ajax gave her a sideways glance. Owen didn't take his eyes off Ajax.

"Everything turned out just fine in Michigan," Owen said finally, after a few moments.

"Did it?" Ajax asked. He turned to Poppy, lifting his hand to gesture. "Didn't Rose Pruette have an agreement with the Vanns? That their story wasn't going to happen in Poppy's lifetime? Where did that get her? She tried to manipulate it, Owen. These stories aren't meant to be interfered with, and when someone tries to change it, it backfires tenfold."

"Wait," Poppy said, her head spinning. "Is that why my grandmother died? Because she tried to prevent the story from happening?"

Both men looked at her.

"He doesn't know that for certain," Owen said.

"Right, I only have about a dozen examples on the very subject," Ajax said, his voice annoyed. "And I do know. The Hood story wasn't supposed to play out in this generation."

Poppy tilted her head, confused. Owen looked at her, and then back at Ajax.

"Excuse me?"

"The Hood story wasn't supposed to play out in this generation." Ajax looked at Poppy. "Rose *did* seek protection from the Vanns, but it was in vain. The story wasn't going to repeat itself until your great-grandchildren. You weren't meant to live it."

Poppy tried to soak up everything she had just been told.

"You mean, this isn't part of the story? My grandmother wasn't supposed to die?"

Ajax shook his head.

"Wait a minute, how do you know that?" Owen interrupted. "How do you know this isn't their story?"

"Look at the facts, Owen. These stories aren't without structure. Hanna was attacked. By whom? The Hertzes, and who were they? Descendents of the Others in her story. Rose Pruette wasn't attacked by a member of the Vann family, and because of that fact, this is not a story. Not in our world."

"So, you're saying this is just a murder case, and not a story?"

"Yes."

"Then why are you here?" Poppy interjected.

"I'm here for Owen," Ajax said. "To keep him on his track. You don't have a story to guide, Poppy. You're one of the lucky ones."

"Lucky?" she said, almost laughing. "Lucky that my grandmother died and I'm in hiding from someone who wants to kill me and it doesn't even have to do with some stupid story that would give me something to blame all this on? I'm lucky because all this just happened out of coincidence? I'm sorry, but I think you meant to say cursed instead of lucky."

"I'm not going to California," Owen said quietly. "Not until Rose Pruette's killer is in jail or dead."

"Owen, I'm not asking," Ajax said. "I'm not guessing either. If you don't go to California, something will happen to that girl you're supposed to save. This is your responsibility. I know it must be tough—"

"How would you know? You're completely free to make your own choices. No one wrote your fate hundreds of years ago."

"But you *know*, Owen. You know firsthand what can happen when people try and change what's written."

"Then what will happen to Hanna? Is she going to eventually become the grandmother of some evil villain? Is the Vann family blood that potent, that no matter what good comes into their world, they're just destined to be wicked? I know William Vann, Ajax. He's not the type."

"I can't say what will happen, because I don't know. The Others aren't my business, but the Good are, and there is a young woman on the other side of the country who needs you."

Poppy could barely digest it all. Owen opened his mouth, as if to argue, but then closed it as his shoulders sagged. Poppy thought he looked as if the wind had been knocked out of his sails. It was obvious he still didn't agree with Ajax, but there seemed to be something in him holding him back. He shook his head, simply disagreeing in silence. Without a word, he turned and opened one of the sliding glass doors that led out onto the porch, nearly slamming it as he closed it behind him. Poppy, awestruck, turned to Ajax.

"What will happen if he doesn't go?" she asked, the words barely registering as she spoke them.

"I can't say for certain," Ajax said, turning as he rubbed his eyes. "I never can, but if history is any indication, it won't be pretty."

"What happened the last time someone didn't follow their story?" she asked. Ajax shifted his stance, as if he didn't want to talk about it. "Please, tell me."

"There have been a number of sorry tales about those who ignore their duty, but the most recent was that of a very intelligent woman, headstrong and beautiful, with all the makings of someone who deserved a happily ever after, but on her own terms. So certain of this was she, that when the time came to follow her fate, she ignored it and grasped desperately at the first thing that would keep her from it. So, in her arrogant youth, she rebelled against her story. Perhaps she honestly believed that he was her gallant knight, freeing her from a life so planned, or maybe she simply wanted to defy everything she had ever been told. Whatever the reason, it didn't matter, because her life from that moment on was plagued with sorrow, until eventually, she took her own life."

"She killed herself?"

"Yes. It wasn't supposed to happen like that, you see. She was meant for such great things, but was far too headstrong to care. It drove her mad."

"That's awful," Poppy said.

"Yes, it is. Owen probably knows that the best."

"Why?"

Ajax paused before giving her a thoughtful look.

"It was his mother, Cynthia. But he hates talking about it. Don't bring it up. Ever," he added. "Listen, I've got to get back to the hotel. I've been driving all day, and I'm exhausted. I'll be back."

Poppy nodded and turned, still in shock. Owen's mother had killed herself? How terrible. How completely devastating it must have been for him. *He must feel like a prisoner*, she thought sadly as she walked out onto the porch. She decided she wouldn't bring it up, though, not ever. Not until he mentioned it. She was unwilling to put him in such an awkward place. Instead, she buried it in her mind and pulled up the mental file on Hanna Loch.

She followed Ajax out onto the back porch and waved goodbye as he disappeared into the dark. It was a beautiful night, warm with a pleasant breeze rolling off the ocean. As Poppy's eyes adjusted to the darkness, she saw the silhouette of a man sitting on the dunes, a few yards off the edge of the porch. She walked down and sat next to him.

"Ajax leave?" Owen asked.

"Yes." She paused before continuing. "Owen, can I ask you something?" She glanced at him and he nodded. "This Hanna girl, is she . . . were you in love with her or something?"

The silence that immediately followed felt like ages. But finally, she heard a laugh. Turning, she saw Owen's smile light the darkness.

"In love with Hanna?" he asked through his laughter. "I don't think I've ever even considered it. No, Hanna's like a sister to me. She was my only friend in Michigan, and I think, being who she was, I felt protective of her. I was worried—hell, I'm still worried about her and the choice she made to be with William, but I can't . . . I can't readily believe that she'll not have a happy ending simply because she wasn't supposed to fall in love with someone like him. They do love each other, and I guess I just believe in that more than in some story."

"Ajax said that if you don't go to California, something bad will happen to that girl you're supposed to be with."

"I know," Owen said, his voice carefully even.

"I don't understand you, then."

"What's there to understand?"

"Well, you were so protective of Hanna, so eager to help those who can't defend themselves, but you know that something bad can happen to this woman you're technically supposed to fall in love with, and yet you refuse to go." Poppy twisted the ring on her finger. "How can that be?"

He looked at her.

"I don't know. Maybe I'm not all that good. Maybe I'm too selfish . . . I guess I'm not as one-sided as the story makes me out to be."

Poppy stared off ahead of her, unable to see the waves that fell quietly on the sand several feet in front of her. She didn't know quite how to feel about Owen now. He had seemed so honorable—annoyingly so—that this selfishness went against the grain of his character.

Yet, who was she to judge? She hadn't been betrothed to anyone since her very birth. For a moment, she imagined a scene with her grandmother and father, sitting in her living room back home, telling her that she was going to fall in love with someone they chose. Poppy couldn't help but smile, knowing that neither member of her family would be able to keep a straight face. The idea was so absurd that Poppy felt a pang of pity for Owen.

"Is your family mad with you?" she asked quietly.

"Yes," he answered. "Or at least, I assume they are. I haven't spoken with any them for almost two years."

Poppy turned to look at him.

"Because of . . . California?"

"Yes." With that, he stood, holding a hand out to Poppy. She took it and he pulled her to her feet. "We should get back inside."

Poppy followed Owen up the steps of the porch and in through the sliding door. In a matter of minutes, Teddy came back, carrying two bags full of Crazy Pete's seafood, but Poppy had lost her appetite. After hearing that she wasn't supposed to be living her family story, Poppy couldn't help but feel like her grandmother's death had been without purpose. At least before, she could blame it on something—magic, fate, or whatever these people wanted to call it. But it hadn't been a senseless act. Now, it seemed to be more malicious than she'd originally felt about it.

Owen sat on the far side of the room, fiddling with the gold badge he had pulled from his pocket. She wondered what he was thinking, if he felt guilty for not going to California. And why did *she* feel guilty about it? It wasn't her problem, and yet, for some reason, she felt bad that Owen had to carry such a ridiculous burden alone. Couldn't he just save the poor girl and leave, if all she needed was saving? Hadn't he thought of that?

Probably, Poppy considered. *He's probably thought of every possible way around it.*

But then, why not just save her and leave?

Poppy thought about it all night, even dreaming about Owen and a faceless beauty queen on another beach far, far away from her little piece of Connecticut.

CHAPTER SEVEN

nother week passed, and Poppy decided she was going mad. Teddy, preoccupied with his phone and computer, enjoyed all his free time talking to his wife, whose virtual presence now felt like a fourth had joined their party. Owen had almost demanded Teddy not chat with his wife so much, but Poppy knew he couldn't get involved in such a matter. Rachel, Teddy's wife, was hardly in a position to be told no.

Poppy had appreciated another female's opinion at first, until she began to side with Owen about safety. Poppy couldn't blame the woman, though; alone, eight months pregnant, and miles away from her husband, the woman had a bit of a right to be paranoid, even though nothing had happened since their arrival at Windgate.

Absolutely nothing, she thought. She sat on one of the Adirondack chairs on the back porch one afternoon, amusing herself by reading one of her geology books from school. Poppy was unintentionally withdrawing into herself as cabin fever set in. She could only talk to Teddy for so long before there was nothing else to say, and she had barely spoken to Owen since Ajax had disappeared a week earlier.

"Can't your brother do it?" she heard Teddy say as he walked out onto the deck, talking into his phone. "Well, honey, I don't know what to tell you. I would have put the crib together before I left had I known."

Poppy winced, feeling guilty that he couldn't be at home with his wife, but Teddy rolled his eyes and shook his head, as if to take the blame off her. "Well, you can always call Mr.

Loch. He's very handy, and Owen says he'd love to help. Yes, he called him."

Poppy put down her textbook and got up to leave Teddy in private. She opened the glass sliding door and walked into the kitchen. Owen stood at the kitchen island, leaning over a paper, his eyes barely flickering up to acknowledge her before continuing to read.

Feeling particularly restless, Poppy stood on the opposite edge of the island and stared at him, almost willing him to look at her. After several seconds, he did.

"Yes?" he said.

She didn't answer right away; she was trying to decide the color of his eyes. She'd thought they had been a sharp hazel-green when they first met the morning after her grandmother's murder, but now they seemed almost a muddy gray. *Can eyes change colors?* she wondered.

"Hello?"

She shook her head, ignoring her own internal question. "I can't stay in this house for another day," she said as he sighed. *He's going to fight me on this*, she thought, but she persisted. "Hear me out. I absolutely cannot read another word or play another game on my phone. I'll go insane. You have to feel the same way. I know Teddy does."

"It doesn't matter what I feel," he began pointedly. "Or what Teddy feels. This is where we stay until they find the guy who is after you."

"But this isn't healthy for any of us. You can't lock yourself up for weeks without interacting with the outside world! It's damaging."

"What would you have me do then, Poppy? You want to go to the beach, where there are tons of people and anyone can see you? You want to go to a movie theater where it's dark, or a restaurant where someone can poison you? It's too dangerous."

"You're being paranoid."

"And you're not being paranoid enough. There is a very real danger out there, and you seem to think that I'm the bad guy for trying to keep you away from it."

"I don't think you're the bad guy," she said, her voice dropping a register. "It's not like I don't appreciate what you and Teddy are doing, but something has got to give. There are plenty of places we can go that are safe. I have to do *something*, some sort of project or workout or anything." She paused for a moment, and then jumped. "I got it! Let's go to a yoga studio. There's one in town, the Lotus-something or other. Can we?"

Owen stared at her blankly. "Are you out of you mind?"

"What? The classes aren't big, you can keep an eye on everyone, and we can go to the night class. It's not deadly or dangerous, I promise."

"Not for you maybe, but I'd probably pull something and have to have surgery."

Poppy stared at Owen for a moment before cracking a smile. He smiled back. *This is good*, she thought. *He's letting up.*

"You wouldn't pull anything," she said, moving around the island and into the kitchen. "It's just stretching and breathing. It's fun."

"It sounds redundant."

"Have you ever tried it?"

"No."

"Perfect! You get to try something new, and I get out of the house, and Teddy. . . . Has Teddy ever tried yoga?"

Owen looked at her for a long moment and sighed again. She thought he would ignore her and return to reading the paper when he suddenly folded it up and crossed his arms.

"All right, here's what we'll do. As comfortable as I am staying in this house until this case is closed, I know it's not mentally the healthiest option. So, for the sake of our health, we'll each get to pick something to do outside of this place, but," he said, as Poppy smiled excitedly, "I'll be informing the local police of each one of these excursions. We'll have a black-and-white parked here before we leave and until we get back. When we're out there, you must be aware of your surroundings, and no wandering off, talking to people, or anything that would compromise our situation. You have to listen to me, understand?"

Poppy nearly bristled at his overbearing protector bit, but she was too excited to finally get out of the house. Instead, she just nodded, smiling her biggest smile.

"Understood, Detective," she said jokingly. "But ease up a little on the commands, will you? You've got to relax."

"I'm just staying safe."

"I know, but how would you like it if someone constantly told you what to do or how to do it?"

"Probably the same way I feel when someone hounds you endlessly until she gets her way."

"I did not."

"I think you did," he said. "But I like that."

His voice was lower and a bit huskier that it had been before, and his smile faded into a sexy side smirk. Was he flirting with her?

Wait a minute—did I just think his smirk was sexy?

Poppy's eyes widened as this realization came over her. Suddenly feeling self-conscious and a little excited, her smile faltered a fraction as she nodded. Without saying a word, she turned around and headed back out onto the deck, almost running into Teddy as he came inside.

"Wow, where are you off to in such a rush?" he asked as she darted past. She heard him ask Owen, "What did you say to her?"

She didn't hear Owen's response, though; she was too far out onto the beach. *What was that all about?* Shaking her head, she hoped he didn't think she was a complete jerk for walking out so abruptly, but what could she do? Normally, when she flirted with guys, it sort of just came naturally, but he wasn't a regular guy. Or had he even been flirting?

Probably not, she thought to herself. Why would he? He was seven years older than her, a detective under whose protection she had been placed. There was no way he was flirting, let alone would even *think* about flirting with her, even though it had felt that way.

Taking a deep breath, Poppy tried to rationalize her heightened pulse. She was excited to be getting out of the house, not because he'd said he liked her. *And he hadn't even said that!* He'd said he liked that she had gotten her way. Why was she making a federal case out of it?

Tucking away her bizarre thoughts, she pulled out her phone and did a search for the yoga studio. Hopefully, they would be able to go tonight, and she wouldn't look like a moron when she went back into the house.

Several hours later, Poppy stretched into warrior pose in a studio hotter than a sauna. She had noticed that this was a hot yoga session, but she had never gone to one. It was the only class scheduled, but she would have done yoga on the surface of the sun if it meant she could get out of the house, which, oddly enough, is exactly what it felt like. Thankfully, Teddy had taken the mat next to her, putting some distance between her and Owen. She hadn't said anything to him since she left the kitchen earlier, but it wasn't her fault. She didn't know what to say, and although he seemed completely normal, she didn't trust herself to say something cool.

How lame am I, she thought as sweat dripped down her temple. Pushing the thoughts out of her mind, she focused on inhaling and exhaling. She hadn't realized hot yoga would be so . . . well, hot.

From warrior, she went into half moon pose and looked to her right. Poor Teddy breathed heavily with his back leg barely off the ground. Looking past him, she saw Owen, who seemed surprisingly comfortable, with his back leg extended straight and his arms perfectly vertical. He wore basketball shorts and a fitted gray T-shirt that was drenched in sweat. Poppy had never seen Owen in anything but a black suit, which she'd almost believed he slept in, until tonight. She stared at his back until they switched poses again. Teddy was red in the face when they moved, looking extremely uncomfortable, but Owen's eyes caught her attention. He looked at her with a mixed expression of awareness and confusion. She felt as though he could see right through her, which was surprising since she was sweating buckets. Her hair was a mess, and she had huge sweat marks all over her tank top, which had originally been baby blue and was now more of a navy. She turned away quickly, hoping she was just imagining it.

By the end of class, Teddy looked near death. His shirt was completely soaked, and he all but ran out of the room, pushing past everyone toward the water cooler that stood in the hallway. Poppy felt bad, and was rolling up both her mat and his when Owen bumped into her.

"That was . . . different," he said, taking Teddy's mat from her.

"You feel good though, right?" she said. "Got all the toxins out."

"I don't know if Teddy feels that way about it, but I didn't mind it."

"Have you done this before?"

"No, why?"

"You did really well. I thought that maybe you were a closeted yogi or something." Owen smiled, and Poppy felt a small thrill go through her. "So, you think we'd be able to come again?"

"I would, but I don't think you'd be able to convince Teddy to come back," he said as he nodded toward the glass doors separating the room from the hallway. Teddy was chugging water as though his life depended on it.

"Poor guy," Poppy said. "I don't think this was what he had in mind."

"Yeah, but he'll get over it. Hey," he said, stopping her as they made their way to the doors. "Are you all right? You seemed, I don't know, preoccupied all afternoon."

"Oh, yeah, I was just . . . thinking about things. School and stuff like that."

"You're studying geology, right?"

"Yeah, I want to work with environmental geology, working to reduce human impact on the world." She was glad her face was already red, because she could feel herself blushing. "It's not all that interesting to most people."

"I've never met a geologist before."

"I'm not one yet." An awkward pause followed, but luckily Teddy was waving at them to hurry. "I don't think Teddy wants to come back in here."

"No, I bet not. We should get out of here."

By the time they made it to the street, Owen had switched back to being the law-abiding detective, looking around suspiciously as they got into the car. Even Teddy, who had been completely beat up from the yoga session, had regained his composure and seemed aware of his surroundings.

They arrived at Windgate in under ten minutes and swept the house while the local officer chatted with his partner. The cops left when Owen gave them a nod that everything was under control. Poppy entered the house and made a beeline for the shower, eager to wash the gallon of sweat off her. After getting dressed, she had lain down on her bed and zonked out before her head hit the pillow.

Visions of snow and roses passed through her mind so quickly she could hardly make sense of them. It seemed she was too exhausted to dream, which surprised her when she woke up a few hours later. She hadn't realized she was so tired. The clock on her phone read twelve o'clock. Stretching, she got out of bed and quietly walked into the kitchen.

Snores could be heard from somewhere upstairs in one of the bedrooms on the second floor. Poppy filled the kettle and turned on the stove before she noticed the sliding glass door was open. Cautiously, she stepped toward the door. It seemed Owen's paranoia had brushed off on her. She peered out and saw Owen sitting on one of the Adirondack chairs, looking out into the darkness. Noticing her presence, he looked up at her with a worried look on his face, his hands gripping the ends of the armrest.

"Everything okay?" he asked.

"Yes," she said quickly and he relaxed a bit. "Everything's good. I just fell asleep too early. I think I'm going to be up all night now."

"Teddy's been out for hours," Owen said. "I guess you're feeling better since you got out of the house?"

"Aren't you?" she asked, taking a seat in the other chair. He nodded. "So, is this what you do on watch? Stare out into the night, waiting for something?"

"No," he said, a hint of defensiveness in his voice. "I'm just thinking about things."

Poppy had a feeling he was thinking about Ajax and the looming trip to California. She wondered if she should bring it up or leave it alone. She didn't want to bother him, even though she admittedly enjoyed annoying him with her relentless questioning.

But not tonight, she decided.

He seemed to notice her hesitation. "What would you do, if you were in my shoes?" he asked suddenly.

Poppy raised her eyebrows, shocked that Mr. Sure-Of-Himself would ask such a question. Of course, it wasn't like he could ask many people for their advice about it. He couldn't ask Teddy without explaining everything to him. She shrugged and shook her head.

"I don't know. I guess I would go if someone was in trouble and needed my help," she said.

"Part of me agrees with that, so much so that I decide to go at least ten times a night. But there's the other part of it, the part of me that disputes the story I'm supposed to follow." He paused, inhaling for a long moment before continuing. "My mother killed herself after she rebelled against her own story. People believe she ended her life because of it, but I don't. She was sick. They wanted to blame it on some mythical reasoning, but it wasn't that. She wanted to live her life on her own terms—and so do I—but that isn't what caused her to kill herself."

Poppy realized this was the first time he had mentioned his mother's death, but she didn't want to focus on it, for his sake. She was sure he had gone over it a million times, and besides, he wasn't asking to discuss it. Or perhaps she wasn't comfortable talking about it.

Our mothers are both dead, she suddenly realized, surprised she hadn't thought about that when Ajax first told her. A chill went through her. *What are the odds?*

"So, if you don't go, you don't think you'll end up in the same mind set as your mother?"

"No. I know her illness wasn't connected to her diverting from her story. Everyone else just thinks otherwise."

"And if you go, you're afraid that . . . what? You'll be magically bound to this girl?"

"Partially."

"Well, besides wanting to live life on your own terms, would it be so bad to live happily ever after?"

Owen was silent for a moment, his stare concentrated on the unseen dark waters ahead of him.

"No," he said finally. "It wouldn't."

Poppy felt her stomach drop slightly. *It shouldn't be a surprise. Guys always seem to go the more difficult way about things*, she thought. *He may have his reasons for not wanting to go, but after all, what guy* wouldn't *want to go to California and fall for some beautiful, mysterious woman he gets to rescue?*

Wow, she thought for a second. *Why am I getting so bitter?* Why should she care what Owen did? She should be helpful and keep her ridiculous opinions to herself.

"So you're going to go?" she asked after a lengthy silence.

He turned to look at her and Poppy could see the same look he had given her at the yoga studio. He looked apprehensive, and yet hopeful. *But that doesn't make any sense*, she thought.

"Should I?"

That was not what she was expecting to hear. A simple yes or no would have done it. *Why do I have to make his decision for him?* He looked genuinely confused and concerned, waiting for her to answer.

"If someone's in trouble, you should help them," she said, hoping her indirect answer would be sufficient.

"Should I go?" he asked again.

Apparently, it wasn't.

"I can't tell you what you should or shouldn't do, Owen. She's in trouble, and she needs your help. If no one else is going to save her, then yes, I think you should go. But I don't think you should chalk it up to some predetermined bond you have with her. Don't do it because you're part of the Good and don't have a choice. Do it because you're a good person."

He nodded, but didn't seem glad to hear her answer. Instead, he shook his head and changed the subject.

"Are you missing out on your studies being up here?"

She wasn't sure why, but she felt disappointed that he didn't want to talk more about his choice. She smiled, though, and continued.

"A bit, but I got the syllabus for the fall semester emailed to me, so I'm on track with that."

"Miss your friends?"

"Yes, but I think by now they've heard through the grapevine about what happened, so none of them are trying to contact me, except for a text here and there with their condolences. What about you? Any friends missing you up in Michigan?"

"Believe it or not, I'm sort of lacking in the friend department."

"No, really?" she said in faux shock. "So you have no one missing you at the moment?"

The minute she said it, she wondered if it sounded too forward. She felt her cheeks heat up when he didn't answer as quickly as she'd expected.

"Well, besides a few friends at the department and the Lochs, no, not really. I guess that's the opposite for you? You must have tons of people wondering about where you are, worrying about you."

"A few people, maybe, but no one in particular."

A light rain began to fall. They got up slowly and for a moment, they stood face to face, only inches apart. Every thought that had been in Poppy's mind disappeared. All she could focus on was Owen's eyes. His mouth twitched, as if he were about to say or do something, but suddenly the kettle in the kitchen whistled sharply and she turned away. Shaking her head, she went inside, took the kettle off the stove, turned off the burner, and pulled out a bottle of water from the refrigerator. She no longer wanted a hot drink and decided to cool down in her room alone, listening to the sounds of the rain falling outside her window.

CHAPTER EIGHT

Several days after Poppy and Owen's midnight chat, the rain hadn't stopped. The outing had helped lift everyone's spirits, though, and as much as Owen wanted to stay in the house, Poppy had been hinting at going out again. She had all but beat him into submission to get her way with the yoga, but he eventually agreed that she had been right. It wasn't healthy to waste away in a safe house, even though it was his preferred option.

And it wasn't that he was against going out that evening—this time to a small diner outside of town—but there had been no leads in the investigation, and Owen couldn't help but feel as though they were sitting ducks. It irked him beyond belief that he couldn't do anything to help, convinced that he should be out there tracking the murderer, but in the same breath, he couldn't leave Poppy alone with anyone, even Teddy. He trusted his partner with his life, but he couldn't explain to him the severity of the situation. Although, if the roles were reversed and someone was trying to kill him, he'd run right into danger. But he could handle himself, and though Poppy was a smart, independent woman, he couldn't stifle the overbearing need to protect her.

He thought back to their conversation for the hundredth time since that night and decided that, whether he liked it or not, he would eventually have to go to California. Every time he made the decision to go, a part of him raged against it. With every passing day, he felt more and more determined to stay, but when he looked at Poppy, his resolve faltered. She had been right: he should help someone who was in trouble, especially when it was his responsibility. But every time he looked at her, he could feel a growing tightness in his chest. He needed to see her to safety first, before he went to California.

"Ready?" Teddy asked, walking into the kitchen from the front foyer. "The black-and-white is parked outside. Where's Poppy?"

"Here!" she said, closing her bedroom door behind her. She wore a sleeveless maroon dress and black flip-flops, with a matching small black purse. Owen must have been staring too long, because she looked at him and asked, "What? What's wrong?"

"Nothing," he said briskly, leading the way out of the house.

He cursed inwardly at himself, annoyed that she had distracted him, even if it was only for a moment. It had happened a few times since their arrival at Windgate, and though it was his own doing, he blamed her for being so, well, distracting. *Why would she wear flip-flops instead of sneakers?* he thought, convinced that he was rationalizing his aggravation toward her because of her lack of proper footwear.

He drove in silence, while Teddy and Poppy discussed the names that Rachel and Teddy were planning to name their baby. If it was a boy, Teddy wanted to name the little guy George, after his father; if it was a girl, Jezebel. Obviously, Teddy didn't know anything about girls' names.

They arrived at the diner, with Poppy agreeing wholeheartedly with Rachel on her choice of Beatrice.

"But that's so old-sounding," Teddy argued as they took their seats in a corner booth. "She'll be a baby with a grandmother's name."

"You cannot name a girl *Jezebel*!" she insisted, smiling as Owen took the seat next to her. "It's uncouth."

"Why? I think it sounds pretty."

"Haven't you ever heard of Jezebel? She was a liar, and kind of a bitch, from the Old Testament."

"Really?" Teddy asked. "Even then, so? I'm not religious."

"It's another word for tramp, Teddy. You cannot name her that, right, Owen?"

"She's right," Owen said, reading over the menu.

"See?"

"You two are just ganging up on me."

"We are not."

Owen was about to delve into the history of the name, when the sound of a gun being cocked echoed through the diner and a woman screamed.

"Open the register, now!" a male voice demanded.

Everything went into slow motion, and yet sped up at the same time. Owen threw himself on Poppy, practically shoving her underneath the table. Teddy pulled his gun from its holster and lay on his back in the booth, his head just barely above the table. Owen pulled his gun out and nodded. With one hand on Poppy and the other on his gun, Owen popped up, pointing his weapon at the masked man at the register as Teddy flung himself up. Before the robber knew what was happening, Teddy had the man on the floor. It happened so quickly that Owen's pulse had barely risen, but he could feel a surge of rage and fear suddenly bubbling beneath the surface.

"Are you okay?" he asked harshly beneath the table. Poppy's hair covered her face, and though he couldn't see it, he could sense her panic. Without thinking, he grabbed her shoulder and squeezed. "Poppy?"

"Yeah," she said, her voice barely a whisper.

"Are you all right?"

She nodded, as if to demonstrate that she was, but he knew she wasn't. It was too soon, too traumatic after what she had already gone through. Anger blistered within him at the robber, at himself for letting them be in this situation. He wanted to pummel the robber, but couldn't bring himself to leave Poppy.

Pulling out his phone, Owen called the local police and within seconds, the entire diner was swarming with police officers. Thankfully, he had notified the cops that they were going to be at the diner before they came. After giving a detailed account of what happened, he took Poppy home while Teddy gave an official statement. Owen sped back to the house, not speaking. Too many things were going on in his head and anything he thought to say seemed inadequate. He stole a glance at Poppy, who sat quietly, a blank expression on her face that he could barely see in the dark. She looked like she was in shock, and it was all his fault.

When they reached the house, he swept the premises with one of the officers who had been sitting at the house, while the other sat on the steps with a catatonic Poppy. The cops agreed to stay outside until Teddy's return and when Owen was finally able to bring Poppy into the house, he had calmed down enough to try to talk to her.

She sat on the couch in the living room, her dark red hair forming a wall around her face, her hands folded in her lap. He knelt in front of her.

"Are you okay?" he asked. Poppy shook her head at first, but then nodded. "Poppy, you've got to talk about it, otherwise it'll eat at you."

After a moment of silence, she spoke in a quiet voice.

"What do you want me to say?"

"Anything. Say something."

"I can't." She looked at him, and he was startled by the distant look in her eyes. "I don't know what to say."

Owen stood up, unable to put his own frustration into words. They shouldn't have gone out. He should have put his foot down from the beginning. *What if my reaction had been slower, or if the robber had shot first? What if it had been the killer?*

"I should never have allowed this," he said, more to himself than to her.

"You couldn't have known," Poppy said, but he shook his head.

"I should have. It was stupid to go out."

"It wasn't stupid."

"Yes, Poppy, it was. Do you hear yourself?" he said, his anger crackling. "You could have been shot. My job is to protect you, and I put you in danger. It was pure negligence to go out—"

"It was not!" she yelled. "You can't keep me here for weeks on end. I'm going crazy."

"Better to be crazy and alive than dead."

"Do *you* even hear yourself? I'd rather be dead than live like this!"

"Don't say stupid things you don't mean."

"You're talking like a jackass!"

"You have no idea the kind of danger you're in, so just sit down and quit talking."

Poppy stood then, rage showing in her eyes. "How dare you? I have no idea? *No idea?* I just buried my murdered grandmother three weeks ago and I have no idea that it could have been me? That it was *supposed* to be me? You don't think that every other minute I think about that?"

"You certainly aren't acting like it!"

"What would you have me do? Hide under a blanket for the rest of my life, locked in my bedroom? That once the killer is caught, I'll be safe for the rest of my life? Anything can happen at any freaking moment and to live forever in utter fear is ridiculous! It isn't living at all!"

"So why don't you just go out and pretend like nothing is going to happen?"

"Fine!" she said, as she stomped toward her room. "I'll leave right now."

"The hell you will."

"Don't talk to me like that!"

"Hey, hey, hey!" Teddy's voice sounded as he walked in from the foyer. "What's going on here?"

"Back off, Detective," Owen shouted, unable to restrain himself. His emotions were out of control.

"Don't yell at him!" Poppy shouted.

"Stand down, Peirce," Teddy said. Owen looked at him, almost challenging. He didn't move. "I said, stand down."

But he couldn't get a handle on himself. He turned and ripped open the sliding glass door, barging out into the night. He tried to beat down the seething rage roaring within him, but it wouldn't subside. He hadn't always been so hotheaded, but it seemed in recent years, especially since Hanna's kidnapping, that every time danger reared its head, he snapped. He had felt a darkness growing within him, consuming him in ways he couldn't understand.

The past year had felt like one long, bitter mood. Every time he became angry, all the anger in his life came to a boiling point, and coupled with that, came the guilt—the guilt he felt about his mother, about his family, about ignoring his duty and fate, everything. He took everything on his shoulders, even the betrayal of his best friend, Roderick, who had stolen a family heirloom right behind his back. That had been his fault, too. He should have known that Roderick's trickster lineage would eventually come into play. Roderick was an Other—of course he couldn't change.

Owen pressed his hand to his forehead, trying to push away a headache. *I shouldn't have snapped at Poppy or Teddy like that.* He inhaled, strangling his anger into submission as he counted to ten. There was no room in his life for such behavior. *I have to get a grip on myself, somehow.*

It hadn't been long, but by the time he got back into the house, Poppy was nowhere to be seen. Teddy sat by the kitchen island, a serious look on his face. Owen instantly felt regret.

"Listen, Teddy—" Owen started, but his partner put his hand up.

"Don't apologize. It's no big deal," he said. "But you have got to get a hold of yourself, Peirce. I can't have a hothead for a partner. That's how good detectives get killed." Owen nodded. "Then, we move on?"

"Sure," Owen said, taking a seat. "Where is she? In bed?"

"Yep. Didn't say much after you walked out." Owen winced at Teddy's choice of words, but nodded again. "The robber was some punk kid, twenty years old, in and out of juvenile detention for petty theft . . . "

Teddy went on to explain what he had learned from the cops. They were able to determine that the robbery was in no way connected with their case. It was a relief, though the coincidence had solidified Poppy's words. She couldn't live the rest of her life hiding under a blanket. Even after the case, there was always going to be a chance of something happening to her, but even as Owen realized this, the tightness in his chest that had grown substantially in the last few weeks seemed almost unbearable now.

Owen sat on the couch and for the next hour, they were quiet, looking up only when they heard the rustling of bedding every now and then. Soon, Teddy stretched and came to him.

"Are you okay?" he asked. Owen, who had been staring at his badge for well over half an hour, looked up and nodded quietly. "Are you sure?"

"Yeah," Owen insisted, trying not to look concerned. "I'll take first shift."

"You sure? You took third shift last night."

"Yeah, I'll be fine. Goodnight."

Teddy shrugged and left the room, which seemed much larger now that Owen was alone with his most annoying adversary—himself.

He looked past the kitchen to Poppy's bedroom door and stared at it for a long time, twirling his badge in his hand. He could almost hear his mind humming as it rushed through the thousand or so conflicted thoughts he had.

Ajax was right. He knew it, but he couldn't accept it. He knew that if he went to California, he wouldn't come back. It would happen just like it always did to their kind: the invisible pull would start in their chests, encouraging them to be close to one another, the auras that lay dormant would shine to life and they would fall in love and live happily ever after, just like the story. He should want that life. He should be glad and happy and ready for it, especially after the last two years, but he couldn't force himself to want it. He had tried to do so, desperately, but there was something deeper, something more he needed to prove. But it wasn't his ego that drove him. It was death.

The suicide had happened nearly two decades ago, and though most people still remembered Cynthia Pechman, no one did so much as Owen. He was only six when his mother jumped from the twenty-first floor of the Alba Hotel in New York City. He had dealt with her death long before he had decided to become a police officer, but Owen had always held tightly to the reason for her suicide; she hadn't followed her story.

He had wished so hard as a child for her to come back, to not be dead, but as his father had warned him and he had later learned, wishing was a dangerous hobby. It kept dreamers in their dreams and forced nature to become unnatural. His mother's death had happened, and no amount of wishing could change that.

It should have shocked him into order, but as much as he tried to be the Prince Charming he was meant to be, a part of him wanted to fight it. He wanted to prove them wrong, to prove that his mother's death had not been part of some recourse for her attempting to live her own life, but because she was sick. He wanted to be free, like she had been, to choose his path and not have to worry about being cursed because of it. It was why he couldn't go to California. If he went, he would solidify his mother's death as a curse to be feared for generations, and he wouldn't do it, even though the other part of him, the inherently Good part of him, wanted to save the nameless girl.

A rare smile crossed his face. What had Hanna said to him during his visit to Charleston that past spring?

"You've got a complex. A knight-in-shining-armor complex."

Owen had promised to visit Hanna after her finals, since she wouldn't be coming home that summer. She'd begged for nearly a month until he had finally agreed to come down for a few days. It had been unbearably hot, though it was only May. Owen wondered how a Michigan girl like Hanna could handle the sweltering Southern summers, but she'd seemed content enough. He'd flown into Charleston and had been picked up by a smiling Hanna, who, after hugging him for several minutes, had declared she was famished and drove him to a famous little eatery tucked somewhere down a brick alley only locals knew about.

During their meal, Owen had mentioned an email he had received from Ajax, informing him that he would be needed in California in the next few months for story guidance. After explaining his ordeal and his reasons behind not wanting to go, he'd told Hanna he had been struggling with his selfish decision.

"It's not selfish, Owen," she said as she ate her sweet potato pie. "It's selfish for this Ajax guy to expect you to drop everything you're doing and run off to California to go help some chick you've never met."

"But I feel like I have to."

"Because you're nuts. You've got a complex," Hanna said, pointing her fork at him. "A knight-in-shining-armor complex."

"Excuse me?"

"You can't help wanting to save every girl who comes along, whether she's stubbed her toe or has three murderous villains after her." Hanna winked.

"Regardless, I think anyone with three murderous villains after them would be glad of some extra help. And since when do I help girls who stub their toes?"

"Remember my friend Carly? You offered to run out and get her gas when she made the joking comment that she probably couldn't make it to a gas station."

"I was being nice."

"Carly probably said that a dozen times a day, at least. She always got around just fine, but you hear of the littlest trouble and you swoop in to save the day." She took another bite of her pie. "See? Complex."

"Must be tough on William with you always being right," he said sarcastically.

"It is," she said, shaking her head. "He forgets sometimes. Like you."

Owen had smiled, and he smiled again as he remembered their conversation. William had joined them soon after, and for three days, Owen had forgotten all about fairy tales and police work. He was content with being just a regular guy, a tourist in a new city, far away from all his troubles.

It was a far cry from where he was now, sitting in a house with his partner and a person in his protection, trying to separate the real world from his own. Ajax's warning was weighing on him, and as much as he wanted to fight it, as hard as he would resist, a part of him knew his struggle would be fruitless. The annoying truth was that his fate was inevitable.

He took another look at Poppy's bedroom door and stood up to stretch. He couldn't stand the confines of this house suddenly. *It was too small or too big*, he thought as he began his first search of the premises.

The night passed quickly, and before he knew it, Owen heard an alarm going off. Confused, he turned onto his side and read the alarm clock, its red numbers flashing 8:00 a.m. Jumping out of bed, Owen grabbed his holster and ran down the stairs. He rushed into the kitchen where Teddy and Poppy stood, talking about her choice in major. Both stopped when they saw him, surprised at his dishevelment.

"What's wrong?" Teddy asked, concerned, putting down his coffee mug.

"Nothing. I thought I had third shift," Owen said.

"I let you sleep," Teddy explained. "You seemed no good when you woke me up."

"You should have mentioned that at two this morning."

"He was just being nice," Poppy said under her breath. Owen glared at her. Seemingly piqued by his stare, she added, "And you can wipe that look off your face."

A slight, almost undetectable Southern accent curled around her words, just touching the edge of her voice. It was a rude statement, a challenge, and he knew it, only he couldn't bring himself to muster up a response. The guilt he felt from last night was still fresh, and though he knew it would be easier to argue with her, he wouldn't. At least, he'd try his hardest not to succumb to his anger. Poppy made him lose his focus too easily and that worried him. *Is it this so-called knight-in-shining-armor complex, or is it something else?*

Owen blinked and shook his head, as the very thought of that question posed too much danger. *It won't do any good thinking about that*, he told himself. Instead, he breathed slowly.

"If we don't communicate, we can be caught off guard, like last night," he said pointedly to Teddy, though everyone in the room seemed to notice his tone was directed toward Poppy. "And people die when we get caught off guard."

"I can't stand it here anymore!" Poppy shouted. "You and your constant attitude! As if you're doing us all a favor by being here. Last night was a coincidence and no one's fault! You can't keep snapping at us every time you feel like it!"

"Poppy, it's fine," Teddy insisted.

"No, it's not. Someone probably told him once upon a time that it was fine to act like that, but it's not. It's disrespectful." Her wording hadn't been lost on Owen, and the surge of her Southern accent grew. "And I flat-out refuse to be kept in this house like some sort of fish in a bowl with a *bully*!"

"Keep your voice down," Owen said, his own voice rising, unable to stay calm. *Damn*, he thought, *how I hate myself.* "I just need to figure this all out," he said, more to himself than to anyone in particular.

It was apparently the wrong thing to say to Poppy, who turned on her heel.

"What is your obsession?" she asked. "Why can't you think of anything else?"

"Because it's my job, and if I can save you, then it was worth it."

"What was worth it?"

He was keenly aware that Teddy was staring at him, but he couldn't say what he meant in front of him. *If I can save Poppy*, he thought, *I can prove to Ajax and Grandmother that choosing to stay away from California is right. That staying here with her was the right choice.*

When he didn't answer, Poppy turned without a word, marched out of the kitchen, and slammed her bedroom door behind her.

Owen could barely concentrate, but he allowed the jumble of emotions to settle in a fog, one he was unwilling to sift through for understanding.

"Owen, what is the damage with you lately?" Teddy asked quietly as he came around the island. "You're not acting like yourself."

"I'm just . . . I've got a lot on my mind, and that girl," he said, motioning toward Poppy's door, "she pushes my buttons for some reason."

"I don't care if she ruffles the Queen of England's feathers, you've got to pull yourself together and quit jumping down everyone's throat."

"I know, I know," Owen said. "I just . . . "

"Listen, whatever it is, get a hold of it. We've got bigger issues."

"Issues?"

"The sheriff from Miner's Way called. There's a situation in Louisiana, something to do with an inheritance."

"What are you talking about? There is no inheritance."

Teddy shook his head.

"Not according to Mr. Pruette. Someone called about an inheritance."

Owen's brow furrowed. There was something strange going on. "I need a copy of Rose Pruette's will."

"I'll call the law offices."

Owen needed some time to think and double-check his facts. He offered to go out and get some doughnuts, and to quickly call Ajax in private. But by the time he exited the coffee shop, holding a box of doughnuts and a carrier of coffee, he was still mulling over what he'd learned.

Something wasn't adding up in his and Teddy's reports. Rose's only living relative aside from her son and Poppy was her sister, a nun who came up from New Orleans and had spent most of the memorial service in tears. *Why would* she *be asking for an inheritance?* He had made a point to make sure Rose didn't have one. It would have made an excellent motive for the killer. Rose had come from a wealthy family before she married, but all that money had dried up long before Poppy was even born. The Pruettes had settled into a middle-class life ages ago, so an inheritance seemed unlikely.

Have I overlooked something, somewhere? A sinking feeling began to grow in his abdomen. *Have I messed up?*

He pulled out his phone and called Ajax.

"Ah, Owen, looking to book a flight? I swear, you people think I'm some sort of travel agent . . ."

"I need the backstory on Roseanna Pruette."

"No, you need to get on a plane."

"Listen to me, Ajax, get me this information, let me catch this person, and . . . " Owen paused and let out an audible sigh before continuing. "And . . . I'll go to California."

Silence followed.

"I know how you feel, Owen, but it's for the best."

Owen doubted very much that he knew anything about how he felt, but he nodded. "Yeah, just get me the information I need, and . . . " Owen trailed off when he saw Teddy beeping in. "I'll talk to you later."

He answered Teddy's call.

"What's up?"

"Is Poppy with you?" he asked, his voice serious.

Owen felt suddenly cold. "No."

"She's not here," Teddy said. "She's gone."

He dropped everything he was carrying and rushed to his car. Making an illegal U-turn, he sped down the road back to the Windgate house while trying to call Poppy.

She didn't answer.

Teddy was waiting in the driveway when he pulled in. "What do you mean she's gone?" Owen asked loudly as he jumped out of the car.

"She's gone. After you left, I did a sweep and tried to get her to talk, but she wouldn't come out. I just thought she was pissed, but when she didn't answer my second knock, I said that if she didn't answer, I'd have to break down the door. No answer, so I kicked it in and she wasn't there. Her bag is gone, which makes me think she left willingly. Where would she go?"

Owen knew she wouldn't go back to Miner's Way, but he suddenly remembered she knew someone only ninety minutes away.

"She's gone to New York City. You get that will and any other information you can. I'll grab her. We'll meet back here as soon as possible."

And with that, Owen was gone.

CHAPTER NINE

It rarely snowed in Miner's Way, yet that year it seemed to be never-ending. Poppy was dreaming. She found herself sitting at her grandmother's kitchen table, painting a watercolor of a horse when she knocked over the gray paint.

"Shoot," she mumbled. "I wish I hadn't done that."

"Wishing is dangerous habit, Poppy. Have a care not to make it one."

Her grandmother had been washing the dishes, gazing out the window that overlooked her garden. It was a rough year for her roses after that winter, Poppy recalled.

"Why do you say that?" Poppy asked. "You always say wishing is dangerous, but nothing ever happens when I wish for things. They never come true. So how can they be dangerous?"

Her grandmother turned around, drying her wrinkled hands with a green dish towel before placing her rose quartz ring back on her finger. Poppy was amazed she could remember such a small detail.

"They could be dangerous for a number of reasons. You said that none of your wishes have come true, correct?"

"Yes."

"Well, do you know there are people who wish all day, every day? They wish for more money, or more power because they think that's what will make them happy. The more they think they want these things, the more they become disenchanted with themselves and their life."

"What's that mean?"

"It means they aren't happy. So they wish for outside things to make themselves happy, but true happiness comes from within."

"So, that's why wishing is dangerous?"

"Yes, and no. Other people tend to wish their lives away without doing anything about it, making wishing a pastime for the uninspired. Then, there's another danger. . . . The most hazardous kind of wishing."

"What's that?"

"When someone wishes for a bad or unnatural thing. It is the worst sort of wishing, especially because those wishes will most likely come true."

"What?" Poppy asked. "Why do bad people's wishes come true?"

"Because they are willing to pay a high price for it."

"So, I shouldn't wish for anything? Not even on my birthday?"

Poppy's grandmother smiled, brushing away a small tear that had escaped, and the memory began to fade. Poppy wanted to hold on to the image longer, but it weakened quickly as she felt the train swing roughly, jolting her awake. She stared out the window of the train as the close-knit homes turned into wires and underground flashing lights.

She had gotten on the train in Mystic and shut off her phone after she received a few calls from Teddy, and then Owen. It was probably the stupidest thing she had ever done, running away from the people who were trying to protect her, but she couldn't help it. The incident from the previous night had nearly shocked her into an early grave. She'd experienced the same horrible, paralyzing feeling that had been bubbling below the surface since her grandmother's funeral. It felt as though her heart would burst and shatter her chest all at once. The only thing that helped her avoid the awful sensation was arguing with Owen. The minute she found her voice, she'd attacked him. If she didn't argue with him, she'd feel the unbearable terror rise in her heart. She felt it clawing at her once she'd stormed off into her room. She needed to do something, go somewhere where she couldn't feel like this. It was why she'd impulsively crawled out of her bedroom window and headed for the train station. She needed to escape, for her sanity's sake.

But her sanity wasn't the whole reason behind leaving. There was something in Owen's words that morning that clung to Poppy. If he saved her, then it would be worth it. He hadn't said what would be worth it, but there was something he was working toward, some goal, and she guessed it had something to do with his other life. He was almost crazed, desperate to prove something, or maybe he just wanted to have it his way. Whatever it was, Poppy didn't want to see it—or him, for that matter. She wanted to get lost for a little while in a big city where no one could find her, and where she could find the familiar comfort of an old friend.

When the train arrived at Grand Central, Poppy must have looked every bit the country girl as she looked up in awe at the massive walls and elegant, Old World ceilings. She stood there, slack-jawed as she slowly spun around, taking in the colossal building. She had never been to Grand Central before and for a moment, she felt very small in the sea of people.

Poppy turned on her phone and scrolled through the missed calls and text messages until she saw Sean's number. Selecting it, she walked toward an exit as the call connected.

"Hey, lady," Sean's friendly voice echoed in her ear.

"Hi, Sean. What's up?" she nearly barked into the receiver.

"Where are you? I can barely hear you."

"Grand Central Station." She paused. "Come get me?"

"What!" he responded excitedly. "I'll be there in twenty! Meet me at the 42nd Street entrance."

Poppy agreed and smiled as she hung up the phone. It took her a few minutes and a few questions to strangers to find the 42nd Street entrance, but when she did, she saw Sean waiting on the street. He was so excited to see her that he never asked why or how she was even there. They drove to his apartment in the TriBeCa neighborhood—a nice section he could never afford on his own. Poppy suspected his family was helping to support him while he attended school full-time and worked. He told her he was lucky to find a paying acting job over the summer while also working as an intern for a private law office.

Once they climbed the staircase to Sean's third-floor apartment, Sean paused and turned to her.

"Listen, Poppy, I know you know that I'm gay," he said quietly. "And I know you're fine with it, but I'm not sure how comfortable I am . . . "

Poppy wasn't sure what he meant. "Sean, I'm not going to—"

"I know, I know you're not. But, I haven't told you—or anyone, for that matter—but one of my roommates, Ryan, he's sort of my . . . I mean, he's gay too, and we are dating, I guess?"

Poppy smirked in spite of herself. He was nervous, and rightfully so, but she had so much on her plate at the moment that she doubted she would have noticed he had roommates.

"Sean, it's okay," she said as she gave him a quick hug. "I promise I won't embarrass you."

"Stop it, I don't think that." He smirked at her. "Only Ava is here right now," he said, unlocking the door. "She's a bit reserved, unlike Nina, who may be the craziest person I've ever met."

"How many roommates do you have?"

"Just three. Ava is pre-law too; we have pretty much all the same classes now. Ryan just graduated NYU and he's in advertising. He's best friends with Nina, who I met at school. She's part of the drama program."

"My goodness, it's like a whole other life up here," Poppy said, a touch of sadness in her voice. How fast their once entwined, inseparable lives had detangled. They walked into the small apartment. It was empty. "Where is Ava?"

"Probably in her room," he said as he dropped his bag on the futon.

The walls weren't very high, and it certainly didn't look like how Poppy imagined had a cool, NYC apartment to look like. Instead of a massive loft with large windows and exposed brick, it was cramped with white walls; throw rugs littered the old hardwood floors. The fluorescent light in the kitchen was almost blinding, but they pushed through what she guessed was a straightened-up living room. Poppy sat on one of the two mismatched recliners and jumped a little when Sean's phone rang, vibrating on the glass coffee table.

"Huh, unknown," he said under his breath before Poppy jumped up. "Hello?"

"Hang up!" she shouted.

"Uh, yes, this is Sean," he continued while mouthing, "Who is this?" to Poppy.

"It's him. It's Owen!" She quickly grabbed his phone and clicked it off. "I'm sorry, but I don't want him to find me."

"Why not?"

"Things got . . . messy. I was going crazy up there."

Just then, the door opened and a very tall, very dark, and very handsome man wearing a gray fitted T-shirt walked into the kitchen. The man, who looked first at Sean, looked back at Poppy and grinned.

"There's no way this is the famous Poppy Pruette of Miner's Way?" he said, coming over and wrapping Poppy in a bear hug. He twirled her around, which she found odd, but couldn't help but smile when she saw how happy Sean looked.

He put her down and kissed Sean on the cheek, making him blush, which in turn made Poppy blush. She put her worries on the back burner as she smiled.

"It's so nice to meet you," she said.

"Let me just get changed and we'll go out to eat. I'm so glad to meet you finally!" He disappeared into one of the back rooms.

Poppy barely had time to congratulate Sean on having such excellent taste when Ryan reappeared. They went out and grabbed a cab to take to Sean and Ryan's favorite pizza place. Ryan seemed genuinely interested in her, and he asked a slew of questions about Sean as well. It was comforting to Poppy; if she and Sean couldn't live near each other, at least he was with someone who seemed to truly care for him.

After the pizza, Poppy wanted to see Central Park. They took a taxi up famous Fifth Avenue, and Poppy's eyes glazed over when they passed all the high-end shops, including Mikimoto, Burberry, and Tiffany & Co. They got out near Central Park Zoo and walked through, all the way to Columbus Circle on the opposite end. From there, they took another cab down through Broadway and wound up down by the river walk.

The sun was setting by the time they returned to Sean and Ryan's apartment. The city was truly stunning at night, so imposing and amazing. New York was the most impressive, beautiful, and frightening place she had ever been. Poppy felt hidden here, and she almost wished she could stay forever, if wishing weren't so dangerous. She felt like a new person, until she ran into Ryan's arm. She looked up and saw he was staring at a black sedan idling across the street.

"What's that about?" Ryan asked.

"Oh, no," Poppy said under her breath.

As they crossed the street, a man stepped out of the back of the car. There, with a stoic look on his face, was Owen.

"Detective Peirce," Sean said, extending his hand. "Nice to see you again."

Poppy noticed the hesitation, but couldn't help feeling at ease when they shook hands.

"Mr. McCray," he said, also nodding at Ryan. "I have come to collect Miss Pruette."

"I thought you might. I'll go grab your stuff—" he said, turning to Poppy.

"Won't be necessary. I already got it."

Ryan looked annoyed, as did Sean, but he shook his head and smiled.

"Well then, Poppy, until next time." He hugged her. "Love you."

"Love you, too. I'll text you. It was nice to meet you, Ryan."

"You, too," Ryan said, giving her a quick hug goodbye.

Poppy turned and walked toward the town car. Owen followed so closely behind her she wondered if he thought she might try and flee. When she reached for the car door handle, she turned to tell him to back off, but was suddenly dumbfounded to find him hovering over her, like some great, looming giant. His angry face was barely inches away from hers and she could feel his breath on her chin. She shivered. His calculating eyes shifted, revealing a new emotion she didn't understand. He looked like he might eat her, just like the wolf who ate Little Red Riding Hood. He leaned in menacingly and Poppy held her breath, her eyes flickering from his to his mouth as it opened.

"You're in serious trouble," Owen whispered into her ear. Her senses went into overdrive, causing a firestorm of emotion to explode within her. Fury, fear, something else? They all rolled into the one as she grabbed onto the most familiar of the three. Fury.

"With who?" she said, her voice unstable. She cursed herself for sounding so shaky. Instead, she put her hands up against his chest and pushed him away, surprised that he felt rather like a rock wearing clothes. Ignoring this, she turned to open the car door. "The law, or you?" she asked smarmily as he got into the car after her. She sat as far away as she could, trying to control her breathing that had suddenly become erratic. She motioned to the driver, who wasn't Teddy as she had expected. "Who is that?"

"West 81st and Central," he told the driver before turning back to her. "We can't go back to Stonington until it's been swept, and Teddy is on a flight to Virginia following up on a lead, which means I don't have any backup. So we're going to the only place I feel like you'll be safe."

"Where's that?"

"My family's home."

CHAPTER TEN

*P*oppy looked out her window as the town car raced uptown, dodging between vehicles at such a speed she might have had some anxiety if she cared to think about it. She felt completely drained of energy as hundreds of artificial lights flashed before her eyes. Owen sat next to her, but he felt a world away. When they hit a bit of traffic, Poppy let herself steal a glance at him.

Owen's eyes were closed and his mouth was slightly open, as if concentrating on his breathing. The lights of the city illuminated his face in way that seemed fitting, almost as if he belonged in a big city. Poppy didn't know why, but she studied his face. She was surprised that even after she had memorized his features, she never noticed the curve of his jaw. It wasn't wide or chiseled, but it wasn't soft or rounded either. It was somewhere in-between, and for the first time, Poppy thought he looked strong. His neck was larger than most, but she bet it was due to some sort of shoulder workout, or whatever gave men big trapezius muscles. He looked bare, primal maybe—she wasn't sure—but she felt herself suddenly in awe of his looks and for the briefest moment, she wanted to touch him before she remembered she was supposed to be mad at him.

He yawned then, and she couldn't help but feel sorry for being the cause of his weariness, though she did take note of his facial muscles as they stretched. When he was finished, he opened his eyes and looked at her. Poppy's eyes widened slightly when she saw the same unnerving look he had given her before whispering in her ear. She turned to look out the window, focusing instead on the passing cars. *There's something sparkling beneath the surface*, she thought, ignoring every warning sign going off in her head.

They arrived a few minutes later in front of a beautiful old stone building that sat opposite to a park. *Central Park*, Poppy remembered, as she tried to see the famous wood. For as dangerous as the city was reputed to be, she didn't really believe it and had nearly walked across the street before feeling Owen's hand on her shoulder. It was just a tap, Poppy noticed, and she followed him up several large, concrete steps to a thick oak door with intricate black iron hinges.

Walking through the door, Poppy could barely see the foyer it was so dark, save for a tiny lamp sitting on a table. It was much cooler inside than it was out in the street, though, and she liked it.

"The guest room is upstairs," Owen said, his voice echoing slightly. "I'll show you to it, and then see you in the morning."

Poppy didn't answer him, just followed him up the stairs, careful not to trip in the dim light. When they reached the second floor, she followed him down the hallway toward yet another set of stairs. *How large is this place? And how much could this home be worth?* She didn't know much about New York real estate, but she had just come from an apartment in the downtown area, where four roommates shared a studio with makeshift walls.

Suddenly, Poppy felt inadequate in Owen's presence. She had always felt a bit like a big fish in her small hometown, but here she was in Owen's town, the biggest city in the world, and he was someone, and she, well . . . she was just a wandering Virginian in a different world.

Poppy felt a wave of exhaustion wash over her as she topped the second flight of stairs. It could have been the hour, but she suspected it was more than that.

"This is your room," Owen said quietly as he stopped in front of a door. Poppy nodded and went to walk by him without a word when he touched her shoulder again. "Poppy, I know it's late and I don't want to start a fight, but don't run away tonight, or ever again for that matter. I can't have you—"

Without warning, a surge of tears flooded Poppy's eyes as she quickly turned, hugging Owen around the neck. It was the first time she had cried since her grandmother's death. She cried uncontrollably for reasons she didn't know. Maybe it was because she felt helpless, finally intimidated by the size of the city, or it could have been the growing anxiety she felt with every step she took, as if something bad was coming and she could only ignore it for so long before it took over her thoughts.

"I don't know," she stuttered. "I don't know why."

"It's okay," he said quickly, holding her tightly. It felt incredibly comforting to be held so. "It's all going to be okay."

"It's not," she breathed, shaking. "I feel like this terrible thing is coming, and I can't deal with it. I can only try to ignore it because otherwise, it's going to get me and engulf me and I don't know what it is. I've never felt like this before."

She continued to cry and hardly even realized that Owen had opened the door behind her. She was huddled under his arm at his side as he moved her into a fairly large room. The floors were a dark hardwood, which complemented the dated bedroom furniture. The wallpaper looked fairly new, with peach- and cream-colored floral patterns done in a modern touch. He pulled her down to sit on a dark wooden chest that sat at the foot of the bed.

"It sounds like you're describing a panic attack," Owen said, his arm still tightly around her. "They're not fun to go through, but in a minute, you'll feel better. I'll get you a glass of water."

"No," she said as he went to let her go. "Don't go yet."

"Okay," he said. "Okay, I'm here."

"I feel like I'm dying," she said through the tears. "I felt like this at the funeral, and last night after the woman screamed in the diner. I hate it."

"I know. I'm guessing you get really warm and your ears start to feel like they're vibrating, and soon, you're convinced that your heart is going to explode."

"That's exactly . . . " she said, pulling away to look at him. "Have you had one before?"

"I used to get them a lot," he admitted, "but I learned to talk myself down."

"It's awful. I want them to stop, but I don't know how to control them. They're the worst thing I've ever experienced."

"Yeah, they can be."

"How do you get rid of them?"

"Well, I found a few websites, a couple of chat rooms, and talked to people. I didn't want to do the whole group therapy thing. I read a few books too, and when I realized that other people could describe my exact feelings during the attacks, I thought I could figure it out. Realizing that I wasn't the only person like this made it a lot easier for me to control it. It took a few years of cognitive therapy, but I got a hold of it."

As he finished talking, Poppy felt her heart rate slow down, back to normal as she wiped away her tears.

"See? It's already gone, isn't it?"

"Yes," she said quietly. For a few moments, they sat silently next to each other before Poppy spoke again. "I'm sorry I ran away."

Her voice was raw and quiet.

"It's all right," he said. "Just get some sleep tonight, okay? We'll talk about it tomorrow."

"I just couldn't handle the walls. I felt like the world was closing in."

"I know. I should have foreseen that."

"There was no way for you to know I had panic attacks."

Owen shook his head as he stood up. Poppy stood up as well.

"Still, you're my responsibility."

Without so much as a warning, Poppy stood on her toes and kissed Owen on the cheek. It seemed to happen in slow motion, as she held herself still for a long moment before dropping back to her heels. Owen stood there, showing neither interest nor disinterest. Confused, Poppy spoke.

"Goodnight, Owen," she said softly before turning toward the bed.

Owen nodded, and without looking, he turned off the light and closed the door. For a moment, she thought she heard him whisper "Goodnight" back on the other side of the door, but unsure, Poppy drifted into a much anticipated sleep.

Poppy was sitting with her legs curled beneath her on the overstuffed, floral armchair that sat in the corner of her grandmother's bedroom, reading a science magazine that wasn't keeping her attention. She looked up and saw her grandmother rub her eyes as she woke. This had only happened a year ago, when her grandmother had the flu and was in bed for a week. Poppy barely left her side the entire time.

"Do you want any water?" she asked, putting her magazine down.

"No, thank you, dear," she said. "But why don't you come over here, so I can tell you a story."

"Gram, I'm in college now. I think I might be too old for stories."

"Well, this one has to do with you," she said, before breaking into a coughing fit. Poppy was instantly by her side, sitting on the edge of her bed, holding her hand. "My, you're attentive."

"The doctor said—"

"The doctor said what he said, and that's his opinion. Now, do you remember what I used to tell you when you were a little girl? About Little Red Riding Hood?"

"Yeah, that we were related to the girl in the story? Or rather, related to the person who inspired the author to write the story?"

"Do you remember the story?"

"Yes."

"Not the Grimm one. The one I told you."

Poppy had remembered her grandmother's version, though she would have loved to forget. It was a gruesome story about a murderous man who mutilated a woman and her grandmother before eating them. Supposedly, the man was crazy, but it still gave her nightmares.

"Yes," she whispered.

"There is a family like ours, from this same story. The Wolf line is bound to cross the Hood line again."

"Why?"

"It's written this way, but I don't want you to ever be afraid of this. I've arranged it for you to never have to deal with them. Do you understand? So, when I'm gone—"

"Don't."

"Listen. When I'm gone, you'll never have to worry about them, but that's not what you need to know. You can see the auras if they approach you, so be wary not to trust anyone with one. Only one will survive, my love, do you understand?"

Poppy had thought she was talking nonsense, but had agreed so she wouldn't become overly excited.

"Yes, Gram. I understand."

The dream faded and soon, Poppy woke up feeling well-rested and alert. The panic attack had knocked her out cold, making for an easy night's sleep.

She looked around the room she was in and noticed the tall, cream-colored drapes hanging in front of a pair of massive windows. She crawled out of bed and walked over, pulling them back to look down onto the street. Though it was just a sliver, she could see a tree all the way to her right and guessed the permanent bedrooms in the house showed a view of Central Park.

Turning, she saw a door slightly ajar that led into a bathroom. Grateful to find a shower, Poppy quickly washed and dressed into a simple patterned wrap dress. Dresses were easier to travel in, she always believed, and it was proving to be a smart choice. After she'd gathered all her things together, she slung her bag over her shoulder and exited the room.

The hallway gave her pause, as it was a tall, impressive corridor with arched walkways and crown molding that looked so incredibly detailed Poppy again found herself feeling less than adequate in this beautiful home.

She found the staircase and began her march down, and then again down the second set of stairs until she reached the foyer. The floor, marble, and walls with white panels all looked like it had been restored to the former glory of a bygone era. Poppy placed her bag by the front door and headed down the hallway behind the staircase. She heard the clanging of silverware and dishes, and hoped to find a kitchen where Owen might be, but instead, she stumbled into a dining room.

Full of people.

Poppy stopped short as her eyes scanned the long, mahogany table, searching for Owen's face, but she couldn't find him. Five pairs of strange eyes looked at her.

"Excuse me," she mumbled as she tried to fade back into the hallway.

"Not at all," the eldest woman said, her voice commanding Poppy to halt. "Come in here." Poppy took a step forward into the dining room, but was sure not to leave the doorway. "You must be Poppy Pruette?"

"Yes."

The old woman, impeccably dressed in a skirt suit and wearing a double-strand pearl necklace with matching earrings, looked wearily at her. Her white hair was arranged in a neat, cropped cut.

"Yes. Yes, you have Rose's nose, I believe. And a bit of her coloring." Poppy's mouth opened a little in shock. Had this woman known her grandmother?

"Yay!" a young woman about Poppy's age nearly squealed. She barely had time to register what was going on when the young woman grabbed her wrist and all but dragged her toward the table. "You can sit next to me. This is so exciting! Where's Owen, Uncle George?"

"He's gone out for something or other, I don't know," said an older man, watching Poppy pointedly.

"Excuse me," Poppy said, looking at the other two who hadn't spoken—a young man, possibly Owen's age, as well as a woman with blonde hair who looked as though she might be related to Owen. "I'm assuming you all must be Owen's family, but I don't know who is who."

"Of course!" the young woman to her right said. "I'm Lynette, Owen's cousin, and this," she said, pointing to the young couple at the end of the table, "is Owen's sister, Ana, and her husband, Jonathan." She nodded at the older man. "Uncle George is Owen's father, and last but not least, Helena Peirce, the matriarch of the family."

A little overwhelmed, Poppy nodded.

"Hello, everyone."

"Poppy Pruette, granddaughter of Rose Pruette, of the Hood lineage," Helena said after a beat. "You've been giving Owen a hard time?"

Crap.

"Uh, well, sort of . . . "

"No need to be afraid of me," Helena said. "I believe Owen deserves to be run through the gamut from time to time."

"Mother," Uncle George—or, to Poppy, Mr. Peirce—said. "There's no need to get on Owen."

"I'm not getting on him."

"I couldn't be happier that he's back," Ana said, smiling. She seemed a bit uptight, but sincere. "He hasn't been home in over two years."

"Coffee?" Lynette asked Poppy, who nodded. "I haven't seen Owen in years," she said, addressing the whole table. "Not since he came with me to school that one year."

"Well, that's what going to school abroad will do," Helena said matter-of-factly.

"Still, he could visit in the summer," Lynette said, leaning toward Poppy. "I'm originally from New Orleans, but moved here after my parents passed away."

"Oh, I'm so sorry."

"It happened years ago," she said, shrugging it off and pointing her fork at Mr. Peirce. "Owen and Ana hounded Uncle George for weeks for me to move here."

"Lynette," Mr. Peirce said warningly, not looking up from his newspaper.

Lynette rolled her eyes, obviously not impressed.

"They're so stuffy," she said quietly, though Poppy doubted that she really cared if the others heard her.

Lynette seemed quite out of place in this room, and Poppy was instantly grateful for her presence. In fact, now that she looked at Lynette, she realized just how different she was from the others. Her eyes were dark brown, with her top eyelids outlined softly in black liner. Her skin was about seven shades darker than everyone else's, but it was her hair that Poppy really loved. There was so much of it, and the natural, soft curls of it made her stand out in the most beautiful way. Maybe it was her cheerfulness in the otherwise gloomy room, or maybe it was because she just looked the opposite of everyone, which was how Poppy felt, but she was glad to be seated next to her.

"Youth," Helena said, almost as a joking insult. Helena turned her attentions to Poppy once again. "I'm sorry to hear about the death of Rose. She was a friend of mine from when we were girls."

More surprises.

"Was she?" Poppy asked. "She never mentioned it."

"No, I suppose she wouldn't have. That was years ago, but I was sure Owen would have mentioned it to you."

"Owen likes to keep me in the dark on a lot of things," Poppy said quickly before she could stop herself. When everyone at the table paused and looked up at her, she felt as though she were going to faint. "I mean, that is, he likes to keep to himself."

Silence followed. *Damn, why didn't I just keep my mouth shut?* She was about to speak again, but the sudden laughter of Helena seemed to startle everyone.

"I'm glad I'm not the only one he takes pleasure in annoying," she said as a door closed from somewhere. Poppy's eyes snapped to the doorway, and when Owen appeared, she felt the air leave her lungs. "Ah, speak of the devil."

Owen's eyes caught Poppy's and although he was on the other end of the room, she couldn't help but feel him assessing the situation. With barely a nod toward her, he turned his attention to Helena.

"I think you're being a little harsh with the nicknames," Owen said as he came around the table. As he reached for a teacup, Mr. Peirce stood up.

"I'm running late," Mr. Peirce said. "I have to go to the office."

"George, it's Sunday. What could you possibly have to do at work?" Helena asked, but her son kissed her forehead.

"Business never sleeps, Mother." He stood up straight and looked at Ana. "I'll see you tomorrow morning?"

Ana nodded. He looked up at Owen, and Poppy could see the tension between father and son. He held out his hand. "It was good to see you, Owen."

"You too," he said evenly.

"I hope everything works out with your case, Poppy," he said. "It was nice to meet you."

"You too," she said as he turned and left.

"We should go as well," Ana said a moment later. "We're supposed to meet the Dawsons at the club at noon," she said as she and Jonathan stood up. She looked at Owen. "I'm on the committee for the Ballet's Fall Gala this year. It's falling on Halloween, so you can imagine the themes getting thrown around."

Though he seemed less than amused, Owen smiled the same tight smile Ana had given Poppy.

"Enchanting," he said sarcastically, but Ana only smiled.

"Maybe you can stay in town for an extra night?" she asked. "We can do dinner."

"I wish I could, but the case . . . "

"Okay." Ana nodded, disappointed. She kissed Owen on the cheek, and then her grandmother. "It was nice to meet you, Poppy."

"You too, Ana. Jonathan."

Jonathan nodded and followed Ana out of the dining room. Owen stood, leaning against the wall as he took a sip of his coffee.

"Sit, Owen," Helena ordered, and then, after a brief hesitation, she added, "Please." Owen took a seat next to her on the opposite side of Poppy. "So, have you found your murderer yet?"

The question was a heavy one, but Lynette perked up.

"Lynette, kitchen."

"But—"

"Don't make me ask twice."

Lynette sighed loudly and rolled her eyes again.

"Don't leave," she said to Poppy as she stood up. "I want to talk to you."

"Why don't I just—" Poppy said before being cut off.

"Miss Pruette, keep your seat."

A bit terrified of the Peirce matriarch, Poppy stayed where she was while Lynette disappeared behind her. Owen was looking at his coffee with an annoyed look on his face.

"Well, Owen? I asked you a question."

"Yes, and it's one you already know the answer to, so I choose to remain silent."

Poppy's brow raised, and Helena seemed to notice.

"You know, Miss Pruette, he wasn't always so hostile toward me. We got along quite well for years before he decided to go his own way." Poppy nodded and looked at Owen, who all but glared at her. "So, you've not caught Rose's murderer. What brings you to New York?"

"I told you last night on the phone—"

"You told me no such thing. You said you were bringing your witness to the house, and when I questioned you, you hung up." She paused. "I'd like to help you with your case, Owen."

"I don't need any help. My partner is following up on a lead and we're getting close to our guy."

"We have connections, Owen."

"This wasn't story-related," he said quickly, his temper mounting. "Rose Pruette wasn't killed based on a story. It was a random act, so really, your connections aren't needed."

This seemed to catch Helena off guard.

"Not story-related? It's just a coincidence?"

Poppy prickled at her tone. This was the second time someone had mentioned her grandmother's death as an accident, even though she had been deliberately murdered. It didn't sit well with her.

"I'm not really at liberty to discuss the case. We'll be leaving in the morning."

"Very well, then on to the matter in California."

"Not. Now."

"May I be excused?" Poppy interjected quickly.

"Yes," Helena nodded, looking at Owen. "And we must discuss it now."

Poppy disappeared behind the same door that Lynette had, which turned out to be a short hallway. She went through another door and found an older woman in a dark gray outfit stirring her tea as she read the paper. She looked up, smiled, and continued to read. Poppy was wondering if she was the maid when she saw Lynette enter from a back room.

"Oh, good! They kicked you out, too," she said excitedly as she hurried over to Poppy. "So, you're from the Hood line? How exciting!" Lynette smiled, seemingly studying Poppy. "I've never met one of the Mid-levels before."

"The what?" Poppy asked.

"The Mid-levels. They're the stories that don't involve princesses and kings and stuff like that. They're the moral stories, the ones actually written to teach people stuff. Well, besides happily ever after. There're only a few of you, I believe."

"Oh," Poppy said, surprised that she had never heard of this term.

"Oh, shoot," Lynette said, suddenly looking crestfallen. "I didn't mean anything by it."

"No, that's all right. No offense taken." Poppy looked over at the maid. "Is there a balcony or something somewhere? I'd like to step out for a minute. I think I need some fresh air."

"Oh, sure, follow me to the courtyard."

Poppy followed Lynette out, and for the first time since entering the dining room that morning, she exhaled easily. The courtyard was small, paved with white stone and a bit of crawling ivy along one of the outside walls. Terracotta-potted plants were arranged with the utmost care, and a sweet little four-top table sat in the middle.

"Thanks," Poppy said. "I'm sorry if I seem a bit standoffish. This is all a bit overwhelming."

"I understand," Lynette said, leaning against the ivy-covered wall. "When I first came here four years ago, I don't think I spoke for two weeks. It's a bit of a different world, New York City, especially this family."

"When you first came here? Oh, after your parents passed away?"

"Yes. I was in eighth grade when they passed away in a car accident. We'd lived in New Orleans my whole life until then," she said as she pushed herself off the wall and began to walk, slowly circling. "That's when Uncle George took me in."

"So, you're Owen's cousin on his father's side?" Poppy asked, trying to map out Owen's family in her head.

"No, his mother's, actually. My father was Aunt Cynthia's brother," she said, winking.

"So, then, are you a princess or something, too?"

"Actually," Lynette said sheepishly, "yes."

"Oh," Poppy said, hoping her sarcasm in her previous statement had gone unnoticed. "Um, if you don't mind me asking, I know Owen is from the Charming lineage, so I'm guessing his father and grandmother are as well, but what is his mother's lineage, and yours?"

"Slumber," she said simply.

"Oh," Poppy said. Then, realizing what she'd said a moment later. "Oh! You mean Sleeping Beauty?"

"I don't like to say that because it's presumptuous," she said, making a face. "I would sound pretty full of myself if I walked around saying I was a beauty."

Poppy smiled.

"Um, how many lines are there?"

"About twenty or so of the Good. Who knows about the Others, though. Bad always seems to outweigh the good. There are ten Highers, families that descend from kings and queens, then about four or five Mid-Levels, like yourself, and a handful of Lows, stories involving a lot of magic or animals. Since magic has sort of died out in the world, their stories are harder to track, and animal stories are even more troublesome."

"There's a wolf in the Hood story, though."

"Yeah, but he's an Other."

"Oh," Poppy said, though she was still confused. "I feel like I should be taking a class on this. My family never went into much detail with the stories. Hey, this is going to sound stupid, but are you tired a lot? Because I'm a redhead and I wonder if it has something to do with this red hood business."

"I never thought about it," she said tilting her head. "Wouldn't that be odd, though? I don't think it works like that with anyone in the Charming line, though," she quipped.

"Agreed," Poppy said. "So, you go to boarding school?"

"I did. This was my last year, so I'm starting college in the fall."

They talked at length about college life, and for the first time in a long time, Poppy felt like a normal twenty-year-old. Everything from television and movies, to hair products and makeup. Lynette seemed like a girly-girl, and though Poppy wouldn't have described herself as such, she was thrilled to completely immerse herself in such a discussion.

Lynette told Poppy that she had gone to boarding school in France and had been fluent in French as it was her first language growing up. Her mother, a nurse, was Haitian and had insisted that Lynette learn French first. Her parents had met at a charity event for the hospital her mother worked at and had fallen in love almost instantly. Lynette always wondered if her father's lineage had anything to do with their love at first sight. She also told Poppy that she had been accepted at Princeton and was excited since it was her father's alma mater. Overall, Lynette seemed to have everything going for her. She was smart, beautiful, and genuinely nice. They talked for so long that Poppy barely realized an hour had passed before Owen found them.

"There you two are," he said, looking slightly beaten down, but happy to see them. He pulled one of the chairs out from the table and took a seat. "*Comment s'est passé le voyage en avion*, Lynette?"

"*Ça va*," she said, shrugging. "I like your friend, Owen. She's cool."

"Yeah, I think so, too," he said, without looking at Poppy. "Mind if I have a private word with her?"

"Sure," Lynette said. "Talk to you later, Poppy."

"You, too," she said as Lynette went inside. She turned to Owen. "I think I like her the most."

"I don't blame you. Lynette's always been the most likeable of the bunch. I feel bad that I haven't seen her or Ana in such a long time. I should really visit them more often."

"I think you should." She paused. "So, what did Helena say?"

"Nothing important," he said, though a shadow seemed to pass over his face. "I'd like to get back to Connecticut as soon as possible. I know I said we'd go tomorrow morning, but I think tonight would be best."

"Oh," Poppy said, a little disappointed.

"Is that okay?"

"Yeah, I just . . . I actually don't know why I feel let down. Maybe it's just the thought of going back to being stationary, you know?"

"I know, but it's the safest place for you. Too many people know me in this city, and word is already out that I'm back." He shook his head and gave her a look. "You couldn't have gone to Boston?"

"Sorry," Poppy said. "I don't have any friends in Boston."

"Well, I guess we'd better get ourselves together. I've got to call Teddy, and you should let your father know you're all right. I have to call my captain." Owen yawned. "And do about a million other things."

"You seem tired. Did you not sleep well?"

"I never did in this house, not since—" Owen stopped himself. "I'll see you in a bit," he said, completely avoiding his previous sentence. "And don't leave the house, Poppy. I'm serious."

"I won't," she said as he left her alone in the courtyard.

Pulling out her phone, she answered a text from Sean and called her father's phone. She was about to hang up when she heard Rupert's voice answer.

"Hey, Poppy, how you doing?"

"All right. Is my dad available?"

"Not right now. He's in a meeting. I'll tell him you called, though."

"Thanks," she said, and hung up.

Poppy spent the rest of the day walking in and out of the mansion's rooms, wondering how amazing it must have been for Owen to grow up in such a place. After dinner that night, Poppy was called by Helena into the living room.

"Do you know the tale of the Three Virtues?" Helena asked.

"Sort of," Poppy said, sitting down. "A fairy tale, isn't it? My grandmother always told me bits and pieces, but never the full story. Why? Is it important that I know it?"

"In a way," she said. "A long time ago, before you were born, there were three sisters known as the Three Virtues. The eldest was kind, the second was beautiful, and the youngest was wise, while also being cursed with fear, vengeance, and pride."

"This is how my grandmother told the story," Poppy said, doubtful.

"Well, it's a popular story in our world. They loved each other at first, more than most. But when the two younger sisters fell in love with the same man, a rift was made. They fought viciously with each other until the man they both loved chose the youngest sister. Wisdom over beauty. The middle sister was so enraged by his choice, so utterly devastated that she decided to get her revenge on both her sister and the man who broke her heart. She wished for her sister to know the same heartbreak she felt. The man she sought out to make this wish wasn't very skilled, but he agreed. Now, because he wasn't a very talented man, he warned the middle sister that such a wish would put into motion a series of tragic events that would ultimately destroy her and everyone she ever loved. Only one would survive. Ignoring his warning, she agreed to his terms, effectively causing a death and creating a life."

Poppy was stunned.

"Who was the one that survived?"

"No one knows," she said, her eyes boring into Poppy's.

"Why are you telling me this?" she asked quietly after a moment of silence.

"The same reasons stories have been told for centuries," Helena said. "It's a warning." Poppy stared. "All three of the sisters loved each other once, didn't they?"

"Yes."

"So they all shared a quality, a spark that we all have within us. When the second sister made her dark wish, her spark was tarnished. Her love caused a curse. She disregarded the first rule that we all must live by."

"What's that?"

"Not to be greedy," Helena said. "We are all given only what we can handle, my dear. When we try to take what isn't ours, in every aspect of our lives, things tend to go badly."

Poppy looked at her hands and tried to understand what Helena was talking about. Why would she tell Poppy a story about greed when she wasn't being greedy?

"Poppy," Owen said, coming around the corner into the living room. "It's time to go." He paused and looked at both of them. "Is something wrong?"

"No," Helena said, and Poppy shook her head to agree. Helena stood and walked over to her grandson. "Good luck, Owen. See you soon."

"Goodbye," he said as he kissed her on the cheek. With that, Helena left the room. Owen approached Poppy, who stood up. "Are you sure you're okay? Did she say something to you?"

"No," Poppy said, tucking her feelings about her conversation with Helena away. *That will need some undivided attention to sift through.* She shook her head and looked Owen in the eyes. "Are we leaving now?"

"Yes."

"I wanted to say goodbye to Lynette."

"She's gone out with a few of her friends," Owen said, "but she told me to give you her number. Ready?"

Poppy nodded and followed him into the foyer and out of the house. With one last look behind her, Poppy turned and walked around the black sedan, to where a man held the front passenger door open for her. She thanked him as Owen got into the driver's side.

They drove for about twenty minutes before the city began to melt away behind them. It was a bittersweet parting for Poppy, who had enjoyed her time there, even though she was still basically under protection.

Protection, she thought to herself. *From what, at this point?* According to everyone, her grandmother had been murdered by someone who had no idea who or what she was, which made the case for Poppy's protection less than arguable. Some random psychopath had killed Rose; no one wanted Poppy dead. She thought as much, but decided to bring it up to Owen in the morning. She didn't want to talk to him at the moment.

The story Helena had told her felt heavy on her shoulders. She felt like there was something there, something to block her from Owen. Had she meant to tell her to dissuade Poppy from having feelings for her grandson? *Because I don't*, she thought to herself. She should have told Helena that. She had absolutely no romantic feelings for Owen and was glad, because she wasn't so sure she'd like going to his family's for the holidays. Except for Lynette, they all seemed a bit much . . .

Of course, it was one thing to naturally not have feelings, but to be told to not have feelings didn't sit well with her. She could see where Owen got his bossiness from. Why did everyone think it was all right to tell her what to do? Owen must have noticed her contemplative stare, because he turned off the highway.

"Where are we going?" she asked.

"A back way," he said. "What's up with you? You seem preoccupied."

"Yeah, I guess I am."

Silence, then, "You want to talk about it?"

"I don't know, I think I'm just feeling a little lost, and meeting your family was a bit overwhelming."

"Yes, they can be."

"Is your father mad at you?" she asked. "He seemed so distant."

"Not as mad as my grandmother," Owen said. "But I'm sure it's up there. Ana works with him at P.D. Peirce and Co."

"Wait," Poppy said loudly, shocked. "P.D. Peirce and Co., as in, the bank?"

"Yes, the bank."

"Oh my God," Poppy said as the catchy jingle for P.D. Peirce and Co. sounded through her memory. It had to be one of the largest banks in the country. She stared at Owen in shock. "You have to be a billionaire."

"Hey, I make a detective's salary. I don't have anything to do with P.D. Peirce and Co. Which is probably why I tend to get the cold shoulder when I go home."

"And you just left it all?"

"Yep."

"Why? It seems like you could have anything in the world you wanted."

"Yep."

"Is that all you have to say about it? Yep?"

"Look, I don't expect you to understand. I don't expect anyone to really understand. I just have a simpler idea of life than they do, and sure, money is great and makes the world go round, but I'm happier doing a job I love and making my own way in the world. I don't think I would have been happy otherwise."

Poppy nodded, trying to understand. "I guess it would feel pretty confining, living like that. Like a fish in a bowl, huh?"

"Suffocating is a better word. I just wish they could appreciate my choice to make my own way."

"Have you tried to talk to them about it?"

"Hardly. The Peirce family doesn't really talk about things like that."

"Maybe they'd be a little more receptive if they knew how you felt about everything."

"I know them, Poppy. They wouldn't understand. They think my leaving is a rejection of them and their lifestyle. They would think I was saying something that I wasn't, and I don't have the time to sit there and be lectured about how I choose to live my life."

"You don't think that maybe it might be beneficial to take a few days off work and try to work it out with your family?"

"When am I supposed to take a day off, let alone a few? Right now? After this case, or before the next one? The few days I get to myself are for me. I don't see why it's such a big deal. I chose this life, and I'm happy with it. My family doesn't understand, and I'm okay with that, too."

"I just think it's a little sad, that's all." Poppy looked out her window, watching lights from little cottages pass by. "Family is supposed to be the most important thing, you know?"

"I know, but every family is different. This is how mine works."

They drove in silence after that and didn't speak until they reached Windgate. Two and a half hours after leaving New York, they pulled up the driveway and saw another black sedan parked in front of the garage. The front light was on, along with a dim interior glow.

"Good, Teddy's here. I texted him before leaving New York. He was on the red-eye back, so I figured he'd beat us here. He said he had some news. I think the field agents may be closing in on our mark."

"Really?" Poppy asked as she got out of the car. "That's great. So this might be over soon, then, right?"

"Possibly," he said as he made his way to the door.

Poppy had looked down to check her phone when she bumped into him.

"Sorry," she said, before seeing Owen's arm stretched out. "Owen?"

"Stay still," he said suddenly, his voice cold and low.

In a flash, Owen had his gun drawn, held out with both hands. He nodded at Poppy to follow him, which she did, her heart suddenly in her throat. Everything she had been thinking about melted away as fear struck her.

As they moved closer toward the door, Poppy noticed what Owen must have much sooner. The door was slightly cracked. It seemed a bit trivial to Poppy. *Maybe Teddy forgot to jiggle it.* But even as the thought formed, Poppy knew that although he was more laid back, Teddy was a stickler for detail, just like Owen.

Owen stood straighter and leaned ever so slightly forward, peering through the crack. Unable to see anything, he turned back to Poppy and motioned with his eyes for her to get down.

As soon as Poppy hunched down, Owen kicked the door open, gun pointed straight ahead.

"Oh my God!" Poppy yelled as she looked up.

Laying completely still on the foyer floor in a small pool of blood was Teddy.

CHAPTER ELEVEN

Poppy's scream filled the air as Owen ran into the foyer, falling to his knees to check for a pulse. The sight before her was all too real. There lay Teddy, a man she had come to consider a friend, his partner hovering over his motionless body. Poppy watched the scene unfold before her in slow motion as she walked into the house, petrified. She knelt gently, her hands out, but she didn't want to touch him for fear she would hurt him somehow. Poppy didn't know what to do. The right side of Teddy's abdomen was covered in a dark liquid and he looked lifeless, but he couldn't be dead. He just couldn't be.

She felt as if the air had been violently sucked out of her lungs. "Is he . . . is he . . . " she stuttered, unable to catch her breath.

"No, he's alive," Owen said, his fingers still pressed against Teddy's blood-covered wrist. "It's faint, but there's a pulse." He pulled his phone from his pocket and dialed a number while Poppy moved closer to Teddy, unsure of what to do. She could feel the tears bubbling up. "I need ambulance at 103 Windgate, Stonington. I've got an officer down."

"Owen, he's shaking," Poppy said in a strangled voice as Teddy's body began to convulse.

"He's going into shock. I need an ambulance now!"

Owen dropped the phone on the floor and leaned over Teddy, holding his head in place so it wouldn't bang against the floor. Suddenly, a crashing sound came from somewhere in the kitchen. Poppy looked up as Owen froze.

"What was that?" she whispered.

"Stay here," Owen said. "Hold the back of his head."

Owen was on his feet in seconds, his gun drawn. He ran down the hallway while Poppy put her hands awkwardly beneath Teddy's head, unsure of what to do, but eager to comfort him. *This can't be happening*, she thought as panic engulfed her and Teddy seized on the ground. She tried to blink away her tears, but it was just so unfair. He had so much going on in his life that he couldn't possibly leave now. His wife and unborn baby needed him. Owen needed him.

"Hold on," she said quietly, her voice cracking with emotion. "You can't go yet. You have to meet George or Jezebel, or whatever you want to name the baby. Teddy?"

Her words felt hollow—ugly, even. He couldn't go, not when he had so much. There were no words for the reasons he needed to stay.

"Can you hear me, Teddy?" she said, her voice a touch louder. "Please stop shaking. You can't go. Not like this."

Tears fell as she clenched her teeth, trying to stop herself from sobbing openly over him. *Where were the cops that were supposed to be watching this place? Why was he here alone?*

Where is Owen?

Guilt rose up within her, but she beat it down as she tried to get her phone with one hand, while still cradling Teddy's head with the other. She'd managed to dial 911 into her phone when two shots rang out from outside the house. Poppy dropped her phone on the tiled floor and let out a strangled scream.

Teddy stopped convulsing and his still body frightened her more than when he was shaking. She gently took her hand back from beneath his head, slowly stood up, and backed away, pressing herself against the wall. Another shot rang out, and she closed her eyes tight, jumping at the sound. *Has Owen been shot? What if he's hurt?*

She looked down at her phone and couldn't bring herself to pick it up. Instead, she began inching herself down the hallway, her back pressed against the wall. When she reached the kitchen, she paused and looked around the corner. The back door was wide open, blowing the sheer curtains in a ghost-like manner. Poppy took a deep breath to steady her nerves. When she heard footsteps on the back porch, she ran into the kitchen and grabbed a knife without thinking. Dropping to the floor behind the island, she tried to stifle her erratic breathing. She almost fainted when she heard Owen's voice call out to her.

"Poppy!" he yelled. She jumped up, startling him. He lowered his gun. "What are you doing?"

"I heard gunshots," she said shakily. "I thought you were hurt."

"Put the knife down and grab some towels," he said as he moved back down the hallway into the foyer.

Poppy grabbed several towels from a drawer in the kitchen and hurried into the foyer to hand them to him. Owen knelt next to Teddy's body, pressing the towels into the side of his abdomen, attempting to stop the bleeding. "He stopped shaking?"

She nodded. "I don't think that's a good thing," she said, realizing how unsure she sounded. Owen pressed the towels into the wound harder than she thought he should. When Teddy groaned, she dropped to the floor next to him. "Stop! You're hurting him!"

"He needs to stay awake, Poppy. He needs to or he might die."

"He can't die," she sobbed. "He can't."

Poppy looked from Teddy's face to Owen's. He seemed so calm, and yet he looked so pale in the dark.

"I didn't get him," Owen said quietly, his voice unsettlingly steady. "I tried, but he was too fast."

"Did you see who it was?" she asked.

"No. I shot twice at him, but I don't think I hit him. It was dark, and before I could catch up with him, I saw taillights on the beach. I shot again, trying to hit a tire, but he got away."

Poppy could see the anguish in Owen's face as he looked down at his partner. She didn't doubt that he blamed himself for this, when in actuality it was Poppy's fault. She looked up when the faint noise of a siren sounded in the background.

"Owen, is he going to be okay?"

"Yes," Owen said stubbornly, looking down at Teddy. "Stay with him, and press here. I'll get the EMTs."

He took her hand and pushed it into the side of his abdomen. Poppy winced when Teddy made an unintelligible sound. She felt like she would throw up.

Owen disappeared out the front door, leaving her alone with Teddy. She kept pressure on his wound until the sirens reached the house. Within minutes, Poppy had been pushed to the side while a team of EMTs worked on Teddy. They loaded him onto a stretcher while one wrapped Poppy in a blanket and took her outside, where she cried uncontrollably for a few minutes. She wanted Owen, but he was on the phone and she knew she couldn't be needy right now. He had work to do, and he was probably going through an awful personal hell. His partner had been shot, and he hadn't had backup.

Poppy liked Teddy, had liked him more than Owen, and now he was being loaded into an ambulance. She didn't know if she'd ever have the chance to thank him for all he had done for her. *He's done so much*, she suddenly realized. *So has Owen.*

A tidal wave of guilt crashed over her as the ambulance pulled away, while several cops went around the house with Owen. She had run off because of what? Claustrophobia? Her panic attacks? She had been feeling so sorry for herself that she had forgotten the world didn't stop just because of her. She was pitiful.

Owen was nowhere in sight when Poppy tried her best to answer the questions the local cops had for her. When he appeared on the opposite end of the driveway, Poppy felt reassured. For the first time since they'd met, he had a bit of a glow around him.

Her grandmother had explained the glow to her once when she had been vocal about it as a child. She'd said that it was a residue, a leftover mark of something that hadn't existed in a long time. It was the last bit of physical magic in the world, at least as far as people like them were concerned. Like most kids, Poppy had stopped believing in magic before she got to high school. It hadn't helped that her father had never seemed to have much of a glow about him, but Poppy had always thought it was because he didn't believe in it either. She hadn't given it much thought until the morning Owen appeared and she'd seen the aura that hung around him, like it was doing now. She couldn't help but feel humbled. Magic, it seemed, had indeed existed and to an extent, still did.

An hour passed before Owen finally found her.

"Poppy—"

"Owen, I'm so sorry," she said, crying again as he looked at her. "This is all my fault."

Owen handed her phone over before wrapping his arms around her. He held her tightly.

"It's all right, Poppy. It's not your fault."

"It is, though. If I hadn't run off to New York, you would have been here, and Teddy wouldn't have been alone."

"It's not your fault—"

"Where were the police? Why was he here alone?"

He let his hand fall away from around her and she suddenly felt cold.

"Poppy, I think you need to go in and try to get some sleep."

"Sleep? I can't. I don't think I can ever sleep again."

"This is going to be a long night, and you already answered all the questions you've been asked. You need to try and sleep so you'll be fresh in the morning. I have agents flying in to go over the case."

"It doesn't make sense," Poppy said. Her head was beginning to feel like it would explode. "It shouldn't have been Teddy. It shouldn't have been Gram. It should have been me."

"Poppy, listen to me," Owen said, putting his hands on her shoulders. "This person is a lunatic, and it's not your fault. Not any of it."

"But if I hadn't left . . . " she said, getting choked up again. She felt the tightness in her chest as the panic began to rise. "If I had just stayed here . . . "

"It's not your fault," Owen insisted, his eyes wide with determination, as if he needed to hear his own words. "Please, go inside and try to get some sleep."

"What about you?" she asked.

"I'll rest after I'm debriefed, I promise."

Nodding, Poppy dragged herself into the house, avoiding the area where they had found Teddy, as it was still taped off. Poppy was grateful for the noise of people walking and talking everywhere. She started a pot of coffee for the cops and went to bed, eager to fall asleep, which she did almost instantly.

It was before noon when Poppy finally rolled over, hearing the voices of what she assumed to be officers talking in the kitchen. She hadn't moved at all during the night and her muscles were sore as she stretched. She checked her phone. The previous night seemed like some bad dream, but it had been very real and was still going on just outside the bedroom door. She wondered where Owen was, looking up at the ceiling of her bedroom. Was he upstairs, sleeping somewhere above her? Had he slept? Was Teddy alive? She almost didn't want to get up for fear that she would learn the answers.

Taking a deep breath, Poppy sat up and swung her legs off the bed. She needed to get up and get through the next few hours for Teddy's sake. She hoped against hope that he was okay.

Poppy opened her bedroom door and saw several people stop what they were doing and look at her. There were two cops from last night, a policewoman she hadn't seen before, and a man in a black suit.

"Miss Pruette?" an officer from the previous night said. "How are you feeling?"

"I feel fine," she said. "Is Teddy all right?"

"Teddy?" the officer asked, looking back at the man in black.

"Detective Fields is stable," the man in black said, covering the receiver of his phone. "He was shot twice in the abdomen. One of the bullets shattered a rib and the force of the bullets ruptured his spleen. He just got out of surgery."

"Oh my God. Does Owen know?"

"Detective Peirce was informed this morning. Your father is waiting for your call."

"And who are you?" she asked, slightly confused.

The man in black didn't answer, returning instead to his phone call and turning his back on Poppy. She was about to start an argument with the man, but couldn't find the strength to fight with him. She didn't even know him and really, wasn't it all her fault that everyone was here right now?

She poured herself a cup of coffee while the policewoman watched her.

"Miss Pruette, will you follow me? Agent Mendez will need to question you."

"Okay," Poppy said, following the policewoman into the dining room, where the police had set up several computers. As she took a seat, holding her coffee close to her chest, she looked up. "I'm sorry, did you say agent?"

"Yes. Agent Mendez works for the FBI."

"Oh," Poppy said as a fresh fear came over her. "Is the FBI usually called in to situations like this?"

The policewoman stared at her.

"Yes. When there are multiple murders across state lines, they are."

Poppy nodded, taking a sip of her coffee absentmindedly. *Now the FBI is involved? They couldn't possibly know about the Others, could they? And where is Owen?* She needed to be coached, to know what to say and what not to say, lest she look insane.

As if her prayer had been answered, Owen walked past the dining room and into the kitchen. Putting her coffee down, she stood up to join him.

Owen looked exhausted, his face slightly puffy as though he just woke up. She wondered how long he had actually slept. The bags under his eyes seemed pronounced, and the disheveled look of his clothes and hair gave her the sudden urge to hug him. Not because she felt guilty, and not because she wanted to feel comforted, but simply because he looked so exhausted. She always liked the feel of leaning into a hug when she was tired and she bet he would to, but she stayed rooted to the ground. When he scanned the room and finally saw her, he made his way toward her.

The man in black spoke suddenly. "Detective?"

Owen turned seamlessly toward the man, his voice quiet but strong.

"Agent Mendez," Owen said. "Have you heard anything?"

"Detective Fields is in stable condition, but they're keeping an eye on his blood pressure. It hasn't returned to normal."

"Any hits on the car?"

"No. Can we speak in private for a moment, Detective?"

Owen nodded and followed Mendez onto the porch, closing the sliding door behind him. Poppy watched as the two men spoke, Owen becoming visibly annoyed with whatever Mendez was saying. She grabbed her phone from her bedroom and called her father, who at first was furious with her for disappearing to New York, but grateful that she hadn't been at Windgate when the man who shot Teddy was there. He expressed his want for her to return home, a sentiment with which Poppy agreed. She didn't want to stay in Stonington any longer, not with what happened to Teddy.

She also spoke with Samantha, and when she finally hung up with them, she heard a thud, as if someone had hit the wall.

Looking up, she saw Owen's hands on his hips, his coat pushed back. He was looking down as Mendez opened the sliding door and reentered the house.

"Miss Pruette?" Mendez said. "Your case has been transferred to my department. Detective Peirce will no longer be working on it."

"Excuse me?" she asked in disbelief, looking past Mendez. Owen still hadn't looked up. "Why?"

"Because Detective Peirce is incapable of handling this case. He's too close to it. It's a conflict of interest."

"If anyone can handle this case, it's Owen," she argued, her anger rising. "It wasn't his fault that Teddy was shot."

"It was."

"No, it wasn't. It was my fault. I shouldn't have left—"

"And Detective Peirce should have been able to handle you," Mendez interrupted. "It's done."

"It wasn't his fault!" she shouted again, when Owen finally stepped back into the house.

"Poppy, it was," he said solemnly. "Agent Mendez is right. I should have had a better handle on the situation."

"What were you supposed to do? Lock me in a room? Chain me to your side? It was my fault. I left of my own free will."

"And I'll take that into consideration," Mendez said. "But as of an hour ago, Detective Peirce is off the case. I'll be driving you back to Virginia—"

"Can't Owen do it?"

"*Detective Peirce*," he said pointedly, as if Poppy's use of Owen's name irritated him, "has proven unable to perform the task."

"This is garbage," Poppy bit out angrily.

"Calm down," Mendez bit back.

"Wait a minute," Owen started.

"I'm not getting into any car without him," Poppy all but growled, ignoring how ridiculous she sounded. She needed to speak with Owen in private, without all these police around.

"You'll do as I say," Mendez countered, not giving an inch.

"Like hell I will!"

"Hold on," Owen said loudly. Everyone in the room looked at him. He inhaled. "Poppy, wait outside a moment."

Feeling betrayed by the tone in his voice, Poppy gave Mendez a nasty look and walked out onto the porch, slamming the door behind her. *Why does he have to be so damn infuriating?* He'd sent her away like she was some toddler having a tantrum when she had been arguing for him. *How could he?*

She walked off the deck and kicked at the ground, letting out a grunt. What was he going to do, leave her? Let the FBI take over when they both knew she wouldn't be fully protected by anyone unless they knew the whole truth? Did he *want* her to tell them the whole truth? She'd be locked up for being insane.

Poppy stomped down to the water, looked out over the choppy sea, and inhaled. It was all she could do to keep herself from going back in there and starting an argument. She needed to get her anger under control. For a few moments, she concentrated only on the horizon, where gray skies met dark waters. *He can't leave me*, she thought. She'd be a dead woman walking without him. For all anyone knew, the killer could still be around, on this very beach, and no one would know.

She looked around and did see someone. A few yards away from her stood a man with sun-kissed skin and dark hair that blew slightly across his forehead. He was staring at her. He wore a light blue button-down shirt, tan shorts, and a pair of boat shoes, looking every bit like a New Englander in the summer.

Ajax.

CHAPTER TWELVE

 $\mathcal{P}$ oppy looked back at the house behind her to make sure Owen was still inside talking with Mendez. When she could see no reason not to walk toward him, she headed in his direction as Ajax walked to meet her. She wrapped her arms around herself as a low rumble of thunder sounded above them. When she reached him, she tilted her head, as if to ask what he was doing here, but Ajax just turned toward the ocean and looked out to sea.

Poppy studied his profile for a moment, taking in his features. When he turned to look at her, she realized he looked tired, noting the bags under his eyes. His tan skin had made it difficult to notice before, but now, as he looked at her, she could see he had been running himself pretty thin.

"Rough night, Poppy?" he asked quietly.

"Teddy was shot," she said, her voice threatening to quake. "Owen's been removed from the case. I'm going back to Virginia."

Ajax nodded.

"What are you doing here?"

"I heard about what happened and I wanted to make sure everyone was okay."

"You could have called."

"I like to do things in person," he said. "How are you?"

Poppy inhaled and shook her head, looking down.

"I don't know. I'm scared for Teddy, for Owen . . . for myself." She paused. "I feel awful."

"Do you know if Teddy is going to be all right?"

"I don't know," she said softly. "This is all my fault, Ajax."

"No, Poppy, it isn't. Whoever is after you has caused all this, not you."

"But if I hadn't left . . . "

"You might be dead," he said matter-of-factly. He sighed, and Poppy looked at him. "You mustn't blame yourself for any of it. Besides, Owen wouldn't want you to blame this on yourself."

"It wasn't Owen's fault, and they're trying to say it was," she countered. "And now, he's getting canned."

"It's better this way, Poppy. You'll see."

"How?"

"Because it's supposed to be this way."

"Oh, good. You're going to be vague, too. I can already tell this is going to be a good day," she said sarcastically. "Why can't he just stay?" When Ajax didn't answer right away, she looked up and saw an expression on his face that seemed to look into her soul. "What?"

"Poppy," he said gently, turning toward her. "Owen's work with this case is nearly finished. When it's done, he'll be leaving and your life will go back to the way it was."

"My life will never be what it was, Ajax."

"Still, you'll go back to college, and in six months, this whole business will seem like a distant dream."

She looked out at the horizon. "What's your point?"

"My point is that Owen's path isn't in Virginia. He called me last night. He's decided to go to California."

Poppy's eyes snapped back to Ajax.

"W-what?" she barely got out. Ajax looked at her with sympathetic eyes, but didn't speak. "Geez," she said, her own eyes closing. "I wish I didn't have to deal with this."

"Oh, be careful," Ajax said quickly. "Wishing is a dangerous—"

"Yeah, I know, a dangerous hobby. Everyone says that, but I do wish. I wish—"

Three of Ajax's fingers suddenly touched Poppy's mouth, stunning her into stillness. She looked at him, wide-eyed.

His eyes were dark, and Poppy saw that there was something mysteriously, hypnotically beautiful about him.

"To normal people," he began, his voice soft, "wishing for something instead of doing something makes for zero gains. But to people like us, wishing can be deadly. I know this is a difficult time, but you have to watch what you say."

Poppy looked at him quizzically as his fingers fell back to his side. Ajax turned back, gazing over the ocean once more.

"Wishes are complicated. There are only two lines that understand them fully. The Fate line and the Ruse line, a Good and an Other."

"What stories do they represent?"

"The Fate lineage is the family of the Godmother."

"As in—"

"No, they weren't fairies, but there is something blessed about them, something unexplained. The Ruse lineage represents the family of tricksters and gnomes—most notably, Rumpelstiltskin."

Poppy was quiet, staring at Ajax as if he were mad.

"Really?" she asked, unconvinced.

"Absolutely, and you can imagine what he might have done to make a wish come true, and the type of wishes he would grant."

Poppy was quiet for a moment as she tried to process everything she was hearing. Her mind whirled as she recalled the story Helena Peirce had told her the night before.

There had been a wish in the Three Virtues story.

"What kind?" she asked suddenly.

"Pardon?"

"What sort of wishes would he grant?"

Ajax looked slightly uncomfortable. He shifted his weight from side to side.

"Bad wishes, of course. It would become something of a curse, really, but desperate people do desperate things. Those wishes never turn out the way they're intended. Wishes are extremely difficult. They require two things to complete, and neither are easy to come by."

"There was a wish granter in the Three Virtues story," she said quietly. The look on Ajax's face was that of genuine worry. "When did that story take place, Ajax? What line made the wish?"

"Forty years ago. Do you not know who they were?"

"No."

"They're family, Poppy. Your family. Rose was the youngest sister."

Poppy looked at Ajax like he had gone crazy. *That's not possible*, she thought to herself. Her grandmother was from Virginia, had lived in Miner's Way all her life. She had had only one sister . . . hadn't she? It was just a story. It wasn't plausible.

"That's not true," she said.

"Of course it's true," Ajax said. "This world we live in, where we come from . . . the old stories were all based on real events. The Three Virtues isn't any different from them, except that instead of four hundred years ago, it happened forty. I thought Rose would have told you."

"She started to, but never finished. Helena told me the rest of the story. What happened after the wish was cast?"

"It's difficult to say. The wish, while not cast successfully, brought about the schism between the three sisters. In that sense, one could say it was a curse that eventually destroyed their family."

Poppy looked at him, her brows furrowed in frustration.

"So, my family has been cursed? Is that what you're telling me, Ajax?"

"I'm sorry, Poppy, I'm not your Storyteller. I'm only working with what my father told me as a boy."

"It's all right," Poppy said, deflated.

"I'll go through my books and see what I can find out. You should head back in," Ajax said as he turned and waved. Poppy turned back to the house and saw Owen leaning over the railing, watching them. "Wouldn't want you to be seen with a suspicious-looking character."

"You are sort of suspicious-looking," she said, giving him a weak smile that Ajax returned. "Will I see you again?"

"Who knows?" he said, shrugging. "It was nice talking to you, Poppy. Safe travels."

"You, too," she said as they both turned away, him toward the beach, her toward the house.

Owen looked conflicted, but remained perfectly still until she reached the porch steps. She turned to see if Ajax was still visible, but he had vanished. *He's a strange sort*, she thought as she climbed the stairs. Owen had turned and was now leaning with his back against the rail, his arms folded.

"What did he want?" he asked harshly.

"He was checking on Teddy, I think, or me. I'm not really sure."

"What did you talk about?" he asked, but then Mendez came out.

"Have you told her?" Mendez asked.

"Told me what?"

"Detective Peirce will be driving you back to Miner's Way, albeit with several undercovers following you, just in case you manage to talk him out of returning you home."

Poppy's cheeks heated up.

"I don't know who the hell you think you are—" she started, but Owen stepped in front of her.

"She understands, sir," Owen said. "We'll be ready to go in an hour."

Mendez nodded, his eyes on Poppy as he turned back into the house. Owen spun around.

"Why do you have to antagonize him like that, Poppy?"

"Me? Why do you let him talk to you like that?"

"Because he's in charge, and I have the decency to show a man in his position some respect."

She was simmering. "He doesn't show you the same courtesy."

"He outranks me, Poppy. He can do whatever he likes. Why would it bother you, anyhow?"

"Because it's rude."

"I thought you'd enjoy seeing me put in my place."

"Why would you say that?"

"Because you like to do it." He spoke as if he was trying to convince her. He looked away. "You seemed to enjoy it when Teddy did it, too."

"Teddy wouldn't cut you down in front of anyone, and he only did it when you would lose your temper. I only did it because I . . . I wasn't being fair." She paused for a long moment, her thoughts on the detective. Owen looked back at her and seemed to deflate. Was her anxiousness over Teddy so obvious? "He'll be okay, won't he?"

"His blood pressure isn't rising."

"What's that mean?"

"It means the doctors could have missed a bleed. He might need a second surgery."

"What?" Poppy whispered, her emotions exposing themselves as tears welled up in her eyes. "This is all my fault."

"No," Owen said softly as he reached for her. He pulled her into a hug and squeezed her tightly. Poppy couldn't help but feel safe, as if she were hugging a friend instead of, well, whatever it was Owen was to her now. "It's not your fault, Poppy. Hey, stop that." His breath warmed the top of her ear. "There's no need to cry."

"No?" she said, muffled into his chest. "Teddy's in the hospital and there's still a madman out there, and I can't stop feeling like this anxiety is going to kill me. And now you're getting kicked off the case. . . . What am I going to do without you?" There was a moment of quiet stillness that made Poppy feel uneasy. Owen slowly put some space between them and looked down at her. She couldn't understand the look in his eyes, but would have sworn she saw it before. "Who is going to understand the level of danger I'm in except you?"

There was another beat of silence before Owen blinked, as if he had been suddenly pulled out of a daze. He cleared his throat and took a step back.

"I'm sorry," he said, his voice a touch cooler than it just had been. "For all of this. I should have done more; I should have been more aware."

"Don't say that. It's not true."

"It is."

"But—"

"It is, Poppy." His voice was as stern as the look on his face. All the softness that had been in his voice and his stance disappeared. He was Detective Peirce again. "Leave it alone."

Isn't that just like him? she thought angrily. *Perfectly normal one minute, and transformed into a jerk the next.* It drove her insane when he was like that.

"Fine, whatever. Excuse me," she said, shoving past him. "I have to pack."

She couldn't bear to look at him at that moment. He had handed over her case without so much as a fight and now, he was telling her to show that jerk some respect when he insulted Owen every chance he got. It made her blood boil, and she looked like an idiot by trying to defend him.

She threw her clothes into her bag without folding them, shoving her books and computer in along with them before she ran out of steam. She sat on the bed and tried to calm herself by breathing slowly. Her emotions were running wild and it wasn't doing anything except for making her stomach upset. For the next thirty minutes she lay on the bed and tried to meditate. She kept hearing Ajax's words about wishes and wondered what it took to make one. *Is there some archaic spell that has to be cast or is it just finding the right person to enforce it?* Ajax had said it took two things to make a wish come true. So, what were they?

Knock, knock, knock.

"Poppy?" Owen's voice sounded. He opened the door and looked in at her. "Agent Mendez has some questions for you, then we'll be leaving. Are you ready to go?"

She nodded and sat up. Grabbing her bag, she followed him out of her room. He nodded toward the dining room and took her bag with him. Mendez sat at the table, typing away, but he paused and looked up as she entered.

"Miss Pruette. Take a seat."

Poppy sat across from him, staring at him as she did. He was a middle-aged man, with dark, cropped hair and a mustache. There was definitely an arrogance about him that she didn't like, but she thought of Owen. He believed that this guy deserved respect, and he had probably worked hard to get where he was. She doubted giving him attitude would help her situation and decided to cooperate instead. The quicker this was over with, the quicker she could get in the car heading home.

"How well do you know Detective Peirce?" Mendez asked, hitting the record button on his phone.

"What?" she asked, surprised by the question.

"Just answer the question."

Poppy bristled at his tone, but shook it off.

"Not very well. I hadn't ever met him before my grandmother's murder."

"So you were unaware of the fact that your families were on friendly terms? For quite a long time?"

"That was something I learned recently."

"Recently, as in yesterday? When you met his family?" Poppy was quiet. "Answer the question."

"Yes, I learned it yesterday when I met his family."

"So, you're aware of the Peirce family?"

"Sort of. As much as anyone else is, I guess." She paused. "What does this have to do with the case?"

"I'll ask the questions, Miss Pruette."

"Then why not ask ones that will help figure out who's trying to kill me?"

"Has it occurred to you that I may be?"

Poppy looked at him, baffled. *What is he insinuating?*

"You think Owen has something to do with this?"

"I think Detective Peirce is an upstanding young officer. I also think he knows more than he's letting on." Mendez's eyes seemed to bore into her. "I need to know everything about this case, and the fact that you two have a shared history makes me wonder if I'm being kept in the dark about something. Now, am I missing anything, Miss Pruette?"

Poppy felt torn. He was right to want to know everything, but to tell him would be suicidal. He'd lock her up and probably have Owen fired. She couldn't let that happen.

"Agent Mendez," she said, her stare unwavering. "Detective Peirce has told you everything. I'm sure of it. There isn't any part of me that thinks he's hiding something from you."

Mendez watched her.

"So you trust him?"

"Yes," she said quietly. "I trust him wholeheartedly."

They stared at each other for another moment before Poppy heard footsteps come to a halt behind her.

"The car's ready, Agent Mendez."

"Very well," Mendez said, his eyes not leaving Poppy. "Until next time, Miss Pruette."

Poppy only nodded as she stood up. She said her goodbyes and thanks to all the officers in the house—except Mendez, though he didn't look too broken up about it.

When she walked outside toward the car, she turned around and looked up at the home that held such fond memories for her and now, a terrible one. She wondered if she'd ever come back to this place as they pulled out of the driveway.

They drove in silence for the next few hours. Time was slipping away so quickly and as every mile marker passed, she knew she was getting another minute closer to having to say goodbye to Owen, presumably forever.

She should apologize for getting him kicked off the case, for causing Teddy to be shot. *I should say something*, she thought to herself, *but what? Hope to see you at the next fairy tale convention?*

Don't leave . . .

She couldn't say that. She had no right to say that, and even if she did, who the hell was she kidding? It wasn't even up for discussion. What did she want from him? What would she possibly gain by asking him to stay? It wasn't for any other reason than that she felt secure with him.

But was that the only reason?

Yes, she told herself. Yet, he was the first person besides her grandmother who had spoken openly about their world, and he had introduced her to so much in their time together. Sure, she had grown fond of him once she got past his arrogance and stubbornness, but he had been rude, too. He had acted unforgivably to Sean and had annoyed her on more than one occasion, but she didn't not like him. If anything, she had begun to have feelings—

No, she told herself. *Stop thinking like that.*

She gave him a sideways gaze, careful not to catch his attention. Surely she didn't care about him like that. She just wanted him close for her safety and nothing more.

Poppy rubbed her forehead. She was giving herself a headache.

"You all right?" he asked, noticing her movement.

"It's just something Ajax said. He told me that one of the Three Virtues was my grandmother."

"Your grandmother?" Owen repeated. "That's not even possible. Your grandmother only had one sister."

"That's what I thought," she said. "It's just so confusing. All of this."

"I know, but I'm sure Agent Mendez will be able to figure it all out."

Poppy looked at him.

"He doesn't know about the Good and the Others, does he?" she asked, worried.

"No, he'd think we were all insane if I told him that."

"Then how will he be able to protect me? He doesn't have all the facts."

"Those facts aren't relevant to the case, Poppy. The killer isn't a Vann, and it's impossible that Rose was one of the Three Virtues. Even if she were, it wouldn't matter, because the killer isn't from our world. We would have known about that."

"So, you're going to California, regardless?" she blurted out.

Silence hung in the car for a moment. What had possessed her to say that? She knew he was going, so why did she need to ask him?

"Yes," he said. "I am." Another moment passed. "I have to."

Poppy nodded, not really sure why.

They drove the rest of the way without a word.

CHAPTER TWELVE

It was a little after midnight when Poppy and Owen pulled into the driveway in Miner's Way. Two other black sedans pulled up almost immediately after them and Owen got out to talk with them. Poppy had tried to think of a reason to get Owen to stay, some loose end that he needed to tie up, but there was nothing. Still, she couldn't help feeling like he was betraying her somehow. When Owen came back from the other cars, she took a deep breath and got out of the car. Her father and Samantha came out of the house to greet them.

"Detective, I'm indebted to you," Mr. Pruette said to Owen, holding out his hand. Owen shook it. "I'm sorry about this whole mess."

"Not at all, sir," Owen said, shaking his head. "It's my job."

Poppy flinched at that.

"Are those the new people on the case?"

"Yes. Agent Mendez will be heading the case now. He'll be here in the morning. These two," Owen said, nodding back at the cars, "will be watching the house tonight."

"It's that serious?"

"I'm afraid so."

"Would you like me to set up the guest room? It's so late," Samantha said as she hugged Poppy.

"I can't, actually. I have a flight." Poppy avoided Owen's eyes when he glanced at her. "I mean, I have work that I need to tend to before I can officially close the case."

"Detective Peirce, please, I insist you come in for at least a cup of coffee," Samantha said, thinking for a moment. "You wouldn't want to fall asleep at the wheel, right?"

Poppy could sense the tension. Owen wanted to leave as soon as possible, but he wasn't the kind to create uncomfortable situations. He took a step forward.

"Sure, coffee sounds great."

"Wonderful. Go get your bag and let's head inside," her father said.

Owen opened the trunk and grabbed Poppy's bag, flinging it over his shoulder as Mr. Pruette and Samantha walked inside, leaving Owen and her alone. Poppy slowed her pace, as did Owen, who looked at her, confused.

"You don't have to stay," she said quietly as they reached the front door. "If you have a flight you have to catch."

"I can take the next flight," he said, following her into the house. "Besides, I probably wouldn't make it to Richmond on time anyway."

They walked down the hallway toward the kitchen, Owen placing her bag on the floor next to the island. Mr. Pruette took a seat at the kitchen table while Samantha arranged a tray full of mugs and sugar. Poppy grabbed the half-and-half out of the refrigerator and turned to see Owen standing by the island, looking displaced. She bet he felt uncomfortable now that he didn't have an official reason for being here.

"How is your partner doing, Detective?" Mr. Pruette asked, breaking the silence.

"He's stable," Owen answered.

"Will you be going back to Michigan tomorrow?" Samantha asked.

"I will, eventually, but I have some business to take care of before I can go home." He turned to Poppy's father. "I'm sorry I wasn't able to better handle the case when it was in my hands."

Mr. Pruette waved his hand in the air.

"I believe she was in good hands, Detective. I'm sorry to see you go."

"Here we are," Samantha said, setting the tray down. She had arranged a few biscotti on a plate. "It was all I could find in a hurry."

"Thank you," Owen said.

A peculiar silence filled the room, then. Poppy looked from one person to the next, wondering if they were all trying to avoid each other's gazes.

"Did your partner tell you what he found in Louisiana?" Mr. Pruette asked, breaking the silence.

"No," Owen said, looking up.

"A lawyer from Louisiana called here a few days ago, asking for me and Poppy. Rupert gave him the house number for Windgate, thinking he might try to get in touch with you up there."

"We didn't hear from a lawyer, just the sheriff," Owen said, his shoulders straightening. "What did he want?"

"There's some sort of inheritance we were supposed to receive from my mother's sister. She passed away a few days ago."

"An inheritance from the sister?" Owen said, his eyes narrowed.

"Yes, Rose's sister, Vilma. My mother hardly spoke of her, and I never met the woman until my mother's funeral. Your partner was supposed to get in touch with the lawyer when he was down there investigating, but we never heard how the meeting went."

"Wait a minute," Poppy spoke up. "How did she die?"

"In her sleep," her father replied. "Why?"

"Don't you find it a little strange? I mean, Gram hasn't been gone two months and her sister suddenly dies, too?"

"She was old, Poppy. It's the natural order of things."

"I know, but she was just here for the funeral, and she wasn't sick then, was she?"

Mr. Pruette was quiet for a moment.

"What are you suggesting, Poppy? That she was murdered? It's absurd."

"Why? Because she was an old lady who didn't have any enemies?" She shook her head. "So was Gram."

"It's getting late," Owen said, standing up. "I really should be going. Thank you for the coffee."

"Oh, of course," Samantha said. "Anytime."

Owen shook Mr. Pruette's hand and gave Samantha a casual hug. Poppy offered to walk him out, but he refused. After a quick goodbye, he was out the door, but Poppy followed him anyway. Once out in the driveway, he heard her footsteps and peered over his shoulder. He stopped and turned to face her, but said nothing. His face looked clouded.

"What do you think?" she asked, certain he was just as suspicious as she was about Vilma's death.

"I don't know," he said evenly, looking back at the black sedans sitting in front of her house. "It can't be a coincidence, can it?"

"It seems pretty strange that Rose and Vilma would both pass away so close together. But then again, I've heard of people who were close and old dying around the same time."

"But that's just it—Rose wasn't close with Vilma." He looked down at the ground and shook his head. "When I was first assigned the case, I went through every possible connection Rose had with our world. She hadn't had any correspondence with Vilma in decades. The Vanns had checked out, and there was no one else in our world connected to Rose. That's why I agreed to come on."

"So, what, you think the sisters' time of death was just by chance?"

"It has to be." He was quiet for a moment before he looked directly at Poppy. "I don't know what to say."

"We should tell Mendez," she said.

"He probably knows, and if he hasn't acted on it yet, there must not be a lead there."

"You don't believe that, do you?"

"I don't see a connection, Poppy. If I did, I would tell Mendez, but it's not my case anymore."

"So, you don't care?" she asked before she could stop herself.

Owen took a step toward her, and she felt ashamed. She realized quickly that that had been an unfair thing to say.

"I do care," he said quietly after a beat. He shook his head. "I care enough to make sure that I don't let my personal feelings get in the way of the investigation. Like in New York."

"New York was my fault—"

"But I went after you, without considering all the angles."

"It was your job to come after me, though," she said. "Wasn't it?"

He gave her a pained look that made her stomach tumble. She felt her cheeks heat up as she kept her eyes on his.

"It was more than that," he said, so softly that she wasn't sure she had heard him correctly. "But it's nothing."

Poppy felt he meant more than what he was saying. But he was still leaving her, regardless of the new information.

"I guess this is it, then." She stood perfectly still, almost afraid to move. "I won't see you again."

"Probably not."

"This isn't right," she blurted out as she looked at her feet, a wave of uneasiness hitting her. "You shouldn't be leaving yet. Something's not right."

"What do you want me to say, Poppy?" he asked, a touch of aggravation in his voice. "I can't stay. I don't have a legitimate reason to. If Mendez sees me trailing his leads or you, I'll get kicked off the force."

"You'll leave the force anyway when you move to California," she snapped bitterly at him.

"We are not discussing California."

"Why not? If this is the last time I'm ever going to see you, it seems like the perfect time to talk about California."

"What does it matter to you, anyway? I asked you your opinion about this weeks ago and you said I should go."

"Then go!" she said loudly, unable to check her emotions. "I don't care! I just think you should finish one case before moving on to the next."

"I'm not moving on to a new case."

"It certainly seems like you are. This case was too hard, so you're just going to fly to California and work on something easier because you can't handle this one."

"I can handle this one," he said hotly. "But I was never meant to. I was meant to be in California."

"Then why has it taken you so long to go there? Why were you even here in the first place?"

"Because."

"Because why?"

"Because I felt drawn here," he blurted out, matching her rising voice. "When I saw you that morning, there was something . . . and I just felt . . . I felt like I belonged here."

Poppy looked at him, shaking as she tried to hold on to her anger. A heavy silence seemed to land around them. *What does it matter, if this is the last time we see each other? In a few weeks, we'll be faint memories to each other and nothing more.*

"You do belong here," she said quietly, looking up at him.

"No," he said, his voice dropping an octave. "I don't, Poppy."

She wanted to say something else, something to change his mind, but before she could, Owen leaned in and kissed her.

It was unexpected in so many ways, most notably the ferocity behind it. His arms wrapped around her back and she felt her spine melt as he pressed into her, kissing with vigor. He kissed her as if trying to prove something and she welcomed it, leaning into him.

He suddenly broke off the kiss, grabbing her wrists that had come up to his chest. Neither spoke, his forehead resting on hers as their ragged breaths evened out. Poppy was watching him, waiting for him to calm down and for her heartbeat to steady.

"Owen," she said, her voice cracking.

"No," he said quickly. "No. Give me your phone."

"Why—"

"Give it to me."

She reached into her pocket and handed him her phone. In a few seconds, he handed it back.

"I have to go," he said, without looking at her.

Poppy's breath hitched as a pathetic sound came from her throat. She felt like she had just dropped off the side of a mountain. Tears began to stream down her face as he opened the door and got into the car without another word.

"Goodbye," she said hollowly, unable to believe he was truly leaving.

The car's engine roared to life and Owen backed out of the driveway. Poppy watched as the taillights disappeared down the road and listened until all she heard were crickets and bug zappers. He was gone.

As abruptly as he had shown up, he left, and she knew a piece of her had left with him. She looked awkwardly around and back at the street before she turned and went inside, disappointed that he hadn't tried harder to pick a fight with her.

"Did Owen leave?" her father asked from the living room.

"No," she said. "Well, yes, but he'll be back."

"Really? I thought he had to catch a plane." When Poppy didn't answer right away, he turned around from the television to see her tear-stained face. "Poppy? Have you been crying?"

"No," she lied again as her father stood up and walked toward her.

"What's wrong?"

"I don't know," she said, shaking her head. "I just . . . don't know why life is so unfair."

Mr. Pruette hugged her.

"I know, Poppy. I miss your grandmother, too."

A new wave of guilt crashed over her. Letting go of her father, she headed upstairs.

CHAPTER FOURTEEN

Ding!

Owen jumped, awoken out of an uncomfortable slumber. He looked up at the lit seatbelt sign and guessed they would be landing soon. Rubbing his face, he sat up, ignoring the displeased woman who looked appalled that he had slept. *Well, if she had been what I had been through, she'd be exhausted, too.*

He took his phone out of his pocket and, seeing no new messages, turned to look out the window. The clouds were spotty, but there was little sign of a city. The ground was brown and dotted with what Owen guessed were trees, but they were still so far up that it didn't look like anything, just blots of muddy color beneath white puffs that melted into a bluish-gray. He lost himself in the scenery for a moment, forgetting about the plane and California and everything, really, except the one thing that seemed to be gnawing at his soul.

Poppy.

What a coward he had felt like when he pushed her away and deleted his number. It was the right thing to do, of course, he always did the right thing, but in that moment, he'd felt like his desire to stay was more right than logical. He wanted to be everything for her, do anything for her, and stop her from crying, and what did he do? He left her without even a goodbye because he knew he couldn't say it. It was pathetic. She was probably cursing him right then. He was surprised how strange and tight his chest felt when he thought of her. It was unlike anything he had ever felt before, as if a new emotion had sprung up within him. But what it was, he didn't know. All he knew was that in thirty minutes, he'd be landing and on his way to meet the other half of his story.

He pressed the overhead button and a flight attendant appeared.

"Yes?" she asked pleasantly.

"Can I have a scotch, neat?" he asked.

"Of course, sir." She disappeared and brought him back two tiny bottles of Dewars and a plastic cup. "There you go."

"Thank you."

Owen cracked open the two bottles and poured them into the cup, all the while eyeing the woman next to him, who seemed downright outraged that someone would have a drink first thing in the morning. It was around seven o'clock with the time difference, but Owen didn't care. Instead, he looked directly at the lady and took a sip. The woman, offended, huffed and pulled out one of the in-flight magazines.

He only drank when he wanted to, which wasn't often. After a particularly hard case, or when . . . well, he really only ever drank after his cases were closed. *The Pruette case is closed*, he thought as he sipped the sharp liquor, but he knew that this wasn't a victory drink. If anything, it was a sign of defeat, a courtesy he was extending to himself before meeting Ajax at the airport.

After the plane touched down in San Diego, Owen walked through the airport carrying only a medium-sized bag that contained two changes of outfits. He met a tired-looking Ajax outside the glass doors of the exit, resting against a white SUV.

"Owen," he said, a hint of annoyance in his voice. "Is there a reason I've been waiting here for five hours?"

"I wouldn't know," Owen said, climbing into the passenger's seat.

"Really?" Ajax said, getting into the driver's side. "Because I'm pretty sure you told me you'd be on the red-eye out of Richmond International, which means you would have been here around 2:00 a.m."

"I switched to the next flight. I had to finish some business in Miner's Way."

"Is the case closed?"

"No," he said.

"I meant your end of it."

"No. Until Teddy recovers, it won't be."

"Will he?"

Owen gave him a sideways glare.

"Yes."

"Good, I'm glad to hear it," Ajax said, pulling out into traffic. "And Poppy?"

"What about her?"

"Is she coping with everything?"

"Why do you care?"

"Listen, I understand that you don't want to go through with this," Ajax began, "but it's where you are supposed to be. Poppy wouldn't fit into your life."

"What do you know about my life? I'm not some big shot playboy boozing it up in cities and mansions across the globe. I'm a cop. I live a simple life in a small town, and I'm not here to follow any story. I'm just here to help the girl, and then I'm gone."

"Her name," Ajax said, sounding slightly perturbed, "is Ileana. Her case file is in the back."

"Case file?"

"Yes, she's, um . . . being held at the San Diego Psychiatric Hospital."

Owen turned to look at Ajax. "Excuse me?"

"Just read the case file," he said, grabbing at the folder on the back seat and handing it to Owen. "Before you judge her, she's had a bit of a rough life."

Not from what Owen read, at least. According to her report, she had been born in California, the daughter of Katharine and Andres Vega. Her father was an Olympian from Mexico and her mother, a physical therapist, had met him after attending the games. It seemed that she had lived an almost charmed life and was attending UCLA to complete her masters up until her father's death last year. While initially ruled accidental, the case was reopened, and a few weeks ago, Mrs. Vega was charged with the first-degree murder of her husband.

"Did she do it?" he asked matter-of-factly.

"Can't say for sure, but Ileana didn't take it well."

"What's that mean?" Ajax didn't answer. "Guess, what do you mean?"

"She went on a bender after the cops arrested her mother. Robbed a liquor store, stole a car and a few other things. Claimed temporary insanity and was taken to San Diego Psychiatric Hospital."

Owen rubbed his face with one hand, pinching his brow as he groaned. "You've got to be kidding me," he said. "Ajax, what am I supposed to do here?"

"Well, you did go to law school, didn't you?"

"Yeah, but I didn't finish. Even if I did, I would need to pass the bar. . . . Is that why I'm out here? To get her out of a psych ward?"

"You have to save her," Ajax said. "It's how this works."

Owen didn't know what to say. This was going to be a bigger problem than he cared for and even though a part of him wanted to help, he knew this was going to take longer than he thought.

"What if I can't help her?"

"You will."

"What if I don't? What if I can't?"

Ajax didn't speak right away. But Owen was beyond caring what Ajax, or anyone, thought of him at this point. It was a vulnerable thing to ask, but he trusted Ajax and waited to hear his opinion.

"I don't know," he finally answered, "but if history is any indication, you will. I don't know how, but fate finds a way." Owen looked at him. "She's kind of remarkable."

Remarkable, he repeated to himself. That was a word he wouldn't exactly use for someone who'd had a breakdown, but what did he know? The only thing Owen seemed to be good at was disappointing people.

They hardly spoke for the remainder of the ride, and when they got to the hotel, Owen checked his phone again. There were no messages, not even from his lieutenant. After he showered, he learned that Ileana's lawyer was waiting for him in the lobby. They spoke briefly about getting Ileana out of the psych ward and into the custody of her aunt. Owen was being used as a reference due to his connections in New York, but it didn't sit well with him. He didn't feel like his name should be the defining element in saving someone, but maybe that's all he was good for now. If he hadn't dropped out of law school, he could have been her lawyer instead of just a character witness, which also didn't sit well with him. He believed Ajax, but to defend someone he'd never met . . . it wasn't right.

After his meeting, he agreed to go and meet Ileana that afternoon. Ajax seemed to finally breathe easily, though there seemed to be something bothering him when they pulled up to the hospital.

"Are you all right?" Owen asked as he went to open the door.

"Yes, I just want you to be nice to her," Ajax said. "She's in a fragile state of mind, and I'm sure that when she sees you, whatever magic will happen will happen, but just remember that she's at a pretty low point in her life."

"I'm not going to bite off her head, if that's what you're afraid of."

"You always bite off people's heads."

Owen couldn't argue, but ignored him as he got out of the car. Ajax stayed put.

"Aren't you coming?" Owen asked.

"I can't," he said. "First meetings have to be done a certain way."

"You're a stickler, Guess."

"Good luck."

Owen turned and walked to the front doors, where he met Ileana's lawyer. They were buzzed in, signed in, and given guest passes that hung on lanyards. As they made their way toward her room, Owen noted the smell of plastic and remembered when Hanna had been in the hospital. It seemed like ages ago now.

They turned down the hallway and came to a door that had the word "PRIVATE" written on it. Apparently, the Vegas could afford to be discreet.

"Shoot," Ileana's lawyer said. "I left my wallet at the front desk. Why don't you go in and introduce yourself, and I'll be right back."

"Yeah, sure," Owen said as he left.

Alone, he knocked and opened the door, not waiting for a response. The room was small and sterile, with white walls and a blue bedspread. There didn't seem to be any life in it, except for when he saw movement in the corner.

Tucked in a corner of the room, on the floor, sat a young woman with long, wavy hair the shade of coffee beans. Her bangs had been cut so short that it looked as if it had been haphazardly done. Owen watched as she stood up, her arms wrapped tightly around her. She was wearing an oversized T-shirt and a pair of black yoga pants. She kept her body pressed into the corner as she rose, her dark eyes heavily outlined with black pencil staring daggers into Owen.

He could see the faintest glow surrounding her, a very pale blue that evaporated instantly. It was the weakest aura he had ever seen.

"Who are you?" she asked, a hint of fear in her voice.

"I'm Detective Owen Peirce, I—"

"No, that's not what I mean," she said forcefully. "Who *are* you?"

Owen exhaled. This was it.

"I'm Prince Charming. I'm here to save you."

CHAPTER FIFTEEN

Two weeks had passed since the night Owen left Poppy in her driveway. The new FBI detail following her since Owen's departure had gone relatively unnoticed—Mendez only contacted her through text messages—though she did catch a black sedan following her from time to time. An official escort had taken her back to Washington and Lee, but besides going food shopping or out to hang out with friends, she didn't notice them tailing her much anymore.

It had taken a week for Poppy to convince herself that Owen wasn't coming back, which was fine since she'd decided to hate him. It had taken another week to finally admit she didn't hate him, and that she wanted to talk to him, but she couldn't as he had erased himself from her phone. It was another day before she was grateful he had done that, because she would have made an ass out of herself.

She had called Sean and confided everything to him, even the kiss that had basically ruined her for the foreseeable future. Never in her life had she kissed anyone like that, and yet she wasn't sure she ever wanted to be kissed like that again. The all-consuming, heartbreaking, breathtaking kiss had shattered her, the emotion behind it too great to handle, yet it was the only thing she could think about whenever she stopped focusing on her schoolwork or ended her shift waiting tables at Gino's. She realized it was going to be hard to let go, but let go she must. So, when a guy named Jared asked her out one afternoon at the school café, she accepted, and tried her hardest not to compare him to Owen.

Her phone buzzed and she put her hair straightener on the desk to see who it was:

Mendez

"Hello?" she answered, a little surprised he was calling her.

"Miss Pruette?" he asked. "It's Mendez."

"Yes, I know."

"Do you have plans tonight?"

"Yes, I have a . . . a date," she said, the words sticking in her throat. "Why? Is everything okay?"

Her roommate Kate looked up from the book she was reading.

"Everything's fine. We've just had a little activity tonight. Had a shady-looking character hanging around the student union earlier that got a few people's attention."

"What sort of character?"

"White male, mid-to-late twenties, longer hair, five o'clock shadow, full sleeve of tattoos on both arms. Sound familiar?"

"No."

"Yeah, I didn't think so. Doesn't sound like a student either, but don't worry, we're upping the detail. I'll be on duty tonight."

"Upping the detail?" she repeated, worried. "Should I cancel—"

"That won't be necessary, Miss Pruette. Goodnight."

"'Night," she said, though he had hung up. She looked down at her phone. "Huh."

"What was that about?" Kate asked, sitting up.

"It was Mendez. He said there was some activity tonight and they're upping the detail on me."

"Are you canceling on Jared?"

"He said I didn't have to," she said hesitantly. She thought for a moment, and then shook her head. "He's right. I'm completely covered and a car will be following me all night. I'll be fine."

"Are you sure?"

Poppy nodded, more to herself than Kate. She used to be so determined not to let the murderer control her life, but the last time she hadn't followed protocol, she had gotten a man shot. *Should I be foolish or paranoid?* Neither was a win in her book. There was an uneasy part of her that desperately wanted to call Owen, but no, that would defeat the purpose of going out on a date with Jared.

"I'll be fine. Goodnight," she said as she opened the door.

"'Night. Have fun!" Kate said as she closed the door.

Poppy walked out of the student apartment complex and saw a black sedan parked right in front. She gave a little wave, though they never waved back, just as a second black sedan pulled up behind the first. Mendez and another man in a black suit got out and walked toward her.

"Miss Pruette, this is Agent Lee. We'll be following you on foot a few yards behind tonight."

"Are you serious?" she asked, a slight panic setting in. "I can cancel if it's safer."

"Won't be necessary. The best thing to do is just go about your date regularly."

"Regularly? I look like the president with this much backup."

"Hardly," Mendez said as a good-looking guy appeared on the sidewalk.

"Poppy?" he said, looking slightly worried at the sight of the agents. "Is everything okay?"

"Hi, Jared. Yes, everything is fine, I think," she said, taking a step toward him. "Jared, this is Agent Mendez." They nodded at each other. "Listen, if you don't want to go out tonight, I completely understand. They're going to be following us on foot."

"Is it dangerous?" he asked, unsure.

"No," she said, just as uncertain. "They say it's not."

"And they're going to be following us?"

"We'll be behind you some yards; you won't even know we're here," Agent Mendez said.

"Okay. Well, if it's safe," he said, holding out his hand. "Let's go."

Poppy inhaled deeply and forced herself to take a step toward him. She took his hand, and they turned to the right. They walked in silence for a few blocks, unsure if they could speak in private. When Poppy saw that Mendez was at least a block behind them, she finally breathed a sigh of relief.

"So, this is different," Jared said. "It's like I'm on a date with a movie star."

"I'm completely mortified about this, by the way," she said, a hint of humor in her voice. "I'm so sorry."

"Don't be. It's kind of fun. Like we're spies or something."

"I guess, if you're optimistic."

"I am," he said, smiling at her. Poppy felt herself blush and instantly hated herself for doing so. "I think you'll like this place. I've only been to it once, when my folks were in town, but it's got a nice atmosphere. Quiet."

"Sounds nice."

"You look pretty, by the way."

"Thank you."

Poppy didn't know why she hadn't let herself like Jared more. He was a nice enough guy, with dark hair, brown eyes, and a knack for making the best out of situations. *Like this*, she thought. He was always quick with a joke or a compliment and he never argued with her, which was a change of pace. It seemed Owen had argued with her every minute of every day, but she would be lying if she said she hadn't enjoyed it. Owen would—

No, she thought. *Don't think about him right now.*

They walked for a few more blocks. The sidewalk had become slightly crowded as they strolled hand in hand into the night. Poppy only turned back twice to see if she could spot Mendez, but to her surprise, she didn't. He really was good at his job, it seemed. Owen wouldn't have blended in so well. He would be breathing down her neck—

Stop it, she scolded herself silently.

"Everything all right?" Jared asked, looking at her. "You're scowling."

"I'm fine," she said.

"Is it that we're being followed?"

"No, it's just . . . I haven't been on a date in a while. It feels weird to be doing something so normal."

"I guess it would, after everything you've been through."

Poppy nodded, not wanting to talk about her grandmother or anything involving the case. She squeezed his hand tightly to try and distract him, which worked because he smiled at her. It was odd, the way he was looking at her. He seemed to genuinely like her, but she didn't feel quite the same way about him yet. Maybe she would grow into it. If Owen was here, he'd tell her she was being stupid or something. She smiled, doubting very much he'd be championing her dating.

"Here we are," Jared said as they came to a stop.

They stood in front of a brick building with large windows. It was dimly lit inside, with deep purple lights hanging from the ceiling and Adele playing in the background. It was rustic and sweet, with tables made out of old cable rolls topped with glass. They followed the waitress to one of the tables near the windows at the front and the waitress handed them menus.

"This is a nice place," Poppy said, looking around. She scanned the room to see if Mendez was inside, but she didn't see him. "I like it."

"I thought you would. Kate said you'd probably like it."

Jared went on about his major and the fall formal that was happening at one of the sororities in two weeks. Football games and parties dominated the conversation, and when he excused himself to use the bathroom, Poppy was left alone to look out the window and watch the people pass by.

She was enjoying her time with him and had hardly thought about Owen. Proud of herself, she watched a couple walk by, holding hands and laughing, then a group of friends crossing the street while a woman hailed a cab. *The world went on about its business*, she thought as she stared, her eyes catching on a man standing on the opposite corner. He wasn't moving, in fact, he seemed frozen where he stood. She couldn't tell, since he had a hood pulled up over his head, but she felt as though he was looking at her. She squinted, trying to see what he was doing, but he just stood there. She felt a chill go down her spine as she leaned closer to the window.

Is he staring at me?

Poppy nearly jumped out of her chair when she felt a hand touch her shoulder. It was Jared, who looked surprised.

"Sorry. Did I scare you?"

"Oh, no, you didn't," she lied.

They continued their conversation, eventually returning to the fall formal. Jared asked if she was going. To her surprise, she said yes, and that they should go together if her detail said the coast was clear. Jared accepted and Poppy smiled, though she felt her gut twist.

Jared insisted on paying for the whole dinner and after a slight argument, Poppy let him—but only after he agreed to let her buy him a drink at a coffee shop close by, where a local band was playing. As they left the restaurant, Poppy saw Mendez and Lee standing on the corner. She gave them a nod, and they began to follow her.

"They're kind of like stray dogs following you home," Jared said as they walked. "I bet we could ditch them if you wanted to."

"Oh, no," Poppy said, shaking her head. "I don't want to be out of their sight."

"I guess you're right. It's got to be a bit frightening in your shoes, huh?" Poppy nodded and he continued. "What was it like? The shooting in Connecticut?"

Poppy shook her head, uneasy at his question. "I don't want to talk about it."

"I understand," he said, but then added, "It had to be pretty awful." She just nodded, looking at the ground as they walked. "I've never seen a dead body."

"Neither have I," she said, suddenly angry. "He wasn't dead. He survived."

"Yeah, but pretty close—"

"You know, I'm tired," she said, stopping in her tracks. "I'd like to go home instead."

"Oh, come on, I didn't mean to make you angry."

"And yet you did," she said, turning around. She saw Mendez and Lee stop.

"Wait," he said as she walked away. "Wait, Poppy, hold on." He reached for her hand, and she stopped. "I really am sorry. I didn't mean to pry. I was just curious and, look . . . " He held up his hands as if to demonstrate his innocence. "I won't ever mention it again. Okay?"

She looked at him, her mouth tight in aggravation. He had killed whatever little mood had been between them, but she didn't want to argue. Not with him.

"Fine," she said coolly. "But I still want to go home."

"Okay, that's cool," he said, taking her hand. "I'll walk you home, then."

"Thanks."

They walked mostly in silence, as Jared's attempts at new topics were shut down by Poppy one by one, but he didn't give up and switched to telling her corny jokes instead. By the time they reached the front of the student apartment complex, her mood had improved slightly and she even started to laugh. She continued to talk with Jared until, out of the blue, he leaned in and kissed her.

Pulling back, Poppy was a little shocked and flustered, which made it pretty obvious that she had been caught off guard. Noticing his displeasure at her reaction, Poppy spoke.

"I'm sorry," she said quickly. "I just didn't see that coming."

"I thought we were having a good time."

"We were, we are, I'm just . . . look, this whole FBI thing has sent me through the ringer. It's not you. I'm just a little jumpier at surprises, even nice ones." He smiled at that, though she knew it was a bald-faced lie. "Thank you for dinner."

"Anytime."

"Next time's on me," she said as she headed to the doors. "Goodnight."

"'Night."

After swiping her card to get inside, she sighed heavily. *That had to be the most awkward date in the history of dates,* she thought miserably to herself. Why had she even agreed to go out with him in the first place?

Because you can't be with the one you want, a tiny voice sounded in her head.

Shut up, she argued with herself. That didn't mean she had to date any random person.

But he hadn't been random, she reminded herself. Jared was nice, funny, a little pushy, but everyone had faults and he was just curious. Wouldn't she be if the roles were reversed?

It was completely unfair of her judge him so quickly. When she reached her room, she took out her phone and texted him.

Maybe we can go out again next week? I owe you a drink.

He replied instantly.

Absolutely.

She smiled, but wasn't happy. Opening the door, she saw that Kate had left, probably out at some party, which was fine with her. She didn't want to talk about her date. All she wanted to do was crawl into bed and not think about anything.

Or anyone, for that matter.

CHAPTER SIXTEEN

That Monday, Poppy was working the closing shift at Gino's when Kate, Jared, and his friend Shane came in for pizza. She didn't mind waiting tables—it was never really busy on Monday nights—and she served her friends with a smile. It was always fun to wait on her friends.

"You coming out tonight, Poppy?" Kate asked as she delivered the pizza to their table. "Lacrosse House is having a party."

"It's Monday," Poppy said.

"It's college," Shane said with a smile, shrugging.

"True," Poppy agreed. "But I've got a ton of work to do on this biology paper. It's due Wednesday and I can't hand it in the way it looks now."

"Come on, Poppy, you're soaring through biology. A B-plus won't kill you."

"Listen to you! I never try to make you skip on your history work."

"That's because history is fun," Kate laughed. "Biology is murder."

The word hung in the air for a moment as the three looked at Poppy. She felt their eyes on her, waiting to see what she would say, but she shook her head and smiled a little too wide.

"Sorry, but you'll just have to go without me."

"You really can't come?" Jared asked. "Even for a few hours?"

"I would, really, Lacrosse throws the best parties, but if I don't want to be going to them for the next decade, I have to get this paper done."

They tried to convince her for another few minutes, but eventually gave up. They left fifteen minutes later after finishing their pizza. Jared gave Poppy a kiss goodbye on the cheek, which made her laugh, as he had warned her beforehand.

After she was done with work, she changed her clothes in the bathroom and pulled her bag over her shoulder. She headed out the back of the restaurant, where her trusty black sedan sat idling. She headed over to it and knocked on the passenger-side window. It rolled down, exposing Agent Lee's face.

"Mind giving me a lift? The library's on the other side of campus."

"Get in," he said, nodding to the back.

She got in the car, and saw another agent she had seen before but couldn't remember his name. They drove in silence and reached the library in under ten minutes.

"Thanks," she said as she got out, walking across the large lawn that sat in front of the building.

They didn't answer. They almost never did. Poppy wondered if Mendez had warned them not to be too chummy with her, considering the last people on her case. She adjusted her bag's strap and walked into the library.

Heading for the back, she passed several students hunched over books. She reached an empty table and pulled her books and laptop out as she took a seat, eager to continue her research paper. *Biology* is *fun*, she thought to herself as she began to scan her notes. *You just have to understand it.*

An hour or so passed before Poppy's eyes became heavy. She struggled to focus on a paragraph about genetics when she finally let her eyes close. *Just for a minute*, she thought.

Poppy was in a room she had never seen before. It was dark, and the only light came from an old glass lamp that sat on a table pushed up against the wall. She looked around, deciding it looked more like the inside of a trailer. It was a small space, with a bed and what looked like a kitchenette on the opposite side of the room, where an old man stood, hovering over the sink. She was startled when he turned around. He had long, greasy gray hair that hung in front of his face. She thought that he saw her, but for some reason, he seemed to look right past her. For a moment, she saw his eyes—his old, frightened eyes.

"I'm sorry," he said in a raspy voice. A pair of hands came through Poppy's chest as though she were a ghost, hands that wrapped around the old man's neck.

Poppy woke with a start, lifting her head off her books. She blinked several times before rubbing her eyes, and frowned. *What sort of nightmare was* that? She hadn't had an actual dream in months. Ever since her grandmother's death, she had only had memories for dreams, not fabricated ones. It could be a sign that she was moving on, but why had she dreamt of *that*? Who was that man?

Rubbing her eyes again, she grabbed her phone and looked at the time. It read 1:00 a.m. She groaned. She had been asleep for hours, but it felt so quick, like she had only been sleeping for a few moments. She hadn't even started typing up her report.

Shaking off the nightmare, she stood up, stretched, and headed for the stacks. She had to get this report done.

"Biology, biology," she said to herself as she walked around the stacks of books. "Bi. Olo. Gy."

As she walked down toward the nonfiction section, she passed the literature section and stopped. *It would be ridiculous to look*, she told herself, and then turned around, walking straight down the literature aisle. It wasn't like she had never read a fairy tale before, but what if she could read something about *him*? She remembered that Owen was constantly trying to not be Prince Charming, but he was, wasn't he? Even if it was only a story she could keep forever, that would be enough for her.

She followed the spines of the books until she found "GR," thinking only of the Brothers Grimm. Sure enough, she found several books containing fairy tales by the famous brothers. She brought them back to her table and looked through the contents, searching for the story about Prince Charming. It took a few minutes for Poppy to realize there wasn't a story centered around Prince Charming, but on the princesses and damsels in distress. *Where was Owen's line?* She looked at her laptop and decided to find out which story he belonged in.

After a few searches, she found a man named Charles Perrault, a 17th-century Frenchman who first collected the fairy tales of his home country. He seemed be the author of Cinderella, until she researched that story and found Giambattista Basile, an Italian soldier who'd put pen to paper almost forty years earlier.

It seemed the more she researched, the harder it was to find Prince Charming, until she found a woman named Jeanne-Marie Le Prince de Beaumont, a woman credited with the most well-known version of Beauty and the Beast. There was something about her biography that spoke to Poppy. She had left France after a painful marriage to become a governess in England, where she supposedly had an affair with a British spy. It was fascinating and familiar.

Owen had spoken French fluently with Lynette in New York. Was it a family tradition of the Peirces to retain their family language? And her maiden name, Le Prince, could easily have changed from Prince to Peirce after three hundred years. Or was she grabbing at nonsense?

Buzz. Buzz.

Poppy looked down at her phone. It was Sean.

"Hey," she said, answering. "It's late. What's up?"

"Just checking on you," Sean said. "I was wondering if you caught the news tonight."

"No," she said, barely listening, she was so absorbed in her research. "Something happen?"

"Yeah, there was a particular story that I thought would interest you."

"Oh?"

"Yeah, are you near a TV?"

"Nope. Library."

"Google Owen Peirce."

Poppy stopped her search and only then began to listen to Sean.

"What? Why?"

"Just do it. I got to go, Poppy, but I'll call you tomorrow, all right?"

"Yeah, bye."

Poppy hung up and pulled up another window to do a search. She typed Owen's name in and hit enter. Instantly, several news hits showed up, all saying the same thing: "Owen Peirce Arrested in Los Angeles."

"What the hell . . ." she said, clicking on one of the links. A news site popped up with the article that read:

Los Angeles, California — Former law student and playboy Owen Peirce, of the Peirce banking family, was arrested in the Hillcrest neighborhood of San Diego last night in an apparent breaking and entering case that has landed the famous Peirce in hot water. He has been released since the ordeal, and the homeowners are not pressing charges, yet it makes people wonder what happened to the former playboy of New York City. It has been determined that Peirce is a police officer in a Michigan police station, though no station is claiming to work with him.

The Peirces have long been held as one of the first families of New York City, rivaling that of the . . .

"Oh, no," Poppy said quietly as the rest of the article descended into the history of Owen's family. With his job now national news, everything he had done to disappear had been ruined thanks to some loudmouth in California. Did this have something to do with *her*? *Why the hell was he breaking and entering?*

Another Google search led to the same article, rewritten several times, with some being more colorful about the Peirce family history.

She looked at her phone and cursed him for deleting her number. The time on her phone reminded her that she had a paper due in less than eight hours. Putting everything aside, she forced herself to go to the biology section and pull the books she needed. She couldn't handle that world right now.

A while later, she heard a door shut somewhere in the library. She sat up and looked around the room. It seemed all the other students had left. Rubbing her face, she began to gather her things and stood up.

Turning around, she saw nothing, nor did she hear anything. She stared into the row of books behind her, not so much looking, but listening for something, anything. *Nothing,* she thought. Maybe she had just imagined a door closing, remembering how her roommate would often wake herself up when she snored, thinking someone was breaking into their apartment. Poppy shook her head and swung her backpack onto her shoulder. She turned off the light above her desk and heard something fall.

Poppy's body instinctively went into fight-or-flight without her. Her legs were already running for the door before she realized that she was bolting. Grabbing at the door, she pulled it open and ran down the hallway, only vaguely aware she was being chased.

A hand grabbed her hair, yanking her back. She screamed as loud as she could as she fell backward, hitting her head on the terrazzo floor. Lights seemed to flash before her eyes as her vision blurred. She saw a hazy figure standing above her, but she couldn't see clearly.

She yelled again before sinking into darkness.

CHAPTER SEVENTEEN

The beeping of machines and voices arguing somewhere in the dark caused Poppy to wake. She felt groggy, and was only vaguely aware of her surroundings. Her eyes shifted around, and soon she realized she was in a hospital room. The lights were off, but she could hear people just outside. She looked down at a sliver of light casting the shadows of two pairs of feet beneath the door.

"She is not safe here," said a deep male voice not familiar to her. His voice was hard, but warm—a strange contrast, and one Poppy wouldn't soon forget.

"I don't care who you say you are, if you don't leave right this minute, I'll arrest you," another voice sounded. It was Mendez. "And since you're so eager to defend Peirce, I'd have him arrested for obstruction."

"You should know—"

"I do know. I'm under direct orders from Mr. Pruette: no one is to see his daughter. Tell Peirce there's a restraining order against him."

"Fine," the hard voice said. "I'll tell him. I'll tell him this wish went wrong."

"What the hell is that supposed to mean?"

Poppy heard a set of footsteps walk away, and the door began to open. She tried to see whoever Mendez had been talking to, but missed him. She shut her eyes, pretending to be asleep before Mendez fully opened the door. She heard him step into the room, and then the door closed again and his footsteps disappeared down the hallway.

What in the world is going on? Poppy thought. *Why had a restraining order been placed on Owen?* She needed to talk to him above everyone else. Owen was the only person who could help her.

Careful not to remove the wires that were monitoring her vitals, Poppy pulled herself up. She wore a paper gown; her clothes were folded neatly on a chair in a corner of the room. Before she could figure out how to get out of bed without being noticed, a searing pain shot through the back side of her head.

Instantly, she wrenched her hand back, yanking the forefinger monitor off in the process. A loud, constant beeping went off and before she knew it, a dark-haired female doctor came into the room, followed by Mendez.

"Hello, Miss Pruette," the doctor said. "I'm Dr. Patel, and you are at Langley Medical. How are you feeling?"

"My head is killing me," Poppy said, letting the doctor clip the forefinger monitor back on. "What happened?"

"You don't remember?" Dr. Patel asked.

"I remember I was in the library," she said honestly, though she began to fight through the foggy memory. "I had a paper in biology due. I fell asleep. When I woke up, it was late, but I had to finish my paper."

"Where did you fall asleep?" Mendez asked.

"At one of the tables, in the back." She looked at him. "Where was the detail? Weren't they there?"

"Agent Lee was there until 12:45 a.m., when he followed a young woman he mistook for you. He and his partner tailed her for about ten minutes before two local black-and-whites cornered him. The young woman had called the police because she felt like she was being stalked. By the time they'd convinced the local police of who they were, they came back to the library and found you, lying in the hallway."

"I was alone?" Poppy felt the familiar panic begin to rise within her. It had been the first time in a month she had been without a detail and she had been attacked? Whoever was trying to kill her had been watching her this entire time, waiting for a chance. "Who was she?"

"A local student."

"But what was her name? Maybe she was part of it," Poppy said, grasping at anything. "Did you talk with her?"

"Yes, and I assure you—"

"No, no. You can't assure me of anything, because I was just attacked, which means behind your detail, someone's been watching me." She was speaking in a rushed tone, her anxiety reaching its peak. "I need to make a phone call."

"To whom?"

"Can I have my phone?" Poppy asked Dr. Patel, ignoring Mendez. She wasn't going to talk to anyone unless it was Owen. "Thank you."

"No problem," Dr. Patel said. "But I suggest you answer the agent's questions. This is extremely serious."

"I'm calling my dad," she lied.

"Do you remember after you woke up? What happened next?"

"I heard a noise," she said, aggravated, until she remembered. "I was being chased."

"By whom?"

"I don't know, I didn't see. He grabbed my hair and the back of my collar," she said, touching the sore spot on the back of her head. "Ripped me down. I hit my head."

"That's where Agent Lee found you," Mendez said. "When did you get to the library last night?"

"I was there after work, around nine or ten," Poppy said. "Agent Lee gave me a ride. Why? Didn't he tell you?"

"He did, but there was also a break-in at your apartment building. No one was hurt, but your roommate was home. It happened around eleven."

A cold, sinking feeling hit Poppy in the gut. *He's still out there.* She looked at her phone before looking up at Dr. Patel. "Am I going to be okay?"

"Yes, you have a nasty bump on the head, but there's no bleeding or swelling on the brain, so you should be fine. You'll probably have a headache for a day or two."

"Thank you, Doctor," she said. "Can I have a little privacy? I'd like to call my dad now."

"Sure," Mendez said as he followed the doctor out into the hallway.

Poppy looked at her phone, desperate. She needed to contact Owen, but how could she get in touch with him? If her father had put a restraining order on Owen, he wouldn't help, but why had he done that? Was it because of what happened in California?

She scrolled through her contacts. There were too many questions, and she needed answers. She was about to call Sean in the hope that he could somehow look for Owen's number in his phone's call history when she suddenly saw Lynette's name. She had completely forgotten about her! She hit dial and waited until she heard it go to voicemail.

Unwilling to give up, she kept redialing until she finally answered.

"Hello?" Lynette's voice echoed in her ear.

"Lynette! Lynette, it's Poppy. Oh my God, I'm so happy I got in touch with you."

"Oh hey, girl, what's up?"

"I need you to get in touch with Owen."

"Oh, no, you saw, didn't you?" she said, her tone worried. "It wasn't what it sounded like, Poppy, I promise. He didn't break in—well, I mean he *did*, but it wasn't his fault, so you can't be mad at him. It's really all Ajax's fault. I mean, it was his idea." A voice sounded behind Lynette's. "Oops. Sorry, Poppy, I'm not supposed to be talking to anyone about it. There's a protocol about these things."

"No, I don't care about that. Lynette, it's an emergency. You have to get in touch with Owen for me—there's a restraining order on him. Tell him I was attacked last night, and that he found me and has been watching me."

"Who?"

"The guy who's trying to kill me," she whispered desperately into the receiver. "I'm at Langley Medical. There are cops here, and I don't know if they'll let Owen in to see me, but you have to tell him. I don't trust anyone but him."

"Geez, Poppy, that's insane! Are you kidding?"

"No, I'm not kidding!" she continued. "I have to get in touch with him. Where is he? Is he still in California?"

"No, he's upstairs. He flew into JFK this morning on the family plane."

Of course, Poppy said to herself. "Can I talk to him?" she asked.

"Sure, just let me—"

Zzzzzzzzzzzzzzzz.

"Lynette? Lynette?" Poppy said, almost in a panic. "Hello?" Lynette's line had dropped. "Shit."

Poppy felt hopeless, and she prayed Lynette would tell Owen about her call. When Mendez returned, he asked a slew of questions. She told him everything she knew, even the guy she thought was staring at her the other night on her date with Jared, but soon her head was hurting again. Dr. Patel gave her some pain medication and advised her to rest. Before Mendez was escorted out of the room, he informed her that he would be at the end of the hallway. Dr. Patel turned on the television and told Poppy a nurse would be by later to check on her vitals.

Once alone, Poppy tried at least a dozen times to call Lynette back, but she only got her voicemail. After about an hour of that, her father and Samantha showed up.

"Poppy," her father said as he came into the room, followed by Samantha. She saw Mendez close the door after them. "Are you okay?"

"Yes," she said, as he took her hand. "I'm fine."

"What happened?"

Poppy went through the details of the previous evening as best she could. After Mr. Pruette and Samantha asked about a zillion questions each, Poppy finally had the chance to ask her father a question.

"I heard Mendez say something about a restraining order set in place for Owen," Poppy said, eyeing him. "Why?"

"There was an incident in California—"

"I know, but what does that have to do with me?"

Mr. Pruette looked at Samantha, who answered her.

"Your father has been working very hard for this election, Poppy. That incident in California, well, it wouldn't bode well if the press knew we had connections with Owen or the Peirce family. They're a very powerful family, and your father's campaign, well, it just wouldn't look good. They're not on the same page as your father's politics."

"So it doesn't have to do with you not trusting him?" she asked.

"No," her father said. "I do trust him, but you know I can't have any connections with him or his family, not only because of the politics."

He gave Poppy a look that suggested he was talking about their other connection. *Will he ever explain to Samantha about our family history?* she wondered. He seemed absolutely determined to avoid it at all cost, and she almost couldn't blame him, at this point.

They stayed until nightfall, when a male nurse came in to check on her. Mr. Pruette and Samantha decided to get a bite to eat and head off to the hotel, saying they would be back in the morning. Poppy was glad they were staying nearby. An officer took over Mendez's watch and he waved goodnight to Poppy as he escorted her father and Samantha down the hall. She dozed off after they left, feeling tired after their visit. It was late at night when she felt her phone buzz in her hand. She looked down and saw a text message from an unknown number:

I'm coming for you.

Her eyes widened. Fear crept up Poppy's spine, draining her of the comfort she had felt since being at the hospital. *I am in police protection*, she reminded herself. No one could reach her without being approved first. She looked out the narrow window of the bedroom door. She saw the back of the officer who had relieved Mendez when her father left.

Who is this?

She texted back, hoping it was Owen. She kept her eyes on the window and the officer. As long as he stayed there, she would be safe. She'd stare at the back of his head for the rest of the night just to make sure.

The moments turned into minutes and her phone didn't buzz. She felt trapped, panicky and oddly calm all at the same time, as if she were preparing herself for an attack. She decided that if she needed to, she would roll to her right off the bed and grab the metal pole holding up her IV bag in the corner of the room. She was on edge, but couldn't run far. If *he* was coming for her, he should have made it a surprise.

An hour had passed before the sound of footsteps down the hall caught her attention. The officer moved slightly as another man came toward the door; the window was too narrow to see his face. She waited nervously, her heartbeat picking up speed on the monitor. Her eyes were glued to the window of the door and her heart nearly stopped when the handle turned. Poppy held her breath as it opened.

The silhouette of a man stood in the doorway, and her fear melted away as she instantly recognized him. The officer closed the door behind him.

"Owen," she said softly.

He hobbled toward her, dressed in scrubs. Without hesitation, he placed his hands to both sides of her face and bent down to look her in the eyes. She was stunned. He seemed to be inspecting her, when it was she who should be inspecting him.

Why is he limping?

"Are you okay? What happened to you?" she asked. "Why are you dressed like that?"

He didn't answer, just held her face a little longer. She sat silently as she watched him. He leaned forward and kissed her so gently she was barely sure their lips touched. His eyes never closed, nor did hers, and when he pulled away, he exhaled, as if he had held his breath the entire time he had been in the room.

"Are you all right?" he asked slowly.

"I'm fine," she said, oddly comfortable at how worried he seemed. "What about you? What happened to you?"

"We have to get you out of here," he said quietly, ignoring her question. "Did the doctor clear you for injuries?"

"Yes, she said I'd have a headache for few days. Owen," Poppy whispered, "did you sneak in here?"

"It was the only way I could get in without being noticed. There are cops all over. Can you get dressed?" Owen took a step toward the corner of the room where her clothes sat folded on a chair. He paused, wincing as his hand went to his leg.

He had *injured it*, Poppy decided.

"Are you sure you're all right? What's wrong with your leg?"

Once again, he ignored her questions, and she felt the return of familiar annoyance. He inspected her machines, tracing where the wires went. Following the cords, he went around the back of the machines and started unplugging them from the wall.

"Are you crazy?" she snapped quietly. "You're going to set them off."

"No, I'm not," he countered.

"Don't even think about trying to boss me around when you're the one breaking into a hospital ward. *Limping*, I might add!"

"We are not arguing here," he said softly, "so keep your voice down, please." He tossed her clothes toward her and turned around to let her dress in private.

"You should want to keep me here, surrounded by police," she said, continuing her rant in a whisper. *Why does he have to press my buttons?* "You walk in here—well, you don't walk, you *hobble*, and don't even *think* to explain why—and jump right into bossing me around. What about California? Yeah, I heard about it, as did the whole country."

"I'm here for less than five minutes and you're already trying to start a fight?" he asked, turning around.

"I'm not starting a fight. Hey!" she said, holding her shirt to her chest. "Turn around!"

Owen rolled his eyes and turned back around. Poppy thought she saw a hint of a smile. *Prince, my foot*, she thought ruefully.

"The officer will be back any minute, so hurry up. Put your hair up in a bun, too. We only have a small window of opportunity to get out of here undetected."

"I'm getting dressed as fast as I can," she hissed, as she pulled her jeans on. "What happened in California?"

"You really want to do this right now?"

"What I really want," she said, pulling her shirt over her head, "is to—"

"Too bad. We've got to go now."

Owen turned, pulling a knit beanie out of his pocket. He pulled it over her head after she put her hair up, and once he was satisfied her hair was covered, he took her hand and drew her behind him. He peeked out the door window. When the coast was clear, he hurried out, Poppy in tow, down the hallway and out of the protected ward. They took the stairs to the first floor, but before they could fully enter the hallway, Owen stalled, throwing them both back into the stairwell. He shook his head slightly and pointed toward the door. Poppy couldn't help but look out the tiny window, and found three uniformed cops blocking the hallway.

Owen led her down the last set of stairs, which led to the hospital's basement. There were only a few doctors and nurses, but no cops. They moved quickly down a hallway toward a side exit door. Poppy kept her eyes down as she followed Owen after an older woman gave her a suspicious look.

Owen opened the door and as calmly as they could to keep from drawing attention, they walked across the parking lot to the major roadway. They passed a busy chain restaurant and finally reached a plain black sedan. Poppy went to open the passenger door, but Owen walked right by it, stopping at the car next to it instead. It was a classic car, painted in flat black. Poppy raised her eyebrows.

"Whose car?" she asked.

"Mine," he said, helping her into the passenger's side.

"What is it?"

"It's a 1968 Mustang coupe." She stared at him as he got into the driver's seat, as if to question it. "What? I like cars."

"Of course you do," she said, with a touch of know-it-all in her voice.

"What's that's supposed to mean?"

Poppy didn't answer. She didn't want to admit to reading all the gossip that had come out about him in the last forty-eight hours.

"Oh, I get it. Did some research, did you? Rich kids like cars, huh?"

"Look, I don't care either way," she lied, hoping she was convincing. "The only thing I'm worried about, besides your stupid leg, which you still haven't told me about, is the fact that someone attacked me last night."

Owen seemed to register the importance of her words and became Detective Peirce again. The transformation was interesting, but Poppy ignored it.

"Are you sure you're all right?" he asked. When she nodded, he took a breath, put the car into reverse, and then drove out into the road. "I cut my leg when I was breaking into that house in Hillcrest."

"So you did break into a house?"

"Yes. We made a mistake, Ajax and I. We were trying to fix it." He shook his head. "Unfortunately, we made a few mistakes. I cut my thigh on a piece of glass. That's why I'm limping."

"Want to explain the break-in?"

"Not particularly," he said. "I want to know what happened to you leading up to the attack."

Poppy explained how she was researching her biology paper, tactfully leaving out the part where she was looking up fairy tales and Googling his family. When she finished, she saw a quizzical look on Owen's face.

"Was there anything else? Did you feel like you were being watched in the days leading up to yesterday? Any auras?"

"No, no auras." Poppy hesitated. "But there was someone looking at me last week. A guy on the corner across the street from the restaurant."

"Restaurant?"

"I was on a date," she said, not looking at him. "I was looking out the window, and there was this guy, but I couldn't really see him. He was too far away."

There was a moment of silence that hung in the air and Poppy felt her cheeks grow warm.

"You didn't get a good look?" Owen asked after a beat.

"No," Poppy said, suddenly wanting to change the conversation.

"Something's not adding up," he said. "If this guy you saw was a stalker and knew you were alone and unprotected in the library, why wouldn't he have finished you off?"

"I guess because Agent Lee was coming."

"No, I mean if this guy who attacked you was the same person who attacked Teddy, you wouldn't be alive. Something's not right." He paused. "Could there be two people after you?"

Poppy shook her head, unsure of how to answer, but he'd made a good point. Why would the person who nearly killed Teddy not try to kill her with the same amount of violence? But suggesting there were two different people after her at the same time didn't make any sense either. "What did I do? Why does he want me dead?"

"The most basic want to end someone else's life is to ensure one's own survival," Owen said, thinking out loud.

"Why? He doesn't even know me."

"We don't know that."

"But you cleared everyone."

"I could have made a mistake," he admitted, which didn't seem to sit well with him. It was evident in his voice and the pained, pensive look on his face. "The devil is in the details . . . I had to miss something."

"There was something else," Poppy said. "Earlier tonight, I heard Mendez talking to someone. Someone who seemed to be in contact with you. Or at least, he said he was."

"What do you mean?"

"Mendez told him to tell you about the restraining order. The man said he was going to tell you the wish had gone wrong."

"A wish gone wrong?" Owen repeated, his voice suddenly distant.

"Yes. What does it mean?"

"It means we're heading south."

"What? Why?" she asked, realizing they were no longer heading toward the interstate. "Where are we going?"

"Charleston."

"Why? Who's in . . . wait." She looked at him, wide-eyed. "Isn't Hanna in Charleston?"

"Yes."

"Isn't Hanna living with William Vann?"

"You know she is."

"Isn't William Vann part of the Wolf lineage?" she asked. Owen didn't answer as she looked straight, the lights of the freeway illuminating her fear.

"It'll be all right," he said.

"I can't believe this," she said, more to herself than to him. "You're leading me right out of woods and into the wolf's den."

CHAPTER EIGHTEEN

Sometime in the night Poppy had drifted off, and when she awoke, the sun was just rising over the horizon. They had gotten off the freeway at some point—probably to avoid unnecessary attention—and were pulled off to the side of the road. She turned her head slightly, only to notice that Owen wasn't in the driver's seat. She sat up and twisted around to see him walking in slow circles as he talked on his cell phone.

Owen is a complex person, she thought as she watched him and, in turn, knew that their relationship was as well. She had wanted so much to be with him over the past month, had

had such a hard time accepting he was gone for good, that when he had showed up back in the hospital, there had been a moment of pure joy and wonder and fear when he kissed her. It had disappeared almost instantly when they started arguing, yet she couldn't help but feel genuinely happy. *But how could this ever work?* There was obviously something between them, but how could there be?

Owen got into the car just as he finished his call.

"Morning," he said.

"Good morning," she said back. "Who was that?"

"How's your head?" he countered.

He's going to be a hard one to figure out. "Hurts, but I think that's to be expected. Who were you talking to?"

"Hanna. I wanted her to know we were on our way to William's house."

"About that," Poppy started. "Why exactly are we going to William Vann's home? Aren't we like . . . sworn enemies or something? What if he sees me and wants to suddenly jump on the 'let's kill Poppy' bandwagon?"

"Nothing is going to happen to you at the Vann home, I promise," Owen said, his tone comforting in its certainty. "But I need William's help. I want to locate the wish granter from the Three Virtues story. If the story is real, and the wish has gone bad, I need to know everything about it."

"But how would William know where to find a wish granter?"

"Because William's worked with the Ruse line before. I'm sure he'll know where to find him. I'll need to call Ajax when we get there, too. I want to see if he's found anything."

They turned down a road with some large, stunning houses. Poppy was impressed. She had never been to Charleston before, but had heard about its beautiful historic buildings. They drove through the city and out toward the coast, where the lawns grew larger and the houses were few and far between, until they pulled up to a brick driveway.

An impressive pale yellow house that stood three stories tall with a two-story wraparound porch sat proudly behind large trees adorned with Spanish moss that lined the square property, giving it a sultry air. Poppy got out of the air-conditioned car, feeling the Southern heat fall heavily on her shoulders. Virginia was humid in the summer, but nothing like this, and it was already the end of September.

"So, this is the Vann family home?" she asked, impressed. "They certainly ended up doing well for themselves." She turned to Owen. "Is every descendent rich except me?"

"No," he answered. "And the Vann family didn't come into their wealth in the most honest way. They're the bad guys, Poppy. Don't forget that."

"Then why are we here?"

"Because I'm owed a favor," he said as they reached the sprawling front steps. The door opened, and a girl Poppy's age with a blonde pixie cut came running out. "And Hanna's here."

"Owen!" the girl who must have been Hanna yelled as she hugged him at the top of the steps. "I'm so glad you're here!"

"What are you doing here?" he asked, taking on a tone that reminded Poppy of a typical older brother. "Don't you have class?"

"Not until noon," she said, rolling her eyes playfully. She turned to Poppy. "Nice to meet you. I'm Hanna."

"Poppy," she said, holding out her hand.

"I know. Owen has told me all about you," she said, winking.

Poppy tried to smile, but her attention was focused on the front door. There in the doorway stood a man capable of things Poppy couldn't understand. She wasn't sure why or how she instinctively knew this, but her body reacted and she began to step backward.

Owen noticed and reached out to hold her hand.

"Poppy, it's okay," he said.

"I can't go in there," she said, her voice shaking. She felt uncomfortably warm and cold at the same time. Her breathing became shallow. "Owen, I . . . I can't go in there."

The man in the doorway came out, closed the door behind him, and came down the steps. He was followed by a large wolf with eyes that seemed to glow. The intense pressure Poppy felt on her chest lifted slightly, but now she could see the dark, hazy aura of the man with black hair and dangerous eyes.

"Shoot," Poppy heard Hanna say. She looked at her. "Owen, are they not going to be able to meet?"

"Mortal enemies, Hanna. What did you think?" Owen said.

Feeling mortified at her reaction, Poppy set her spine and shook her head. Taking a step toward the stairs, she tried her hardest to smile, ignoring the growling wolf.

"Wyatt, heel." The animal stopped. "Go find my mom."

The wolf trotted down the wraparound porch and disappeared behind the corner.

"Hello," she said, even holding out her free hand as the man came toward her. Owen held tightly to her other hand. "I'm Poppy."

"William," he nodded, not taking her hand. "I'm sorry, but I don't think I can touch you."

"Will!" Hanna yelled in embarrassment.

"No," Poppy said quickly, "I agree with you. I was just trying not to be rude."

"Maybe this was a bad idea," Hanna said sadly.

"No, it was the only choice," Owen said. "Mr. Vann is the only one who poses a real threat, but he's out of town." William eyed him. "And I'm not here to argue about good and bad. Poppy was attacked two nights ago, and we think the killer may be hunting her."

"Who would want to kill her?" William asked, though Poppy had the distinct impression that he wasn't so much worried for her as he was that someone might beat him to it. *Stop it*, she scolded herself. He was willing to help her, and even though her future descendants were destined to fight with his, she needed to at least make it to the point where she had descendants.

"Good question," Owen said. "I have to make some calls." He entered the house without permission.

"Oh, yeah, sure, go right in," William said sarcastically to his back. He turned to Hanna. "Polite guy."

"He's stressed out," she countered. "I think about . . . *him*."

"Oh."

"Excuse me," Poppy asked. "Him who?"

"Him, as in Roderick Hobbs," Hanna began. "Owen's best friend. Well, not anymore. Not for a long time."

"Who is he?"

Hanna looked at William.

"He's not Good," William said slowly. "Not like you or Hanna or Owen. He's an Other."

Poppy was a little shocked. "You mean to tell me that Owen was good friends with an Other? No way," she said. "No offense, but I don't think he much likes you and you're dating his cousin."

"She has a point," Hanna said.

"Regardless of how he feels about me, Roderick and Owen were the best of friends for a long time before Roderick betrayed him."

"How?" Poppy asked.

William shook his head.

"It's not important," he said, though Poppy felt like he was deliberately avoiding her question. "What is important is that Roderick is of the Ruse line, and he had an uncle who had a bit of a reputation back in the day. He was known for getting things done in unethical ways."

"Friend of your dad's?" Hanna asked, her eyebrows raised.

William gave her a look, as if acknowledging her teasing, and Poppy saw it: an honest connection between them. For a second, his dark aura appeared, but it had lightened.

She was making him different.

"I'm telling him you said that," William teased back.

"And Owen thinks that Roderick might have something to do with this?"

"No," William said, his brow furrowing. "He must know that Roderick doesn't have anything to do with this."

"Why?"

"He's been in a French prison for two years, and I believe he has two more to go."

"Prison? For what?"

"Roderick's a professional thief," William said. "He would get hired by big wigs to recover things they couldn't obtain legally. He got pinched two years ago in Paris for something. I can't remember for what, though."

"Do you think his uncle had something to do with this? The murders and the attack?"

"I doubt it."

"Why is that?"

"Rumor is no one's heard from him for at least five years. Think he fell into a bottle of booze and never came out."

Poppy couldn't focus long on William's dark stare and instead turned to Hanna, who looked almost sympathetic. Poppy wondered if she ever felt the strange effect William seemed to emanate. Was she the only one who could feel the threat that hung in the air? Did Hanna feel it too, and just ignored it? Poppy doubted she would be able to, since she was becoming increasingly uneasy in his presence.

"I'm sorry," she said quickly. "I have to wait on the lawn."

William nodded, and she hurried down the stairs. She heard hushed voices behind her and by the time she was on the grass, Hanna was behind her.

"I'm sorry," Hanna said quickly. "I know how you must feel."

"Do you?" Poppy asked, suddenly feeling the throbbing in her head. Her nearness to William made all the horrible feelings magnify. "I don't know how you could stand it if you did."

"I do, or rather, I did," she said. "Whenever the Hertz siblings were close, I felt nauseous and dizzy, like I had vertigo or something, only it was suffocating. I would pass out whenever they were near."

"You don't feel like that when you're next to him?" Poppy said, looking up the stairs.

Hanna shook her head.

"How?"

"I don't know. Maybe because I love him," she said quietly, as if knowing her feelings were almost like a contradiction. "I don't think he's quite like his family, though. He's not his father, and believe me, he's a man who makes normal people's skin crawl."

"How will it work?" Poppy asked quickly. "How can it possibly work?"

Hanna was quiet for a moment, as if arranging her carefully thought out beliefs. She nodded slightly and exhaled.

"I think, and this is only an opinion, that one of us will give up our line. Not consciously, but since blending families like ours isn't done, I guess I've always assumed we will come to a point when one of us will have to relinquish a bit of ourselves for the other, so the integrity of our lines can continue. At least, that's what I've come to believe."

Poppy pondered this for a moment.

"You think he will have to give up the Wolf line, don't you?" Hanna nodded slowly, looking down. "But how can you be sure?"

"I can't," she said. "I can only hope. The Vanns are actually a very nice family and save for William's father, I've always felt welcome. Yet, there is another Vann to carry on the Wolf line. I'm the last of the Golden."

"You're sure of it?"

"I am. I've searched high and low for relatives. I'm the last."

"But what if you're wrong? What if you have to give up yourself?"

"I guess I just have to be willing to take that chance. I hope that it will go my way, or maybe we'll be thrown out of this bizarre sideshow of a world and get to live normal lives, but if it doesn't go my way, I'm willing to do it. What the fairy tales don't tell people is that there is a constant give and take. He doesn't always read my mind, but he does often enough, and I'm not always perfect in his eyes, but he's the end to my beginning." She paused, looking up at William's turned back, and then back to Poppy. "He's really not that bad, you know."

Just then Owen appeared at the top of the stairs, searching for Poppy. He said something to William, which caused him to give Poppy a disturbed look. They exchanged a few more words before William turned back to enter the house. Owen walked down the stairs.

"Hanna, can you take Poppy to your apartment?" he asked.

"Of course," Hanna said as William reappeared, putting on a black jacket as he hurried down the stairs. "What's going on?"

"William and I have to take a drive," Owen said, his eye on Poppy. "Try to keep a low profile, okay?"

"Sure," Hanna said as William came up to her. "Where are you going?"

Poppy blushed in spite of herself as they kissed. The look in William's eyes seemed rather intense and for a moment, Poppy wondered if Hanna could do any wrong in his eyes.

"Owen just got off the phone with Ajax," William began. "According to one of his father's old ledgers, one of Poppy's great-aunts did make a wish with Randall about forty years ago. Andrew Guess marked it down, but nothing ever came of it, so he left it alone."

"So, what does that mean?"

"We're going to find out," Owen said.

"Where?"

"Roderick's hotel room. He's been tailing you for weeks."

CHAPTER NINETEEN

Owen and William's trip was silent as they drove toward the outskirts of North Charleston. It had been at least five years since he last saw Roderick, and he had believed the last time was the final time. Hell, when he had heard that Roderick was in France three years ago, he'd flat-out denied it. He had accompanied Lynette to school her sophomore year to see if he could find him, as he had some unfinished business with him still, but all he was able to do was help the local police with a few tips. Roderick may have been as shady as a shadow and quick to disappear, but he was only human.

Owen had already been in Michigan when he heard of his arrest and subsequent sentencing to at least three years in prison, which made this trip to the Econolodge all the more bizarre. *Did Roderick escape? Why has he been tailing Poppy? Why hasn't anyone called about it?* Owen had connections all over the country and abroad on the lookout for Roderick, and yet here he was, according to Ajax, who had heard it from Pearl La Roux, a Storyteller who was more elusive than Roderick, mostly because she was so forgettable.

"I have to tell you something, Owen," William said as they pulled into the Econolodge parking lot. "You're not going to like it."

Owen glared to his right. He hadn't liked William when they first met, and he was still at odds with him from time to time, especially when Hanna wasn't around. Owen had long believed that William helped Roderick in his betrayal five years ago, though William had never admitted it.

"You helped him steal it, didn't you?" Owen asked as he parked, turning off the engine. "Is that it?"

"I didn't know you then. I didn't know any Good ones and only a handful of Others. Roderick's uncle was a friend of the family. When he asked a favor, I felt honor bound to him."

"There's no honor in Others," Owen said icily.

"I'm sure you think so," William countered, "but I didn't know you, or what I was doing, even afterwards. All he asked was for me to drive."

"I knew it was you beneath that mask. I knew."

"I know you did, but I couldn't admit it, not in Michigan. You had it out for me."

"With good reason."

"And you were wrong, remember?" He paused. "Anyway, I thought I should tell you it was me that helped Roderick. That's all."

"And now seemed like the best time?" Owen nearly snapped. "Before we go kick in Roderick's door?"

A cool shadow passed over William's eyes.

"I'm only here to make sure you don't kill him. Whatever your business is with him, it will have to wait another day. A wish was made, Owen. Hanna and Poppy don't understand the severity of wishes, nor the consequences that can come from them. Rose Pruette's killer is still out there."

Owen didn't say anything. He got out of the car and made his way to the front desk. William was right. Whatever his gripe with Roderick, it would have to wait until after they'd caught Rose's killer.

Owen showed his badge at the front desk and gave the lady a description of Roderick instead of his name. She gave him the room number and returned to her newspaper. William opened the door and Owen walked in. It was a dingy room, with an unmade bed and an old television showing the local news. A door was closed at the opposite end of the room. When it opened, a man with a dark, trimmed beard and his hair combed back walked out, wearing a pair of faded jeans and drying his hands with a towel. His arms were covered in tattoos down to his wrists, as were parts of his chest. A murky smirk crossed his face as recognition dawned on him.

"Peirce," he said, his voice deep. "I wondered how long it would take you to find me."

Without realizing what he was doing, Owen strode toward him and hit him in the jaw with all his might. The man flew back into the wall as Owen grabbed his fist, cursing as he rubbed his knuckles.

"Damn it," William shouted, lunging toward Owen. He tried to pull his arms back to confine him, but Owen shook him off.

"I'm fine, I'm cool," Owen said as he looked at the man he once knew as his best friend sitting on the floor.

"Geez, Roderick, are you all right?" William said, looking down at him.

To Owen's surprise, Roderick started laughing as he stood up, touching his jaw. Blood dribbled down the corner of his mouth.

"I guess I had that coming," Roderick said, finding his footing. "Hell of a hook. Been practicing?"

Owen lunged at him again, but William stopped him. It was incredible how much fury Owen felt for one person.

"We don't have time for this," William said, pushing Owen back. "Roderick, we have a problem. Your uncle created a wish forty years ago." The laughing ceased. "What happened with that wish?"

Roderick let out a curse as he exhaled. His hand moved from his jaw to the back of his neck.

"So that's what this is all about?" he said loudly, almost in a groan. "I guess this has to do with the Hood girl, then."

Rage engulfed Owen so suddenly as he began to see red. He went to attack Roderick again, but William pushed him away forcefully.

"Knock it off," he growled at Owen.

"Why have you been stalking Poppy?" Owen asked.

"I wouldn't say I've been stalking her," Roderick started, his gaze falling to his feet. "Keeping tabs on her, maybe, but not stalking."

"Whatever you want to call it," Owen bit out. "Why have you been following her?"

Roderick kept his gaze low, as if he didn't want to meet either pair of eyes looking at him. He shifted his weight from one foot to the other before answering.

"Look, I don't know what's going on," Roderick said. "My Uncle Randall was a drunk. He wasn't the kind of guy you depended on for anything. I got sent his old journal a few months ago."

"What does an old journal have to do with Poppy?"

"I don't really know. It's not very legible, except for a few scribbles here and there. Something about a wish gone wrong, but it wasn't easy to read. 'Follow the Hood line,' it said, and, 'Only one can survive.' I didn't think much of it until I heard about Rose Pruette's death."

"Who told you she died?"

"I hear things," he said, smirking a self-satisfying grin as he finally looked up. "I keep in touch with some people who keep me up to date."

Owen looked at William, but his face was blank. *No doubt a skill of his*, Owen thought.

"So, Rose died and you thought to follow her granddaughter around?" Owen asked.

"Yeah, I mean, I heard him ramble about a bad wish from time to time. I just didn't know what he meant by it. I never really took anything he said seriously."

"Why?"

"Randall wasn't all that skilled, and wishes are incredibly difficult to accomplish. I don't doubt he did one, but I don't think it could have worked."

"Why not?"

"Because he was a drunk. Would you want someone with the shakes to try to grant you a wish?"

"Where is he?" William asked. "Maybe he can help."

"That would be impressive since he's in a graveyard somewhere outside of New Orleans," Roderick said.

"He's dead?" Owen asked. Roderick nodded. "How? When?"

"About two months ago. A neighbor found him in the woods behind his double-wide in the trailer park. They say he'd broken his neck somehow. Probably tripped over a log or something in a drunken stupor."

"You don't seem too broken up about it," William said suspiciously.

"Oh, I'm sorry," Roderick said, sarcastically. "Do you have a script for how I'm supposed to act?" He shook his head. "The guy was a loser."

"He was your family."

"He was a drunk, talentless crook that never gave a damn about anyone but himself."

"A broken neck?" Owen said, his mind still on the facts. "Was there an investigation?"

"No, why would there be?"

"You don't think a broken neck is something to investigate?"

"To be honest, I'm surprise he lasted as long as he did. I've seen that man cheat death so many times. I'm just glad he didn't take anyone out with him, like in a car wreck or something."

"Something isn't adding up," Owen said, almost to himself. "Rose, Vilma, and Randall all died within weeks of each other. As far as anyone knows, their lives were altered that night the wish was made." He looked at Roderick. "Did Randall ever tell you how to make a wish?"

Roderick held Owen's deadly gaze for a moment before speaking. For a fleeting second, Owen thought he saw something—pity, maybe, or sadness—but it had disappeared too quickly to discern.

"Of course," he said quietly, almost as if he were ashamed. "The only time he ever even mentioned it was when I was a kid. Even then, he could barely string words together to make a single coherent sentence. Said he needed to get it off his chest. That he did a favor for someone in that family years ago, but it was all wrong. Ursula went mad from it."

"Ursula?" Owen said. "Who is Ursula?"

"Rose and Vilma's sister. That's who made the wish. Randall tried to mend her broken heart with a broken heart. Said only one could survive."

"What's that supposed to mean?"

"Nothing. It was nonsense. He only spoke nonsense," Roderick said, agitated. "I mean, yeah, you need a broken heart to cast the kind of wishes we make, but you can't mend one with another. It didn't work out how he meant it to."

"Why do you say that?" William asked.

"He said it went horribly wrong. He couldn't do it himself and . . . he sought out help." Roderick rubbed his hand over his jaw, his fingers covering his mouth almost as if he were trying to physically hide his words. He looked at both William and Owen. "From someone in the Gabriele line."

A sudden, faint ringing sounded in Owen's ears as he felt the blood drain from his face. The Gabriele line was the lineage of witches. All the witches in all the stories, good or bad, but they were lost to history. The Gabriele line was thought to be too magical to have survived in the modern world. He looked at William, whose eyes had darkened significantly.

"That's not possible, Roderick," Owen said. "The Gabriele line is dead."

Roderick startled at hearing his name, but his sad eyes seemed to disagree.

"Supposedly," William interjected, still looking at Roderick. "No one has heard of a descendent in over a hundred years, but even if there was a surviving descendent, I thought wishes were granted by only two families."

"They are," Roderick began. "The Ruse line and the Fate line, but they're two different kinds of wish granting. The Fate line can only grant wishes made by one's heart. My line can grant anything else."

"Then why would he seek out someone from the Gabriele line?"

Roderick inhaled and exhaled slowly. "I don't know. All he said was that it wasn't finished. It wouldn't be finished until they were all dead, except one."

"They who? The sisters?"

"Everyone that wish affected. Everyone in that Hood family line."

"Everyone? Including Poppy? What about her father? He hasn't been targeted."

"Her father?" Roderick repeated. "Why would her father have anything to do with this?"

"He was Rose's son."

"Rose never had a son. She had a daughter."

"No," Owen said, sure of it. "Rose Pruette. She had a son, Poppy's father."

"I don't know why you think that," Roderick said. "Rose Vertu had a daughter."

"Vertu? But why would they . . . " Owen said, the wheels in his mind turning. "She changed her name. She didn't want her family to find her." He looked at Roderick. "She must have changed it after her daughter's car accident. But she must have known that a wish like that would have seen through a name change."

"People do strange things when they're scared to death. Scared *of* death." Roderick went to grab a red-and-black flannel on the bed. He took out a pack of Camel cigarettes and lit one. The smoke curled above their heads, and Owen suddenly wanted to hit him again, but refrained. "So now, there's just the two. Poppy and the boy."

"Boy?"

"Ursula's son."

The three of them stood, absorbing the information.

"So it's got to be this guy," William said. "What was his name?"

"Brom," Owen said suddenly, remembering those first few days in Miner's Way. Some of the Good had been in town, but so had some of Poppy's remaining family, their auras all smashed together. Vilma had come, yet there had been another man who never strayed too far from her, both at the service and the reception. He and Teddy had collected the names afterward. "His name is Brom. He was at the funeral."

A sudden rush of lines began to connect in Owen's mind. The deaths in Louisiana, the phony inheritance that no one seemed to know about, the attack on Teddy in Connecticut after he went to investigate. It was Brom.

"He knew how to find out about Windgate. If he followed her to school and has just been waiting for her to be alone . . . "

William's eyes snapped to Owen.

"Do you think . . . ?"

"Let's go," Owen said, even though William was already out the door. He was right behind him before he paused and looked back at Roderick. "This isn't over."

Roderick looked as though he was going to say something, but stopped. He nodded, and for the first time in over five years, Owen believed that he would see him again.

CHAPTER TWENTY

Poppy sat on Hanna's yellow futon, sipping her iced coffee as she smiled at her newfound friend.

"And then, they started brawling," Hanna said, her cheeks turning red at the memory. "Right on my front lawn."

"I can't believe that." Poppy laughed. She crinkled her nose and shook her head, her cheeks hurting from smiling so much. "Owen's always so reserved, so in control of his emotions. I can't see him actually hitting someone, and William nonetheless. They seem to get on pretty well."

"Well, yeah, now, but not in the beginning," Hanna said. "I can understand you saying that, though. Owen always appears to be in control of himself, but I think he just likes being in charge of everyone else instead."

"Now that might be hitting the nail on the head," Poppy said. "But still, he doesn't like to show any vulnerability." Hanna's eyes seemed to question her. "I mean, I know he's supposed to be in California and everything, and from what Ajax says, Owen has obligations that he has to attend . . . I mean, I understand why he doesn't show people certain sides . . . wait, no."

"Poppy," Hanna said softly. She looked up. "Do you, well, do you like him?"

"No," Poppy said quickly, and Hanna seemed crestfallen. "No. It's not that. I don't *just* like him."

Hanna's face lit up and Poppy blushed, shaking her head. As much as she wanted to get back to her normal life, Poppy was truly enjoying Hanna's company.

"What's with the wolf?"

Hanna waved her hand in the air. "I don't know. I can't figure it out myself. All I know is that everyone in the Vann family has a wolf that basically goes wherever they go. It's some sort of magic from the old days," she said, rolling her eyes, "if you can manage to believe that."

"It's definitely hard to believe."

Just then, a phone buzzed.

"Oh, that's me," Hanna said, looking at her phone. She frowned upon reading the text message. "Huh."

"What is it? Is everything okay?"

"Yes," Hanna said, standing up. "It's just . . . it's Mr. Vann."

"William's father?"

"Yes, he said he just arrived home and that Mrs. Vann has food poisoning. She's violently sick. He's worried and wants me to go over to the house." Hanna looked up. "I'll tell him I can't."

"Oh, no. Go," Poppy said, standing up. "I'll be fine."

"Are you sure?" Hanna said.

"Of course."

Hanna stood in place. "I don't know. I feel like Owen would kill me if I left you."

"I can go with you," Poppy said, though it sounded more like a question. "I'll stay in the car, and if it's serious, you can stay and I'll . . . I don't know . . . drive around until Owen calls."

"You think?" Hanna asked. "That actually might be safe. That way you're not at any one place and you're constantly moving. But you don't know any of the roads down here."

"We'll figure it out," Poppy said.

They got into Hanna's silver Honda Fit and drove back to the house they had just come from a few hours earlier. There was a silver Mercedes in the driveway and Hanna pulled in right behind it.

"Here are the keys. Do you want to wait a moment or just go?"

"I can wait," Poppy said.

"Okay, if I'm not back in five minutes, just go ahead without me."

"Sure thing."

Poppy waited, playing on her phone until she received a text from Owen.

Where are you?

She frowned.

At the Vann house. Why?

She waited a moment before she got her answer.

Stay there.

Confused, she started to get out of the car when a black Mercedes pulled in behind her. Suddenly uncomfortable, she waited until a large man with a receding hairline and light eyes got out of the driver's seat. He smiled, and she shivered. He looked familiar.

"Well, hello," he said, his voice scratchy and dripping with a deep, Southern accent. "Who might you be?"

"Poppy Pruette," she said nervously.

The man paused in his steps, his smile becoming wider.

"A Hood on Vann territory? Has hell frozen over?"

Poppy did not like this man. "Who are you?" she asked, noting the rudeness in her tone.

"A bit disrespectful, aren't you? I'm Mr. Vann." Poppy lifted her chin slightly, which made him laugh. "High and mighty, are we? That's fine, but I wouldn't be worried about the big bad wolf, Miss Pruette. Word on the street is you've got bigger fish to fry."

That caught Poppy's attention. "Who?"

A flash of anger shone in the man's eyes, but it disappeared as soon as it showed.

"You don't know?"

"No."

"Have you ever heard of the Three Virtues?"

"Yes," she said quickly, noting his continuing steps toward her.

"Would you walk with me, Miss Pruette? I promise I won't eat you." The man's crooked smile irked Poppy. She didn't trust him. "Come now, you're not afraid of the big bad wolf, are you?"

His voice mocked her.

"No," she said defiantly.

She took a step toward him, and they began to walk with a good distance between them toward the waterline.

"So you know about the Three Virtues? Tell me, do you know whatever happened to the jealous sister?"

She shook her head.

"She died. In an asylum. She went crazy after her one true love died, especially since it was all her fault." Poppy nodded, a grimace on her face. "She bore a son while she was there."

"Was her son mad, too?"

"Oh yes. Extremely so. Her son was the product of a wish. A terrible, vengeful wish. He wasn't actually wanted when he was born. He was conceived in spite. Wouldn't it be nice if we were all wanted from conception? Can you imagine the kind of man he would become, not being wanted like that? Not a very sane man, right?"

"I don't know," she said warily, afraid of his answer.

"No, not sane at all. In and out of foster homes, teased mercilessly about his insane, dead mother and absent father. It's a shame he didn't have a family to go to, an aunt or someone to take him in," he said.

Poppy paused in her steps, both from surprise and the fact that the waterline was only a few feet away.

"But that mad son . . . he found out he *did* have a family after all, but they didn't want him. Who *could* want someone like him? A curse, they called him, and you know what? When you call someone something long enough, they eventually become it. And that's what he did. He became a curse and decided to destroy everyone that had had a hand in his creation. The unfinished wish."

"How is that possible?" Poppy asked.

"His mad mother wasn't a smart woman, just a desperate one. She didn't read the fine print, it seems. See, everyone affected by that wish would have to die for it to be complete . . . all but one."

Poppy turned back and saw him holding something that reflected in the sun. "Everyone in the Hood line would have to pay the price for it. This little ring is supposedly a trinket passed down to the Hood descendants."

"That's my grandmother's ring," she whispered as all the air in her lungs left. Cold fear seemed to hit her in the face as every hair on her body stood up on end. "That's my ring."

"No," he said loudly, the fake smile finally disappearing off his face as an eye twitched. "No, this is mine. My ring. My line."

"Your line?" she said, confused. "But you're a . . . " A sudden wave of realization crashed over Poppy as she looked into the man's cold, familiar eyes. He looked nothing like William, and there was no wolf in sight. "Who are you?"

"I'm the unfinished wish. I'm the last member of the Hood line, or at least, I will be," he said, stalking toward her.

"Will be?"

"Do you know how I found all of this out?" he said, ignoring her. She shook her head, mesmerized by every word he said. "The wish maker told me. After Ursula died, I went looking for an inheritance, anything, but then I found out about Vilma and Rose and Randall. I found him in his trailer, and you know what he said to me?"

"I'm sorry," Poppy said, remembering her dream. This seemed to startle him, and his eye twitched once more. "You strangled him."

"What was I supposed to do?" he growled, white-hot fury in his voice. His eyes looked lifeless. "He did this to me. He told me only one would survive, could survive for the line to carry on, but I didn't believe him, so I killed him. You'd think Vilma, a nun, would have been kinder to the nephew she abandoned, but all she did was pray, sob, call me a devil. I don't like to be called names."

"And Rose?" Poppy asked, shaking. "What did she say to deserve to die?"

"She called me a curse," he said slowly, the words falling from his lips like droplets of venom. "Said only one could survive and it wasn't going to be a freak like me. I was blasphemy incarnate."

"She did not—"

"Yes, she did!" he yelled. "She said it and kept saying it, even when I wrapped my hands around her throat and looked her in the eyes as she left."

For a moment, Poppy just stared at him, awestruck as she saw red. She wanted to kill him. She had never felt like this before and couldn't help but be consumed by it. The idea had barely registered in her mind when she lunged at him, but he had been ready for her and ran into her like a football player, hitting her so hard with his shoulder that the air was knocked out of her body. She hit the ground hard, trying to scream without breath. By the time she inhaled again, his hands were around her neck, squeezing so hard that she could barely see. Her legs flailed wildly, kicking as hard as she could, but he didn't seem affected. His round, red face hovered over hers, shaking with an unspeakable rage. Was this the last image she would see? The last eyes she would look into? They were empty, void of a soul.

It was getting harder to fight as the oxygen struggled to fit down her constricted airway. The sky behind him was blue, and she tried to focus on the wispy clouds, trying to find comfort in the peacefulness she had ignored almost every day since she had looked for shapes in the clouds as a girl.

Her vision began to darken, the edges touched with blackness. All of her senses struggled to keep going, but it was her hearing that was truly heartbreaking. For a moment, she could have sworn she heard Owen calling her name. The blue sky turned fully black as she slipped into the deep, and the faintest popping sounds surrounded her.

It could have been days or hours, but it felt like only a short minute before Poppy felt her body ripped out of a peaceful, floating space, and thrust back into the loud and harsh world. Air was being forced down her lungs, which felt painful at first, but was then welcomed. She coughed harshly, gasping as her eyes opened.

"Poppy!" Owen said, his head hovering above hers. "Poppy . . ." He brought her up forcefully into a sitting position. She felt weak and welcomed Owen's strength. A large body lay in the grass and a strange, deep red color covered his stomach. Poppy noticed the wolf, Wyatt, growling at the body, but before she could take in anymore, Owen's hands were on either side of her face. "Poppy," he said again, and she wondered if he was invoking some sort of Old World magic.

"What?" she said finally.

For a moment, she thought she saw a twinkle in his eye, but it disappeared almost instantly.

"You scared the hell out of me," he said, his voice rough. His one hand moved to curl in her hair at the nape of her neck, while the other rubbed her cheek. "Are you okay?"

"I think so," she said uneasily. "No. No, I'm not. Where is he?"

"He's dead," he said, his voice shaking. "I thought you were dead. I thought he killed you. I just shot and prayed . . ." He paused, emotion strangling him.

"He killed her. He killed all of them."

He nodded, still too choked up.

"I know. I know—"

"OWEN!" a male voice shouted. "Get her over here, now!"

Owen turned, though all of Poppy's attention was still on him. She had wanted to kill him, but what did that make her? Could she be a monster, too?

Before she knew it, Owen had picked her up, carrying her toward the driveway. It was then that Poppy heard the faint sound of ambulances. She looked at William standing at the end of the driveway, waving his arms as if trying to flag someone down. Hanna and an older woman were hugging each other and looked to be crying.

"What happened?"

"Brom. He attacked the Vanns."

Poppy's head bobbed slightly as guilt washed over her. This was her fault. The Vann family wouldn't have been attacked if she hadn't have come here. As the reality of the situation settled in, so did her panic and tears.

"I wanted to kill him," she whispered, her voice shaking with emotion. "I wanted to end his life like he ended hers . . . "

"Shh, don't cry," Owen soothed as two ambulances appeared, followed by a cop car. "Don't cry."

The next hour flew by as the EMTs checked her vitals. William's father had been taken away on a stretcher from inside the house. Mrs. Vann had her head bandaged up and rode with her husband to the hospital. William and Hanna stayed only long enough to make sure that Poppy wasn't seriously injured, and then talked to the police before going to the hospital. Owen had been chewing out the cops for a half hour for no reason until Poppy coughed loudly to get his attention, which worked. The EMTs left them alone.

"Are you okay?" Owen asked. "You're going to the hospital."

"I'm fine. Really, I am." She paused for a moment, looking around to make sure that they were alone. "He said he was a curse, and that only one of us could survive. He told me how he killed my grandmother and I swear, Owen, if I'd had the chance, I would have killed him."

"I know."

"No, you don't know. I don't think like that. Yeah, I have a temper, but I feel ill over it—sick to my stomach because I wanted to kill him. I don't know that I could have lived with myself if I had. It would have been out of rage and revenge, and I wouldn't have been any better than him—"

"Poppy, that's not true," he interrupted. "You were in danger—"

"But it wasn't a survival thing, Owen. I wanted revenge." She looked away, tears running down her cheeks. "Why didn't she tell me any of this?"

"To protect you, Poppy. She wanted to protect her family."

"He said . . . " she began, emotion choking her. "He said she called him a curse. That he was blasphemy incarnate, but I can't see her ever saying that." Owen began to speak, but she stopped him by shaking her head. "What if it's true? What if she wasn't the nice, loving person I thought she was?"

"Whoever Rose was in those last moments shouldn't take away who she was to you your entire life. Sometimes, people lead a hundred lives in their lifetime. You can't blame them. It's just survival."

She shook her head, unsure of anything.

"They abandoned him. They made him a curse."

"It wasn't Rose's fault. If it was anyone's fault, it was Ursula's."

Poppy shook her head.

"No. They could have taken him in, raised him right and raised him not to be some terrible, incomplete wish. They could have saved themselves."

They stood in silence for a moment. Owen found Poppy's hand and squeezed it. She looked back at him.

"It's over, Poppy. There's no use dwelling on the past."

"But—"

"Please, just this once, listen to me," he said. "Think about it tomorrow, or next week, but not today." He kissed her forehead as his free hand touched her face. "Just be glad that it's over."

She nodded and leaned into him as he held her tightly to his chest. After several moments of just being there, she pulled away slightly.

"I should probably call my dad."

"Already did. He's on his way," Owen said, slightly disheartened. "I don't think he's going to be too keen on me, though. I did take you out of police custody."

"I don't care," she said breathlessly. "If you hadn't, Brom would still be alive, watching me. My dad might be more forgiving now that it's over with." Owen smirked and looked down at his hands. "There's just one thing I don't understand."

"What's that?"

"Why didn't Brom try to kill my father?" Poppy watched as Owen's face scrunched.

"What?"

"I think you and your father need to have a long talk when you get back to Virginia."

"Why?" she asked. "Do you know something?"

"I know I'm done with fairy tales for today. The only thing I care about right now is you."

"But—"

"Poppy, please," he said. He seemed to be deep in thought all of a sudden and Poppy waited for him to continue. "This isn't going to work."

The shock and hurt came together and hit her in the gut.

"Owen—"

"Let me finish," he said, holding up his hand. "This isn't going to work if we argue all the time."

"But we always argue. It's our thing," she said.

"I know, but everyone in my family is going to hit the roof when they find out, and I wouldn't be surprised if your father wants to ring my neck," he said, looking into Poppy's eyes. "But we can't argue all the time with each other if everyone's watching, waiting for us to make a mistake. They're all going to be, too."

"What are you saying?" she asked, confused.

"I'm saying that I don't want to be away from you. Everyone is going to tell us it's a mistake, being together, and if we argue all the time, we're just going to give them all reason to tell us not to be together."

The corner of Poppy's mouth curved as she wiped her cheeks dry. "Be together?" she repeated. Owen looked, for the first time, sheepish. "You aren't . . . I mean, what about California?"

"Don't worry about that."

"I am not going to be in one of those relationships where we have to be all pleasant and perfect on the surface, Owen. And I'm certainly not going to be kept in the dark about things like California, and—"

He kissed her suddenly, stopping her words. The intensity was almost too great after the day she'd had and she felt a little wobbly on her feet. But when he finally pulled back, he held her in his strong hold.

"Don't think I'm going to forget everything every time you kiss me," she said breathlessly.

"You're impossible," he said, grinning.

"You are, too," she said as she kissed him again.

For now, Poppy would live only in this moment. They'd deal with her father and their families later, but for now, she was completely and utterly content kissing him.

CHAPTER TWENTY-ONE

Three weeks later . . .

Poppy tried hard not to concentrate on her breathing. If she thought about inhaling and exhaling, but she swore her throat would get tighter and before long she would trick herself into a panic attack. Just then, a hand came down on her shoulder.

"Easy," Owen whispered into her ear as she turned to look at him. He looked like a completely different person, dressed in a crisp new suit. His hair was freshly cut and the tiredness she had often seen displayed on his face had all but disappeared. "It won't be that bad."

"I don't think I can handle this many people," she whispered as his hand dropped to the small of her back, pushing her gently forward. "I've never been to one of these things before."

"Believe me, they're boring," he said, glancing at his watch. "Where's Ana? She said she'd meet us at the front."

Poppy had driven up to New York Thursday after school. The past three weeks had been excruciating while Owen had been in Michigan and she had been figuring out her family history. Her father had explained that Rose had become paranoid after her daughter's death and had insisted on becoming a Pruette, acting as though she was his mother. Since Poppy had only been four at the time of her mother's death, it was easy for them to cover up, since Poppy's father was an orphan. He had wanted to tell her the truth when he got into politics, but Rose had insisted it was a matter of life and death. Her father hadn't truly believed in the Good and the Others, and had decided not to indulge in it often, which explained his aversion to it every time Poppy brought it up. He knew of it, but nothing more.

Randall had indeed been murdered, but without enough evidence, they couldn't link Brom to it, though Poppy knew otherwise. She had dreamed of his death in the library the night she was attacked. She had been worried about the dream for the past few weeks, until finally, she'd told Helena about it when she arrived the night before.

Helena had told her that auras weren't the only bits of leftover magic in the world. When people dreamed of future events or conversations they were never a part of, that was magic. When people would take a different road to work and ended up avoiding a major collision, that too was magic. The little synchronicities in life that couldn't be explained were little traces of magic from a time when magic thrived in human history. The mystery and allure of it kept it alive in the corners of the world, and Poppy was glad to hear it, though she hoped never to have another dream like that again.

Shaken from her thoughts, Poppy looked around. They were standing below one of the archways at Lincoln Center as a crowd of people dressed in fabulous clothes moved around them. Poppy's hair had been pulled up into a high ponytail and her makeup had been done by a professional. Surprised by the exciting hum in the air, she glanced around, searching for Owen's sister while self-consciously touching her dress. She wore a deep cream-colored dress that cut at the waist, flowing down in a most elegant way. The bodice was beaded, the straps forming a V-neckline that called attention to the ruby necklace—on loan to her from Ana—draped around her neck. It was frightening at first, but Owen had assured her that no one would try to rob a detective's girlfriend. Especially at an event like this one.

The word "girlfriend" had made Poppy blush and, unable to stop herself, she smiled at the memory.

"What?" Owen asked suspiciously before smiling as well.

"Nothing," she lied.

"Stop worrying," he said, kissing the back of her knuckles. "You look stunning."

"Quit ordering me around," she said teasingly. She patted her dress. "I've just never been in a dress like this. We're going to look insane meeting up with Sean later."

"I'm actually looking forward to that more than this," he answered, fidgeting with his collar. "Lucky jerk, sitting at a bar, not choked by a tie."

"Stop messing with your collar."

"Who's bossing who around now?"

"I swear, Sean should have come instead of you. He would have loved this."

"What about you? Do you like all this?"

To be honest, Poppy was feeling panicky and wished they could go grab a burger somewhere instead, but she smiled.

"It's okay," she said, looking up at him. "It'll be fun."

"Here I am!" Lynette said, popping up behind them, arms dramatically in the air. She was wearing a mint chiffon gown. "Poppy! You look beautiful!"

"Thanks, Lynette. You look amazing."

"Posh," Lynette said, waving her hand. She looked at Owen. "Looking for Ana?"

"Yes, where is she?"

She pointed behind her into the crowd. "Over by table twenty. She was wearing a headset last time I saw her. So," she said, turning back to Poppy. "How's his partner doing?"

"Good. Great, actually. The doctors said he'll be able to get back to work by the end of the month. He had a son, too. They named him George, so he's been able to spend time with his family for a while before getting back to work."

"How's the job hunt?" Lynette asked quietly.

Since the incident in California, Owen had decided to resign from the Michigan State Police and was thinking about moving back to New York, since he had connections there. Poppy supported it, especially since the drive to New York was a third of the time she'd have to drive to get to Michigan, but she was genuinely excited to hear he wanted to start his own private investigator business. He just hadn't told anyone about it yet and was keeping it secret until all the details were ironed out.

"It's going," Poppy said. "I'm not too worried about it. Plus," she added louder, glancing over at him. "I like this Owen. So relaxed and calm. I think a break has been good for him."

"I think he looks much better when he's well-rested."

"Idle hands," he murmured, still searching the crowd.

Lynette rolled her eyes.

"Can't take a compliment," she said, shaking her head. "How are you? Still sore from that lunatic?"

Poppy had suffered a few deep bruises, but had made out much better than Mr. and Mrs. Vann. Mr. Vann was still in the hospital, and the outcome didn't look good. He had suffered a major blow to the head, and the last Poppy heard, there was some swelling of the brain. She knew it was bizarre to hope that he was all right, especially since they were mortal enemies, but she couldn't find it in herself to want anything for him except a full recovery.

Brom had also attacked the wolves. He supposedly fed them dog treats soaked in antifreeze, which caused them all to be violently ill. Once the wolves were out of the way, he'd attacked the Vanns without warning and had used them as bait to lure Poppy and Hanna there. Despite all that, Hanna had invited Poppy back for a visit, though William seemed a bit uneasy at the idea. Poppy agreed, noting that since Brom had technically been a member of the Hood line, this incident had caused a bigger rift between the two families. Poppy had wondered if they would always be enemies, and had even asked Helena about it.

"As long as the world needs stories, there will be stories told." Helena spoke in just as many riddles as Owen did.

"I feel great," Poppy answered Lynette. "Except the anxiety, but that's getting better. I've actually started seeing a therapist about it."

"That's great! Get help when you need it, right?" Her voice dropped a few octaves as she leaned in closer to Poppy.

"I heard Helena mention something about Owen having to go back to California?"

Poppy's smile faltered a bit.

"Yeah, I think Ajax may have bit off more than he could chew," she said quietly. "He's not doing too well."

"Which reminds me," Owen said pointedly. "I have to call him."

"Eavesdrop much?" Poppy said.

He laughed. "You're both a foot away from me."

Poppy smiled and turned to Lynette.

"He's right, actually . . . Lynette?" Lynette was staring with purpose across the sea of people, her mouth slightly open and a stunned look on her face. Poppy tried to follow her gaze, but saw nothing of importance. "Lynette?"

"Huh? What?" Her focus changed, and she looked back at Poppy.

"What were you looking at?" Poppy asked.

"There was some guy staring at me like crazy," she said. "I don't know why."

"What guy?" Owen said, suddenly falling into detective mode. Poppy liked when he changed back and forth between soft and hard, relaxed and alert. "Where?"

"Over there," Lynette said. "Or at least, he was there." She shook herself and smiled at Poppy. "Complete hottie, though. Dark eyes, possibly a neck tattoo. Had a five o'clock shadow, and I don't even like facial hair. Maybe I'll go find him."

"Absolutely not," Owen said decisively, alarmed at her description. "There are always a bunch of famous idiots who attend these things. You don't need to end up some mediocre rock star's girlfriend for a week. Let's go find Ana."

"Fine," Lynette said, rolling her eyes as she started across the room. "You know, Owen, there's a name for guys like you."

"Hero complex?" he said nonchalantly. "I've heard that before."

"I was going to say grandpa," Lynette said, causing Poppy to laugh. "Oh, there she is!"

Owen went to follow Lynette, but Poppy held him back with her hand. He looked at her, his eyes questioning her motive.

"Are you sure you're not in trouble with Helena?" she asked softly. "I don't want to be the cause of some major family rift."

"I already told you, Helena will get over it. I'm happy, and she can't be angry at me because of that. We'll drive ourselves crazy if we keep worrying about it, and that's not healthy, believe me." Poppy nodded, but didn't speak, waiting for him to continue. "You know why Helena was so insistent about California, don't you?"

"Because of what happened to your mother."

Owen nodded. "She still thinks my mother's death was caused by her decision not to follow her story, but she was sick. I don't think my grandmother can accept that."

Poppy's brow scrunched in concentration. "Owen, if Lynette's father was your uncle on your mother's side, that would make her from the Slumber line, right?" He nodded. "And your father is from the Charming line. Why didn't it work? I thought Sleeping Beauty married a Prince Charming."

"Well, they were together, and in love," he began, "but they were never married. Helena didn't know about Ana and me until after my mother's suicide."

"Really?"

"Yes," he said. "My mother was betrothed to someone else when she fell in love with my father, but even then, she wasn't a stable person. He loved her so much, though, that he couldn't help but do what she wanted, and I think he blames himself. When she died, he told Helena about us." He inhaled and let out a sigh. "The rest is history."

Poppy let this information sink in as she pieced together Owen's family in her head. "So that's why Helena was worried."

"Yes, but that's why we can't worry about California or Helena. We've made a choice, Poppy, and it's the right one."

"How can you be sure?"

"I can't be, but I think if we're both willing to work at it, how could it be anything but right?"

She knew that, despite his words, deep down he was still worried like she was, and though it wasn't in her nature to ignore the problems they might face, she thought that, for tonight at least, she would try.

"Okay," she said, squeezing his hand and smiling. "Let's go find Ana."

Owen looked over the crowd and saw his sister wave at him. He waved back, but paused, hand still in the air. Poppy watched as the siblings exchanged some sort of devious look. Ana rolled her eyes and smiled as she turned away. Owen spun back to Poppy.

"You want to get out of here?" he asked her.

"But we promised Ana to meet a zillion people and Helena isn't here yet. I haven't even seen your dad." Her words fell on deaf ears, but she barely cared due to the broad smile he was flashing at her. For a guy who had been so hell-bent on acting the right way and following the rules, he kept making her want to break them.

She smiled at him. "Let's go."

Owen kissed her hand again and held it tight as they maneuvered through the crowd. Poppy tried to apologize for bumping into almost everyone as Owen dragged her through, fighting toward their freedom. With each step, Poppy felt a bit more alive, especially with so many disapproving eyes on them. Owen turned back, a huge smile appearing on his face, and Poppy laughed. Their escape was so silly, but so much fun at the same time.

Soon, they were free, hurrying down the concrete stairs and onto the sidewalk. Finally liberated, Owen pulled Poppy close to him and kissed her, and Poppy couldn't help but dip a little. Despite everything, this was the right choice. *Things are going to end just like they're supposed to*, she thought.

Happily ever after.

ABOUT MELINDA

Melinda Michaels is the author of *Golden* and currently lives in Milford, Pennsylvania. A self-proclaimed historian with a rare sense of humor, Melinda finds an immense amount of joy in knowing useless facts, exploring historical places and drinking copious amounts of coffee. When she's not writing she can be found researching obscured time periods for her own amusement or refurbishing old furniture.

Melinda loves Philadelphia and visits often to enjoy the city with her husband Andrew. Together they have three rambunctious pets. Archie the Beagle, Winston the Boston Terrier and Beatrice the cat. *Golden* is the first in a Young Adult magic realism series.

ACKNOWLEDGEMENTS

I'd like to thank my amazing husband, Andrew, who has always been the foundation of my work. I'm especially grateful for the hard work of Virginia DeFeo and Michelle Hoehn and to the fantastic people at Reuts Publications. Thank you all so much!